AFTER ALL

A NOVEL

KARINA HALLE

METAL BLONDE BOOKS

Feel it.
The things that you don't want to feel.
Feel it. And be free.
-Nayyirah Waheed

You'll never find peace of mind
Until you listen to your heart.
- George Michael

PROLOGUE

EMMETT

PAST

*E*mmett Hill had just turned ten years old a week before everything changed.

He wasn't a happy kid by any means. But the life that he had was the only life that he knew. And even though he often dreamed of the better life he'd glimpse on the right side of town, it seemed like a fairy tale to him. Something he knew would never happen, something to tuck away in his dreams. Life outside the dirty, mean streets of east Vancouver was all a movie, a film, a play on a stage. He was stuck behind the scenes.

But, like most kids, he was resilient. And being stuck was a way of life. Every day was exactly the same, which made all the hardships that much easier to take.

He'd wake up in the mornings in the tiny one-bedroom apartment he shared with his mother and she'd bring him breakfast in bed, delivered with thin and shaky hands. Usually it was just sugary cereal with water instead of milk, but sugary cereal was like having candy in the morning so he didn't care.

Then he'd get ready for school. His closet was full of clothes that were either too big or too small, clothes that had the names of other kids written into the collar, but at least he had variety. His school kept an eye on him and were always the first to give him, and other kids in slightly-too-big shoes, clothing that was donated. His mother was always looking for clean clothes for him too, when she wasn't trying to get her medicine.

His mother would usually walk him the ten blocks over to his school, though sometimes it was his mother's friend, Jimmy, and Emmett always likened that walk to being in a teleporter or a bridge through time. He read books all the time and one of his favorites was *A Wrinkle in Time* and sometimes he thought the way to school passed through a tesseract. They would leave the depravity of Hastings and Main and the other streets where lawlessness ruled and hope was squashed, and travel through Chinatown, where the vendors were always up bright and early, putting their colorful displays out, the air filled with the smell of hot meat and spices. Then Chinatown would give way to small row houses where Emmett assumed rich people lived, people who could afford an actual house and had tiny slices of a yard, the grass usually waist-high, rusted toys out front.

Of course, these weren't rich people houses at all but anything other than Emmett's apartment (where there were always a few people sleeping in the hall outside his door, some who used the stairwell as a toilet), seemed like it belonged to royalty.

Once at school, his mom would go off to her job as a waitress at a local diner, and he would disappear into the building to learn and play with his friends. Putting on plays during recess–where he was always the hero–was one of his favorite things to do. At some point during the day, usually just after lunch where he scarfed down his usual granola bar, one of the teachers would pull him aside. They'd ask him how he was today, how his mother was, if there had been any problems. Then they'd give him a piece of fruit, sometimes a sandwich (once, his teacher Mrs. Marsden, brought him a Happy Meal from McDonalds down the street–he never forgot that day).

He never really knew why the teachers doted on him but they'd often call him handsome and smart and tell him he had a bright future, so he thought maybe he was just special. He liked feeling special.

Then school would end and he'd always be a bit sad. Everything was so bright and cheery and fun and even learning the crappy subjects like math didn't seem so bad.

But his mother, or Jimmy, would be around the corner waiting. Neither of them liked to go right up to the school to get him and when he asked why he got two different answers. Jimmy said "it would look bad, they don't know I'm your friend," and his mother said, "there are too many people." She said this as if she didn't like crowds when their whole life was so darn crowded with people always in their apartment, on the street, everywhere.

But they were their kind of people.

The junkies. The addicts. The thieves. The homeless, the hopeless.

Those were the people who surrounded them every day.

And Emmett wasn't an idiot. Even though he grew up in that crappy apartment and saw the same scenes day in and day out, he eventually realized that the medicine his mother took, that everyone else took, was heroin and other drugs.

But even so, even as his mother stopped going to her job, even as she was flopped out on the couch more and more, even as the people who came over got dirtier, scarier, he figured everything in his life would be okay in the end.

Until it wasn't.

One day his mother didn't show up after school. He walked around the corner to the same old grey mailbox that she'd wait for him at, but she wasn't there. Jimmy wasn't either.

Since he was now ten years old, he figured he'd wait for a bit and then walk home, alone. Ever since his birthday when he hit the double digits, he felt a little bit older, a little bit wiser. After an hour, he adjusted the straps on his well-worn backpack, the heavy science textbook weighing it down, and took off for home.

He knew his way and wouldn't get lost. In fact, as he walked, no one even looked at him twice. That was the thing about the area. As dirty and scary as it was, the people there weren't known to kidnap or assault people. They just wanted money for drugs. And being that Emmett was just a kid, with obviously no money on him, no one paid him any attention.

By the time he was getting close to the apartment, Emmett started to feel more like a man than ever. Not only did he walk home alone, through the tesseract, but people ignored him. He didn't even feel like a child anymore. He felt invincible.

It was because of this that he stopped being worried about why his mother didn't show up. He ran up the stairs two-by-two to the top floor of the apartment building and burst in through his door, wanting to tell his mother all about his walk.

But she wasn't there.

He tried to think if maybe she had gone back to work–that would be nice, it had been a while since he had a good, hot meal–and then went over to Jimmy's door down the hall to see if he knew where she was.

4

He knocked and knocked and finally a guy who was napping on the floor by the stairs looked up at him and said, "He's not home. Do you have a dollar, son?"

Emmett shook his head. "If I had a dollar, I'd be getting a pop right now. Have you seen my mother?"

The man squinted at him for a moment and then said, "Yeah. Emily, right? Last I saw she was outside the butcher."

That didn't sound too bad. There was a meat store a block up that provided cheap meals if you had the extra change. Sometimes his mother was up there getting them food. Maybe he would have a nice meal tonight. He hadn't gotten anything special for his tenth birthday.

So Emmett put that thought into his head, pushing his worries aside, and went back into his home. He sat on the couch and watched the clock and waited.

Hours passed.

Night settled in.

And still his mother didn't come home.

He searched the cupboards for something to eat and found a packet of stale crackers that he wolfed down. Then he decided to go and look for her.

Everything is scarier in the dark. In the day time you can see the horrors around you but at night, they were shadowed, half-hidden, which made them even more monstrous. Emmett felt like he was being very brave by doing this, the time when things got a little wilder, a little more out of hand. But he remembered that people had ignored him earlier and he knew that he couldn't just wait for his mother forever. What if something had happened to her?

And for once, the reality of *"what if"* was hitting home. As he ran around the streets, asking for his mom, looking for her, dealing with people who scared him half to death, he started thinking about death. The worst-case scenario. His mother was using more and more, looking sicker and sicker every day.

What if, what if, what if?

It wasn't until he forced himself into the back alleys that he knew he was close to death.

He could smell it back here, feel the dark, oppressive vibe.

The brick walls were covered in graffiti, the ground littered with shit, vomit, plastic baggies, discarded needles.

There were people back here too, but not many of them were moving.

Most were slumped here and there, the needles in their arms shining under the dim lights.

He peered at each one of them.

They were alive, but barely. Lost in the dreams of the drug.

And he kept going.

Because now he knew, he knew in his young, small heart that his mother would be one of them.

He walked the alleys for what seemed like forever. It wasn't until he was in the one right behind his apartment that he saw a familiar pair of dirty tennis shoes poking out from behind a dumpster.

His breath caught in his lungs. Bile filled his mouth.

The feeling of pure, undiluted dread was incapacitating, a living, breathing thing that pushed down on him until he felt he was drowning.

His mother's legs weren't moving at all.

In the cold light, they almost looked blue.

He didn't know how long he stood there for, frozen in fear, his heart crumbling inside him. For all her flaws, she was his mother and the only person in the world he truly loved. He didn't want to see her like this. He wanted everything to go back to the way it was earlier. If he could go back through the tesseract, back to when his mother wasn't lying in the alley, before his life changed forever, he would.

Be brave, Emmett told himself. *You're a big boy now.*

And he was. He straightened up his shoulders.

Took in a deep breath.

And peered around the dumpster.

That night everyone heard the cries of that boy.

They seemed to bounce off the alley walls forever, drowning out the sirens and the chaos of the streets.

A horrible wailing that could have woken the dead.

Only it didn't wake his mother.

CHAPTER 1

EMMETT

28 YEARS LATER

"*Y*ou know if you touch me, he'll kill you."

Her words hang in the air. A little too long for my liking but I react as I'd planned.

"How do you know *you* won't like it if I touch you?" I ask her, bringing the appropriate amount of sneer to my voice. I take a menacing step toward her back, her side profile lit just right, until I'm standing behind her. "It will be our secret."

I wait a few beats, counting in my head, then lower my voice as I lift her hair off her shoulder. She smells like hairspray and my hand practically sticks to the strands. "I know you've been wanting a walk on the wild side for a long time. Now is your chance. Give in to me."

At that she stiffens and it's almost realistic. Is she really this repulsed by me in real life? She definitely wasn't a few weeks ago when I was screwing her in her trailer.

"Cut!" Jackson yells, his voice booming across the set.

"Sorry, Emmett, the line is walk on the dark side, not wild side."

I roll my eyes, stepping away from Madison and look over my shoulder at him as he stands next to the playback screens, tired and frustrated. It's eleven p.m. on Friday night and we're into overtime once again. Everyone wants to go home, myself included, especially since I've got to be up bright and early for my friend Will's wedding. I feel bad enough as it is, having to miss the rehearsal dinner tonight.

"I know my line," I tell the director of the week, trying not to sound snippy. "But walk on the dark side is a little too Darth Vader for me."

"I know. But look who our audience is," Jackson says. "This is the CW network here. People get who Darth Vader is and they need to associate him with you. You're the villain here, you're the one that everyone wants to watch."

"At the moment," Madison mutters under her breath. I give her a sharp look and she can't even be bothered to put on her fake smile in return.

"Of course, they're here to see Madison, too," Jackson offers. "But don't hold back here, Emmett. You're Cole Black. Doctor Death. People expect the puns, they expect you to be over-the-top. You know this by now."

I sigh. Serves me right for trying to do this properly. Seems all those years in London's West End theatres don't count for shit when you're playing the bad guy on a super-hero show for teens.

I'm definitely not complaining though. I haven't been on the rise for a good ten years. Hell, until six months ago, I was written up as a has been in the Canadian media. I mean, you know your career is going downhill when fucking *Canada* starts taking shots at you.

But ever since I landed the role of Doctor Death in the

world's most ridiculous superhero show, *Boomerang*, my life has completely turned around.

For the better, of course.

At least, I'm fairly sure.

You know when you've dreamed about something for so long, craved it so fiercely, that when you finally get it, you're not sure what to do with it, or even how to feel?

That's what I'm going through.

Some people might even say I'm not handling it all too well.

I try not to listen to them–the media especially.

The only problem is Autumn, my new publicist, is starting to say the same thing too.

But aside from sleeping with Madison and having it out with one of the script supervisors, I'm trying to be a fucking angel on set. It's just that everywhere else, trouble seems to follow me.

With that in mind I take in a deep breath, swallow my pride and give Jackson a winning smile.

"All right, let's do it again," I tell him. "I'll follow the script. Promise."

Madison scoffs beside me. She knows as well as I do that following script hasn't been my strong suit. That's a metaphor that can go a million different ways.

Luckily I pull through, summoning as much cheesiness as I can manage to bring Cole Black to the edge of caricature and in another hour it's time to call it quits.

I say goodbye to the crew and leave the North Vancouver studio in my Audi, a recent purchase. Though I'd saved up a pretty big nest egg while working for most of my twenties, which resulted in my waterfront home, I'd also been especially frugal with my money.

But with the role on *Boomerang* has come the big bucks and more opportunities, especially in advertising. It wasn't long ago that doing ads as an actor was frowned upon, unless you were doing them overseas for things like Japanese whisky. Now Matthew McConaughey and his damn drawl and Lincoln car has made it acceptable. Danny DeVito and George Clooney smiling about Nescafe then pushed it into the *encouraged* department.

So a popular show plus a few ads here and there and I'm finally making money I'm not afraid to spend. Hey, I've been the 'it kid' and then I've faded into obscurity. At thirty-eight, I know more than anyone how quickly everything fades and I'm not just talking this business. It's life, in general. Over in the blink of an eye.

I'm not sure why my thoughts have taken a turn for the negative but I feel myself being pulled into the liquor store hoping to pick up something for tomorrow morning when Will and Ted come over before the ceremony. It's an excuse, really, since I have a fully stocked bar but I've got it set in my mind. Naturally, being that it's late and everything in this damn city closes early, it's closed.

I probably should keep going, get in my car and head over the Second Narrows Bridge towards home. Grab a bottle of rye from the bar cart, put my feet up and relax. Pass out in front of the TV. That sort of thing.

But there's a fire building through my veins. I don't get back in the car, instead I walk across the parking lot, past the grocery store and shops that are all closed for the night, right to El Rodeo.

Don't ask me why it's called El Rodeo. It doesn't serve Tex-Mex or any food, nor does it have a western décor. If anything it looks like a nautical joint. But it is a bar and one usually frequented by actors and crew who work at the studios.

Being Friday night, there's a few people inside, some that I vaguely recognize, but I keep to myself and take a seat at the bar. I try not to do a lot of drinking at this place since there are usually some autograph hounds, gossip bloggers and paparazzi around, plus the drinking and driving laws in British Columbia are very strict and the last thing I need is to be tossed in jail.

But for some reason I find myself pounding back the rye like it's water and by my fourth one I know I'm taking a cab home. Maybe it's that I'm feeling increasingly frustrated lately, which reminds me that I probably should schedule another meeting with my therapist, Christine. Or it's that Will is getting married tomorrow and while I'm happy for my best friend and Jackie, his sweet, pregnant and young bride-to-be, it reminds me that while my career might be moving forward again, my personal life isn't. It's as stagnant as ever. One step forward in one direction, two steps back in the other.

Whatever it is, I stay until the bar closes and the bartender calls me a cab. My head is foggy but my heart rate is doing a dance. I still feel this vague frustration and anger even though I don't know why or what to do with it. The alcohol hasn't masked it, it's only encouraged it.

"Hey buddy," someone says from behind me after I stumble out of the bar and onto the street. The cab isn't here yet but I'm obviously not alone.

I turn around to see a rotund guy with a paunchy gut staring at me, phone aimed in my direction, a dick-ish smile on his fat face.

"Are you talking to me?" I ask him. I shouldn't even open my mouth, especially when I'm drunk.

"Look, he thinks he's the next De Niro," the man laughs to his phone, obviously recording this exchange.

Take in a deep breath. Don't engage. The world is full of people waiting to pull you down and that says more about them than about you.

I go over the things that my therapist has taught me.

But right now, none of that matters.

"Are you recording this?" I ask dick face, trying not to slur my words.

"Hey buddy, how does it feel to go from Cruiser McGill to Bruiser NoChill?" he asks snidely.

Bruiser NoChill.

My new nickname.

And I know exactly why he's saying this. He's trying to provoke my reputation. Trying to make me say something stupid, something he can capture on his phone and sell to fucking TMZ.

Somehow I manage to corral the instinct to give him what he wants. AKA, put my fist into his nose. Two weeks ago I did that to a bouncer at a bar downtown, probably where the fucking nickname Bruiser NoChill came from. Or maybe it was from the week before when I told a paparazzi who took a photo of me and a young actress leaving her house to go fuck himself and threatened to break his camera.

I'm not really Mr. Popular as of late.

I put my back to him, my fists balling, and wish the damn cab would show up. There's nowhere else for me to go and this guy is still right fucking *here*.

"You're, like, forty, dude," the guy keeps talking at my back and he's getting closer. "You really think playing Doctor Death is going to help your career? That was over when you left Degrassi, you Ryan Reynolds wannabe."

I swear I don't have anything against Ryan Reynolds.

But those words set off a bomb inside me.

I spin around and almost clock the fucker right in the face.

Lawsuit, lawsuit.

Those words, flashing in my head like a siren, are the only thing that saves me.

Instead, I grab his phone and throw it down to the pavement, then take the heel of my boot and slam it down on the case until I hear the glass crack.

"Holy fuck!" the guy exclaims and then I bring my eyes to his and I know I look drunk and crazy but it's enough for him to back up while shaking his head. "You broke my phone! You fucking broke my phone!"

"You need a social media break," I tell him dryly, something that Doctor Death would say.

Fucking hell, what's wrong with me?

I need to get out of here.

Just then the cab pulls into the parking lot and I wave my arm frantically, jogging towards it.

I get in and give the driver my address. I can't help but stare out the window at the guy trying to pick up the pieces of his phone.

Sighing, I run a hand through my hair and lean back in my seat as the interior of the cab begins to spin.

What are the chances all of this will go unnoticed?

* * *

"WELL, well, well if it isn't Mr. Movie Star," Ted Phillips says to me as I open the door to see him and Will standing on my stoop in tuxedos, squinting in the sunshine.

"TV star," I correct him with a smile, always happy to see Ted. "And a pretty mediocre one at that."

"Ah, false modesty," Ted says, patting me on the back and strolling past me down the hall, looking around the open living area of my house. "But damn what false modesty can buy you."

"You should try it sometime, Ted," Will calls after him.

I let Will step in, looking him over. The man has always had an old school James Bond way about him, though more

15

Roger Moore than Connery. He's tall, dashing, with a jaw that needs its own postal code. Naturally, he looks extra dapper now that it's his wedding day.

"I'm not sure if it's the groomsman's role to tell you that you look good, but you look good pal," I tell him.

"Well, it's sure as hell not the best man's role, is it?" Will says, directing his words at Ted yet again as Ted slides open the glass doors of the living room and steps onto the patio that overlooks the bay.

"How are you doing? Are you nervous?" I ask Will, heading to the kitchen.

"Not one bit," he says smoothly. He's so damn unflappable. The opposite of me.

"Need a drink?"

"Why the hell do you think we're here?" Ted asks with a grin, stepping back inside. "We can't get properly boozed at the wedding without raising a few eyebrows."

"You mean I can't," Will says. "If you don't have a glass in your hand at all times, someone is going to check your pulse."

"You seem you like you need a drink too," Ted calls out to me. "Make it doubles all around."

"Single, please." Will is trying to be the responsible one here.

"Ah, not in a few hours," Ted says, wagging his eyebrows.

"Why do I seem like I need a drink?" I ask Ted as I start pouring the Crown Royal. I did wake up with a hangover but after a shower and a quick run of the beard trimmer (I have it in my contract that I can't fully shave–part of the doctor's charm is having permanent stubble which is harder to maintain than you'd think), I cleaned up pretty well. My brain fog cleared on the cab ride back to North Vancouver where I had to pick up my car before they towed it. The last step to looking and feeling presentable is the tuxedo and no one can look lousy in a tux.

"Don't pretend, I've seen the news," Ted says. "TMZ, Perez, Just Jared. That asshole is pissed that you broke his phone. He deserved it, no doubt, but he's livid."

I close my eyes and groan. Ted is in his sixties with a shock of white hair but his charming smile makes him seem much younger and he keeps up-to-date with all the Hollywood gossip more than anyone I know, like he reads Variety and the Hollywood Reporter in his sleep. Being the owner, along with Will, of Mad Men Studios, which does animation and visual effects here in Vancouver and in their LA office, I guess he prides himself on being the first to know everything, even if it has no direct connection to his business.

"Maybe you should be my publicist," I tell him, handing them both their drinks. "You take this sort of news a lot better than she does." In fact, it's kind of strange that Autumn hasn't called me yet but then again she did say she was going hiking all weekend and I'm sure cell reception is scarce. Maybe the whole thing will blow over by the time she gets back. Maybe she won't know at all.

Wishful fucking thinking.

"How bad was it?" I ask him with a wince.

Ted cocks a brow. "Well, it was on Instagram live."

I groan.

"Which was actually a good thing because people were able to see what an asshole the guy was being. Like I said, he deserved it. People are on your side this time. Still think he's going to raise a fuss and get you to pay for his phone though. Luckily if you can afford this house," he notes, looking around him again, "you can afford a new phone."

That doesn't change the principle of the whole situation. Why should I have to buy him a phone when he was in the wrong? Why do the boundaries of being a decent human being fail to exist when you're a celebrity? The moment you become a public figure you cease to have feelings, cease being able to express yourself without getting shit on. You cease to exist as a person, you're just a pixelated image on a screen.

I exhale loudly and get myself my own glass before turning to face them. "Well, that's enough about me, then. Today is Will's day. Let's focus on that."

"Also, it's my day since I'm the father of the bride," Ted adds, raising his glass.

"Every day is your day," Will says under his breath before breaking into a grin.

I guess this wedding is a little different from the usual. Not only are Will and Ted business partners and friends but Ted is Jackie's father. Will and I have been friends for a long time, even when I was living in London and doing theatre and he was at the LA office with his ex-wife. We both helped ourselves through some messy breakups and now he's finally met the real love of his life. Of course there were complications, since she was his employee and the daughter of his best friend. But true love prevails and all that fucking bullshit.

Stop the cynicism, I have to remind myself. Some people are built for love and long-lasting relationships. Some people aren't. I know which category I fall into, it's time to start owning it.

With that slightly bitter thought lingering in my head, the three of us cheers and finish our drinks outside on the patio, the waves of English Bay lapping against the rocks beneath the house. When we're sufficiently buzzed–at least Ted and I–I get on my tuxedo and the three of us leave. The wedding venue is at the Royal Vancouver Yacht Club down the street, about a fifteen-minute walk from my place.

We must make a peculiar trio, all dressed to the nines under the late July sunshine, enduring some honks from passing cars and I swear a few snaps from the paparazzi, though I'm probably just paranoid. After last night it's hard not to be. We stroll around the corner to the yacht club and head down the driveway to the ornate building.

A small crowd of wedding guests have gathered outside beside the large, white columns that surround the front steps. Jackie, thankfully, is nowhere in sight. Will is old-fashioned enough to believe in that "not seeing the bride before the wedding" superstition.

And then I see a sight for sore eyes.

It's hard not to.

For one, she's in a hot pink dress that's nearly blinding in the sunlight, beaming against the white building like radioactive bougainvillea.

For two, she's got the nicest set of tits I've ever seen.

For three, her face is fresh, glowing and sweet, and yet her eyes are full of snark and sass.

She's got that "bitch-hot" vibe down pat.

Poor girl doesn't know I'm a sucker for that.

"Who is *she*?" I ask Will, nodding at her as we make our way towards the group.

"Which one, the tiny Asian one, the blonde, or Jackie's grandmother?"

"The blonde," I tell him.

"She's off-limits," Will says, giving me a stern look. "I mean it."

I jerk my chin back. "Says who?"

"Says me and it's my wedding."

I narrow my eyes at him. "Is she your long-lost sister?"

"Are you talking about Alyssa?" Ted speaks up.

Alyssa. She has a name.

"If she's the blonde," I tell him.

"She works for us," Will says quickly.

"And she's a handful," Ted says. "And not in the way you

think I mean. Because believe me, those seem more than a handful. Maybe two handfuls. Depends on the size of your hands. I wouldn't know of course."

I give Will a curious look.

He rolls his eyes. "Neither would I. But she's my employee and Jackie's best friend and the maid of honor and I really want to get this marriage off on the right foot. You…doing your thing that you do now, it would make it that much harder. Plus, I'd have to murder you and honestly I just want to get on our honeymoon."

I scoff, shoving my hands in my pockets. "I'm just asking who she is. She's pretty." Pretty fucking hot.

Will laughs. "She might be pretty but she can do without the likes of you."

"What? Just yesterday you were telling me I needed to go out and meet women outside of the dating app world and here I am, enquiring about that hot pink blondie at your wedding of all places, in the real world, and you're telling me to back off. She have a boyfriend or something?"

Ted laughs. "I think she scares the pants off most men."

"Why?" I like a challenge and the closer we get to her, the more I realize how enticing she is. There's something almost delicately cute about her face that lends an air of vulnerability. Combine that with the take-no-shit look in her eyes as she talks to the other bridesmaid, and I feel heat coursing through me, a nice change from the anger of last night.

"Because the guy I gave dating advice to was Emmett from last year," Will points out, lowering his voice. "Emmett before he became Doctor Doom or Death or whatever you are. The Emmett who wasn't sleeping with every starlet or model within a ten-mile radius and becoming gossip mag fodder."

I wave at him dismissively. "You can't believe everything the media tells you."

Will lets out a caustic laugh. "I'm believing what *you* tell me. Don't think I haven't been listening."

He's got a point. While Will's been stuck in pre-matrimonial bliss, I guess I have been giving him a weekly rundown of who I've been screwing. I have to blame the fact that we're usually at a bar and I've had one too many when it happens.

"What Will is trying to say," Ted says, slapping me on the shoulder, "is that this is his wedding. And I'm the father of the bride. And the two of us have vested interest in Alyssa. Without her, the office just doesn't run. So, for our sake, back off and behave yourself tonight."

"Fine, fine, I promise to behave," I mutter as we approach the group.

Everyone lights up when they see Will, but I'm watching Alyssa. Her features become warmer when she sees him. It might bother me a little but the man has the effect on everyone. Fucking bastard.

Of course I have my own effect. I don't have a name for it yet. It's a mix of nostalgia and awe whenever people see me and right now every single person in the group is staring at me with either that "I know that guy from somewhere" look or "It's Cruiser McGill!" Despite *Boomerang*'s success, people still resort to my character from that damn TV show. As long as my nickname doesn't come up, I should be okay.

But Alyssa isn't looking at me with either of those expressions. She's looking at me like she's completely unimpressed. It's not that she doesn't recognize me and I know I look fucking good in a tux. It's that she can see right through me–and she doesn't like what she sees.

I feel my smile falter, just for a moment, and tear my eyes away from her. It's probably for the best. Any longer and I would have been caught in a war between staring at her tits and her face, both absolutely mesmerizing and vying for my attention.

21

"Everyone," Will says, addressing the group. "You all know Ted here as my best man. I'd like to introduce you to my groomsman, Emmett Hill. You may remember him from such TV shows as Degrassi: The Next Generation and Boomerang."

"It's Degrassi the *New* Generation," the other bridesmaid corrects him before wiggling her fingers in excitement. "I can't believe I get to walk down the aisle with Cruiser McGill."

Damn. I was hoping for the blonde.

And then everyone starts talking about the show and my character and what a good ol' boy I was, how the old *Degrassi* was better than the new *Degrassi*, and of course everyone's favorite topic, Drake.

Fucking Drake. After being on the show for ten years, everyone always wants to know if I know Drake personally. And the answer–no, I don't, I left before he joined the cast– always disappoints them.

The only one who isn't interested is Alyssa–in fact she seems like she's trying to look everywhere but at me–and looks just as relieved as I feel when a woman in a blue cock-tail dress shows up from around the corner, clapping her hands together.

"All right, we need you all to get in your places!" she cries out.

"That's the wedding planner," Ted says beside me. "She's also a handful. Best to just let her do her job. She seems nice until you ask if you can have a karaoke machine."

I stare at the woman, her mouth too wide, her teeth too white. There's far too many people like her in my life at the moment. I feel like wedding planners and publicists are the same thing right now, one tries to plan your wedding, the other tries to plan your life.

The wedding planner isn't dicking around either and

soon we're all ushered around the building to the grassy area at the back of the club overlooking the docks, the sparkling waves of English Bay and the towering North Shore Mountains in the distance. My own sailboat is moored below which is the reason why Will and Jackie were able to have the wedding here. Lord knows someone oughta take advantage of that perk.

It's not long until I'm paired up with the Asian bridesmaid who introduces herself to me as Tiffany. She's cute, young, and smells like champagne. From the way her face is going red, I can't tell if she's embarrassed or just has a low tolerance for booze, though the more she talks to me, the more I realize she probably doesn't embarrass over anything.

"Wait a minute," I say, pulling away from Tiffany and addressing Will as he stands beside the minister. "Who is walking Alyssa down the aisle if Ted is walking Jackie down the aisle?"

"This is what you get for missing rehearsal dinner," Tiffany says, yanking at my sleeve. "You're walking us both down the aisle."

"Lucky me," I tell her, looking around for Alyssa. "So where's the hot blonde?"

"Did you just call her a hot blonde?" Tiffany asks.

"I might have."

"Well hot blonde went to the washroom. Do you have a name for me?"

Tiffany is staring up at me with warm, slightly tipsy eyes. I play this carefully.

"Hot non-blonde."

"You Hollywood types are all the same," she says with a roll of her eyes.

"Oh, you have experience with Hollywood types?"

She gives me a pointed look. "I'm a receptionist for a movie studio. D'uh."

"But you deal with VFX and animation. Those aren't Hollywood types. Those are stoners and nerds."

She sighs. "Don't pop my bubble. Pretending those nerds are Hollywood royalty is the only thing that gets me into the office most days. That and the donuts."

"Places, places," the wedding planner calls out, trying to do this thing with her voice so it's a yell and also a whisper. It just sounds like she has laryngitis. She frantically waves at me and Tiffany to come join her behind the rows of seats, some guests still filtering in.

As we approach, she also manages to snag Alyssa as she comes back from the washroom.

"Remember your cues," the wedding planner says to us, her eyes lingering sternly on me for a moment too long before she jets off somewhere.

"What are the cues?" I purposely ask Alyssa, trying to get her to say something.

But Tiffany pipes up. "Follow our lead. That's what you get for skipping."

"Skipping?" I repeat, looking at her. "This isn't high school, non-blonde. I was working."

At that Alyssa makes a scoffing noise that eerily reminds me of the noises Madison makes when she's unimpressed. AKA when she's not in the bedroom.

That puts a bad taste in my mouth.

Of course the bad taste goes away when I start imagining what other noises Alyssa might make. You know. In the bedroom.

I stare at her openly and she holds my eye contact for just a second. Just long enough to see that her eyes are a very clear blue. "Something in your throat?" I ask her.

She just frowns at me. She's a tough nut to crack.

"Anyway," Tiffany says loudly. "We're supposed to wait for the cue and then we walk down the aisle. You in the middle, us on either side. Like this." Tiffany sticks her arm around mine and then grins up at me. "You know I love your new show," she says.

She sounds completely sincere. "Thank you," I tell her.

"Alyssa and I were just discussing earlier that you should have a male/male scene with you and Boomerang."

This isn't the first I've heard this. Lots of *Boomerang* fansites ship the hero and the villain together. What does interest me is that Alyssa was roped into this conversation.

I give Alyssa a smirk. "Oh really? You were discussing me? You know, I don't think we've actually met. Maybe I should introduce myself before I give you the privilege of my arm."

I can tell she's trying not to roll her eyes. "Will introduced you already."

"Are you always this prickly?"

Her frown deepens.

"Like a cactus," Tiffany says.

Then the music starts up. The slow romantic strains of a piano playing...the theme song to *Jurassic Park*?

"Interesting," I comment.

"It was Ty's choice, Jackie's son," Alyssa says, keeping her eyes forward to where Will is standing by the minister at the end of the aisle.

"Ah, she speaks," I remark.

Her eyes flash to mine. "I just spoke to you two seconds ago."

"Uh," Tiffany says, looking between the both of us. "Have you guys met before or something because there's enough animosity and unresolved sexual tension to fill a million episodes of Moonlighting."

"You are way too young to know about Moonlighting," I tell her. "And, as you can see, I haven't quite met her yet." I stick out my hand and say. "Hi Alyssa, I'm Emmett. It will be a pleasure to walk you down the aisle today."

But before Alyssa can shake it (if she was even going to), a hush comes over everyone and the music changes from the plinky plunky piano part to sweeping strings.

"That's our cue," Tiffany says.

I offer my elbow to Alyssa.

"You have to take it now. It's the rules," I tell her, strangely determined to win this prickly bitch-hot blonde over.

Once she does, I press her hand harder into my side and lean into her. "You know they both warned me to stay away from you."

She turns to face me and this close I can see the streaks of grey in her eyes. There's also fire in them. Rebellion. Just what I wanted to see. "Who did?"

Now I have her attention.

I just shoot her a grin and I start down the aisle, a girl on each arm.

CHAPTER 2

ALYSSA

"*J*'m going to throw up."

I roll my eyes at the statement and put the window down so some fresh air gets in the limo.

"Oh, please, *please* don't," Jackie says, gathering up the hem of her wedding dress and staring at Tiffany reproachfully. "The last thing I need is to get vomit on my dress at one p.m."

"As opposed to vomit at one a.m.?" I ask, reaching for the last of the champagne so that Tiffany isn't tempted. I can see her wavering eyes focus on the bottle, momentarily distracting her sorry ass from the fact that she wanted to throw up a second ago.

"I'd like to keep my wedding as puke free as possible, thank you very much," Jackie says, then reaches across to grab the champagne from my hand.

"You know," I say, watching as she pretends to drink straight from the bottle. I put my thoughts on hold as I grab

27

my phone and take a picture of the delightfully unladylike sight. Will is going to get a kick out of it. "I have to say I thought you'd be the one feeling sick."

She frowns as she hands the bottle back to me. "For the last time, I'm fine. I'm not nervous. I'm cool as a cucumber."

It's true. And it's annoying. And probably a sign that her and Will are really meant to be together, as if that wasn't already apparent.

In fact, Jackie has to be the most chill bride I've ever come across and I've been to a hell of a lot of weddings over the last few years. Your late twenties is prime wedding season where everyone you know, from high school frenemies to family friends and random co-workers, are tying the knot and you get to go to every single one of them.

Alone.

Yeah, that's the other problem. During the summer months, finding a date to a wedding is next to impossible. I'm starting to think there's a business idea in men and women as wedding dates for hire, of course in this city the males would be in high demand. I'm not sure if there's more women than men here or that the male dating pool sucks (and I can attest that it does) but all the guys have to do is snap their fingers and a woman will be conjured up in front of them. It's *I Dream of Genie* but with sex. Meanwhile all the women are fighting over a remotely eligible man like they're duking it out over the last ham on Christmas Eve.

But, I promised myself I wouldn't dwell on it. Not today. Today is Jackie's day. And despite our friend and co-worker Tiffany having too many mimosas at breakfast, everything is working out beautifully. It's a sunny and warm summer afternoon with not a cloud in the sky, Jackie is looking absolutely stunning in her designer wedding dress (low-cut Grecian style top with a poufy skirt), her golden-brown hair flowing in sleek waves over her shoulders.

As her bridesmaids, Tiffany and I don't look half-bad either. Even though Tiffany's head is currently half-hanging out the window, her updo is staying intact and her makeup is perfect. Jackie's colors for the wedding are blue and hot pink, so we were able to pick whatever style of dress we wanted so long as the color was an exact match. Tiffany is thin and tiny, so she's rocking the classic strapless cocktail dress while I've got an empire waist and fluttery sleeves to hide my fluffy arms and stomach. The only problem is that my cleavage is bordering on vulgar so I have to keep reminding myself to pull up the neckline and make sure the girls are in check.

"I'm feeling better!" Tiffany suddenly exclaims, straightening up and looking at both of us with wide eyes.

"Did you just do a line of coke when we weren't looking?" I ask her.

She looks at me absolutely horrified, which was the point. Tiffany is twenty-one, still lives at home (which is actually smart in Vancouver's vicious housing market), and for all her bluntness, dry humor and quirks, there are still a few things that shock her. Mainly drugs, co-ed changing rooms and farting. When you work with a person for a long time, you end up learning a lot about them.

"I don't think I've ever done day-drinking before," she says as way of explanation.

Jackie and I exchange a look. As the oldest of the group, my look is the most weighted.

"No day-drinking? How did you survive high school? Or college?"

"I studied and got good grades. You try having my parents. I didn't even have a sip of wine until I was seventeen and at my Uncle Lin's wedding."

"Oh Tiffy Whiff. What are we going to do with you?"

"You can start by not calling me Tiffy Whiff."

I shrug and sit back in my seat. Despite being the oldest,

I'm still the one who is single. Tiffany has a long-term boyfriend, Ken, and Jackie of course is getting married today.

She's also pregnant. No, it's not a shotgun wedding. They only found out last month or so. Of course, I'm absolutely thrilled. Everyone is, especially Will and most especially Jackie's nine-year-old son Tyson, whom she has from a previous relationship. The baby wasn't expected at all but sometimes the best things in life catch you by surprise.

I look Jackie over again, beaming at how beautiful she is, how radiant she looks. If anyone deserves eternal happiness with a sexy gentleman like Will, it's her.

"Make sure you eat enough," I tell her. "You barely touched your avocado toast."

"Did you know avocado toast is why I can't afford to buy my own house?" Tiffany pipes up.

I'd heard that shit before. Newspaper articles blaming everything from avocado toast to social media as the reason why millennials can't afford a house. In Vancouver it's because a tiny tear-down house in the city is worth over a million dollars. I have a job that pays well and yet I still have to live with a roommate. And no, I don't eat my weight in avocados, even if I look it.

"I'll try," Jackie says. "I haven't had an appetite."

"Too nervous?" Tiffany goads.

"I told you, I'm chill," Jackie reminds her. "I'm chill. I'm good. I'm great. Cool as a cucumber."

I narrow my eyes thoughtfully. The lady doth protest too much.

"As cool and cucumbery as you are," I reassure her, "you have nothing to worry about. The rehearsal last night went fine. The ceremony will be over before you know it and then it's time for you guys to have fun."

"I never said I was worried."

"I know you didn't…"

"Do you think Ty is too old to be a ring bearer?" she suddenly says. "What if he doesn't want to do it and is only trying to make me happy?"

"He's not too old and you can tell he likes the responsibility. He wants to be a part of it all."

"What if Emmett does something stupid?"

"Cruiser McGill!" Tiffany exclaims, clapping her hands together.

I sigh. I've never met Emmett Hill, Will's friend and fellow groomsman. I have, however, heard a lot about him. I mean, everyone in Canada knows who he is. He was on the reboot of *Degrassi* as Cruiser McGill, the nice boy next door, for what seemed like forever. I never actually watched the show but I saw his face a lot.

And I never really thought much about it. That's kind of the way it is with Canadian TV. Lots of faces on mediocre, poorly-lit shows, faces you don't bother attaching to any names.

That's not to say Emmett still has the same face. He was always cute but he's managed to get sexier as he's gotten older. Now he's on some ridiculous superhero TV show and everyone is swooning over him left, right and center. Granted, as I said, he's sexy. He's got this permanent smirk and sexy stubble and light brown hair you just want to run your fingers through. Plus, abs for days since the network tries to show him as shirtless as possible (which doesn't really make sense when the guy is a villain and it's not *Baywatch*, but whatever).

But regardless of him being hot, he's still a dick. I know I don't know him enough (or, you know, at all) for this judgement but meh, I'm going to do it anyway. Maybe there's some gossip site or media bias, but all I see of him now is news of him dating this actress or that model or whatever and then just acting like an asshole to the public, like swearing at the paparazzi and being an overall doucheburger. I'm not always for this country's tall poppy syndrome wherein we like to cut down those on the rise to keep them humble, but if Emmett is a poppy, then someone oughta start plucking his petals off.

Also, he wasn't at rehearsal dinner last night and he has the task of walking both Tiffany and I down the aisle since Jackie's dad is also the best man.

"He'll be fine," I tell her. "That's not for you to worry about anyway. He's Will's friend, that's Will's problem."

"Will's problems are my problems," Jackie points out, not looking convinced. "That's how relationships work. Hey, give me the champagne. I want some for real this time."

"No way," I tell her. "You're pregnant."

"But my doctor said a glass—"

"You're pregnant and you need your head on straight so you can remember every detail of the wedding. You're as cool as a cucumber, remember?"

She nods at that.

I drink the rest of the champagne.

By the time we arrive in front of the grand building of the yacht club, Jackie is back to pretending everything is okay again. I have to admit, as much as I like seeing her be real and human before the wedding, it's easier when she pretends she doesn't have a care in the world.

We are ushered inside the building to a chartroom upstairs where we're briefed by Janice, the over-zealous wedding planner with big teeth, while Jackie talks to the minister. Then Ty comes in and provides child-like relief from the vibe that's growing more serious by the second.

Finally, Tiffany and I are sent downstairs to wait for further instructions. We decide to stand around in the front with some of the more important wedding guests like Jackie's grandparents and catch some sun while we're at it.

"So have you seen that show, Boomerang?" Tiffany asks me.

"No," I tell her. "You know I don't have cable."

"It's on Netflix."

"I'm sort of over the superhero shows. Plus, that one sounds dumb. What's the guy's power again? Being Australian?"

"Being a hot Australian. And he can turn back time for one minute. Hence the title. And the catch phrase. *The world can change in one minute*." She says the tagline in a throaty and terrible Australian accent.

"Right. And Emmett is the villain."

"Yes. You would love him."

"I doubt it."

"You would. I think I know your reading tastes by now to know you're a sucker for the alpha anti-hero. That's what Emmett plays. Doctor Cole Black. Or Doctor Death."

"He looks cheesy," I tell her, neglecting to mention that he also looks hot.

"You think he's hot though," she says, studying me with pursed lips.

I shrug my shoulders. "I'm not a fan of blondes." I know his hair is really light brown but I tend to swoon over the darkly handsome types. You know, the ones with thick, dark hair and dark eyes that make them look all hot and brooding.

"He's got brown hair, Alyssa. He's not blonde. And he's hot. I can show you a million pictures of him with his shirt off."

"I've seen them."

"Have you seen the pictures that people have Photoshopped of him and Julian Crane together?"

Now this has my attention. Aside from being a sucker for romances with a brooding alpha asshole, I also like my m/m novels. "What?"

33

She reaches into her pearl-trimmed clutch and pulls out her phone. I watch as she scrolls through her photos. She legit has folders for every TV show, comic and movie. Also one for WWE wrestling which is weird.

"Jeez Tiff." I whistle. "I had no idea your fandom was this bad."

"Oh yeah," she says proudly and she stops on some very well edited images of Emmett Hill in compromising positions with Julian Crane, the rugged, Australian actor who plays Boomerang.

Damn. That is hot.

"If the show was about them two hooking up, then I would watch it," I tell her.

"Speak of the devil," Tiffany says in a hushed voice and I look up from the pervy images to see Will, Ted and Emmett walking toward us from the end of the driveway.

They look like a trio of James Bonds out to fight crime and find pussy. I know, it's a weird (okay, inappropriate) thing to say when two of them are your boss but hear me out. For one, Will is absolutely gorgeous. Tall, striking, with thick dark hair (what did I just say about darkly handsome types), a beautiful smile and a real python in his pants. I'm not being a perv, it's just the way he is and I dare anyone not to notice when he's wearing certain materials. Even from all the way over here I think I can see the shadow of the thing. Then again my eyes are trained to search for it.

Don't tell Jackie.

For two, Ted, also my boss, and Jackie's father, and Will's best man, defines the term silver fox. He's like Anderson Cooper's older, straighter cousin. He's handsome in the way Cary Grant got handsome even when he wore thick, black-rimmed glasses and had hair the color of snow.

For three...well, damn. It's not like Emmett can tell that I'm giving credit where credit is due, but in person, here, now, I can totally understand the appeal and the hold he has, not only on the hot actress of the week, but on all the people I know who constantly fawn over him.

He's taller than I expected too, since most people on TV are short. Maybe six feet, which is perfect for me even when I wear heels. He also has this way he moves that's hard to put my finger on. I pick up a lot on that with people, their walk, the way they operate their body, how they occupy the space they're in. Emmett has a strut that's borderline cocky, yet there's a fluidity about him that's unmistakable. My brain trips over itself as it tries to recall something I'd read somewhere, how he was doing musicals in London for a long time before he started up his career again with *Boomerang*. He must know how to dance.

So yeah, he moves like his body knows how to move and then there's his body itself, which looks perfect in his tuxedo, with broad shoulders like a swimmer (did he compete in swimming before he got the role on Degrassi or was it hockey?), a slim waist, long legs.

And, as he gets closer, I really take in his face.

Gone is that boy-next-door. Oh, there's traces of it with his wavy, shiny hair and winning smile, but there's a look to his eyes that's far more man than boy. Brooding and primal in one moment, playful and mischievous in the other.

Of course the closer he walks to me, the more I have to look away. The man obviously has an ego I don't want to add to. I don't know what it is about actors and models or just guys that ring an eleven on the handsomeness scale, but I have some kind of aversion to them. Actually I have an aversion to cocky men in general. I've seen firsthand what damage an ego can do.

Will makes the introduction and everyone around us immediately starts talking about *Degrassi*. I've never been so proud to have not watched the show before. Admitting you don't watch it is akin to saying you don't like Bryan Adams or ketchup chips and you think Justin Trudeau's butt is just "okay."

I mean, don't get me started on Bryan Adams. The song "Run to You" makes my blood boil. Have you ever listened to the lyrics?

But we're obviously all here for a wedding, not to talk about Emmett, and soon Janice comes back and tells us to get in our places.

As Emmett and Will walk ahead of Tiffany and I, I get a whiff of Emmett's scent. It's fresh, like soap or shampoo, and something a bit herbal. Rosemary? Whatever it is, it's bracing and I like it, enough that it awakens the heat between my legs.

Crap. When was the last time I got laid? I start counting back the weeks to my last date, a guy named Nels I met on Tinder. The date ended in sex but it didn't end in an orgasm. Not for me, anyway. It was just as well, the guy was all sorts of intense in an abrasive, creepy way. I sure know how to pick 'em.

Still, even though I have no real interest in Emmett, it doesn't mean I shouldn't look good for Jackie's wedding. I steal away to the bathroom for a moment to freshen up my face and give myself a good once over.

I look better than I normally do, I'll say that much. The makeup artist Jackie hired is a total professional and did an amazing job. My blue eyes look even bluer thanks to the rose-gold tones of the eye shadow and my pale skin looks warmer with the strategic layering of bronzer and highlighting. My normally thinner upper lip looks plumped up with nude lipstick and liner and I swear she's done some magic with contour powder under my chin.

But when I look away from my face and at my body, I wince. Even though the dress is super flattering, I didn't wear

Spanx and you can see every lump and bump if you look closely.

No one is going to look closely, I remind myself.

But it's hard not to be critical. In a city where everyone is thin and fit and perpetually wearing yoga pants, I feel like I standout like a sore thumb. I'm currently a size ten after working my ass off for the last six months trying to drop two sizes to fit in this dress and I still don't feel good enough. I've got muscle and I'm stronger but I've got a layer of fluff that won't budge. And most of the men here don't want the fluff. I'm a Marilyn in a Gigi Hadid world.

Luckily I know how to fake confidence. I throw my shoulders back and strut out of the building and to the grass where Tiffany and Emmett have gathered with Janice.

What's interesting about Emmett is the more I try not to look at him, the more he looks at me. I know this because I have well-honed peripheral vision. I can practically read out of the corner of my eye. That said, I honestly can't say why I'm having such a hard time taking him in–maybe I think if I stare at him too long I'll get sucked into some hot guy black hole where I'll lose all sense of self-worth.

Actually, I'm correct. Because when I finally do meet his eyes for a moment, I'm momentarily stunned. Unable to look away. And my heart does this funny skip and a hop, like I've got some newborn bunny in there taking its first stumbling steps.

At this range his eyes are vivid, ice-blue, like the lake water in New Zealand where I backpacked when I was twenty. They're beautiful.

And he knows it. I can see that self-awareness in his eyes too.

I try not to look at him again, even when he asks me questions and makes small talk and especially when he calls me "prickly."

Fuck yeah I'm prickly. I wear my cactus badge with pride.

Then the romantic strains of *Jurassic Park* start to play and it's our cue to start walking down the aisle. I reluctantly take Emmett's arm as Tiffany gleefully takes the other.

Then he leans in close, so close (too close) I can smell the mint on his breath.

"You know they both warned me to stay away from you," he says, his voice low and rough enough to make the hair on my arms stand-up.

What?!

"Who did?" I ask.

The bastard just grins at me like he's got a secret he can't tell.

CHAPTER 3

ALYSSA

*W*ho told Emmett to stay away from me? Is that more for my protection or for his?

It's got to be Will and Ted. Jackie wouldn't say that. Would she? Then again, she said in the limo earlier that he might ruin shit.

I'm thinking all of this while Emmett, Tiffany and I are slowly walking down the aisle like some celebrated ménage.

I try to snap about of it, pasting a big smile on my face as we pass by all the guests. I'm still smiling even when I look at handsome Will at the altar, nervously waiting for his bride.

Was it you? I think to him but he's got a big, shit-eating grin on his face and I know I'm the least of his concerns right now.

I take my place with Tiffany and keep glancing around Will to see Emmett, hoping he'll give me a hint. For once, he's not looking at me.

In fact, he's doing the right thing and looking straight down the aisle as Jackie and Ted make their appearance.

And just like that, I force myself to pull my head out of

my fat ass and concentrate on the big moment, the main event, the couple of the year.

Beautiful Jackie slowly making her way down a rose petal strewn aisle on the arm of her father. Ted is grinning from ear to ear. And beside me, Will is stiffening up. I sneak a glance at him and see tears building in his eyes.

Oh my god. Is this going to make me cry? I've been to a dozen weddings over the last few years and none of them made me even remotely tear up. It's not that I have a black heart or I'm soulless. I'm just...what was it again? Prickly. Thorny. And those are only because of a build-up of cynicism. Eventually the prickles will build up enough to become a coat of armor. Or something.

But this time my emotions don't stand much of a chance.

The ceremony is absolutely beautiful.

It doesn't matter that Jackie picked the shortest version because she didn't want to bore people. It could have been two hours long of them up there, staring at each other, holding hands and talking and I wouldn't have complained. I can't think of a more romantic couple out there. Even their vows–which they each wrote, of course–had me tearing up.

Especially when Jackie promised to be "all in" for Will and Will promised to forever be her Prince Charming.

Cue the waterworks.

Then they kissed–one hell of a deep, sweet, emotive kiss–and everyone clapped and hooted and hollered and the flood down my face just got worse.

"Oh my god," Tiffany whispers to me as Will and Jackie hold hands, going down the aisle and waving at everyone with Ty in tow. "Your makeup is getting ruined."

"Oh no," I mumble and notice Emmett and Ted making their way over to us.

To Ted's credit he looks extremely misty-eyed which is probably why he doesn't fire any zingers my way. Emmett, however, is raising an eyebrow as he glances me over. Amused.

I turn away from him with a scowl and grab my clutch I'd placed on a chair. While everyone starts getting up and heading into the building to the reception area, I slyly check my face in the compact. The makeup artist had the intuition to put on waterproof mascara but there are still tracks where my tears ran over my blush and foundation. I discreetly touch up my makeup while sniffling and try to get a hold of myself.

Stay prickly, I remind myself, only because I know if I'm getting weepy and emotional over Jackie and Will and their ever-so-sweet romance, I know it's only a matter of time before I get depressed and hopeless over my own dating situation.

I should probably stay away from more wine, that's for sure.

Luckily, the next hour or so is distracting while we watch Will and Jackie take their wedding photos. At one point, Emmett takes us down to the docks so they can pose on his boat.

It's a nice looking sailboat, I have to admit, as far as sailboats go. I mean, it's not sinking and it has a mast and looks like it cost a lot. That's really the extent of my sailboat knowledge. Emmett seems completely at ease on it too. The boat's name is called Sick Buoy which I know is a Social Distortion song. His humor in naming the boat catches me off guard and endears him to me for just a second.

Then it goes away when I remember what he said earlier.

When we all start heading back along the dock, I impulsively reach out and grab the sleeve of Emmett's tux, pulling him back so we're the last ones.

"Hey sunshine," he says to me, raising his brows at me in

surprise. "Feeling better? You cried more than Will did up there."

I glare at him. "I'm fine. Just caught up in the moment. Hey, what did you mean they warned you not to talk to me."

"Actually they said to stay away from you," Emmett says, lowering his voice, his eyes darting up toward Will and Ted. I knew it!

Also, his eyes are kind of dreamy.

Also, shut up Alyssa.

"Will and Ted," I say, gritting my teeth as if they're the names of a life-long nemesis. "Did they say why?"

He shrugs. "They only had nice things to say about you. Don't worry."

I feel a little bit better. "Then why did they say it?"

"I don't know. I guess they think I'll corrupt you."

I don't want to smile but I am. I'm strangely touched by Will and Ted's possessiveness. And like reverse psychology, the fact that they want me to stay away from Emmett actually makes me want him. Not enough to do anything about it but I have rebellion in my blood.

Then there's the fact that if Ted and Will warned Emmett to back off, that means Emmett must have shown some interest in me. Right?

"Do you think I should listen to them?" Emmett asks with a cocksure smile that makes my limbs feel all hot and gooey. His eyes skirt all over my face, resting on my lips. "Or try and corrupt you anyway?"

I can feel my face burn up. I should have worn sunscreen today.

"What are you guys talking about?" Tiffany says, staring at us suspiciously over her shoulder as she walks, now starting to trail behind.

"Nothing," I tell her, starting to walk faster to catch up with her.

But my dress is long.

The docks are rough.

It catches on a splinter of wood and then I'm stepping on it in my heels and pitching forward, trying to stop myself from falling, the movement sending me sideways.

Falling over like a tree into the cold, dark water.

Only I don't hit.

An iron grip wraps around my forearm, keeping me in place.

I stare down at my reflection in the water for a moment, my face pale and shocked against the charcoal-blue, and it's like I'm suspended in time. I imagine everything around me paused while I'm hanging between the dock and the water.

And then I'm yanked back to reality.

I'm on the dock and Emmett is pulling me to him. It was his grip that saved me.

How the fuck did he manage to pull my heavy dead-weight back on the dock without going over himself? Is he more superhero than villain?

"Are you okay?" he asks, brow furrowed in concern. The breezy quality of his eyes has changed to one of intense focus.

I blink at him, my heart racing.

Tiffany looks horrified as she comes over. "Oh my god, Alyssa, you were this close to getting eaten by a shark."

"There are no sharks here," Emmett tells her.

"Wanna bet? She has the worst luck with animals. If there are no sharks, she'd at least be molested by a porpoise. *At least*."

While they talk, I glance over her shoulder at the others and they head up the ramp. So far no one noticed how I almost ruined everything. It's not like I had a spare bridesmaid dress in case this one went for a swim.

"Yeah," I say, wetting my lips before my gaze drops to his

hand still tight around my arm. I kind of like the fact that he's still holding onto me. Which is why I say, "You can let go of me now."

"Are you sure?" he asks. "Because you seem like you might fall over again. Can't say you're the first woman to fall for me."

I narrow my eyes. "Don't flatter yourself. It's this stupid dress. It doesn't belong on a dock."

"I think maybe you don't belong on a dock," Tiffany says, taking my hand and pulling me toward her until Emmett lets go. "Come on, let's get on dry land before something worse happens."

We head up the ramp toward the building and as we walk I can feel Emmett just behind me and my arm is still throbbing where he grabbed me. Man, he must have the strength and balance of…well, I hate to use the superhero adjective again. But that was impressive.

So he saved you from falling in the ocean, I tell myself. *So what. Anyone would do that.*

I know I'm telling myself these things so I don't fall for his charms.

And it seems to work.

My raging hormones don't stand a chance against the jaded landscape of my brain.

"I think he likes you big time," Tiffany whispers to me later as we get our food from the buffet table. I wish Jackie's nervousness had passed on to me because I want to eat everything here and I think I just might. It's too bad I don't like working out as much as I love eating.

"Who?" I ask Tiffany, scanning around the reception room. Everyone at their tables is staring at us longingly since we get to go first for food. I feel like I should pile my plate extra high, just to rub it in. Heh heh.

"Your hero," she says, using a crab leg to point to me for emphasis. "The villain."

I roll my eyes. "He is not my hero."

"I just saw him save you from drowning."

"I know how to swim, Tiff."

I look past her down the table to where Emmett and Ted are starting to pick at the salad selection. Just as I suspect, Emmett takes a huge heaping pile of lettuce, enough that it takes up most of his plate. He probably has to eat really well to stay in such good shape. How boring.

I decide to grab extra dessert later out of some weird kind of spite.

"Why don't you like him?" she asks.

I glance at her. "What do you mean?"

"You bristle every time he's near or I'm talking about him. It's like you're a shifter and all the hairs along your back are poking out."

"You really do paint the strangest pictures."

She shrugs. "Anyway, I think he wants to get in your dress."

I don't know why but what she's saying is bringing out so many conflicting feelings. On one hand, of course he does, he's a womanizer. On the other hand, I'm a far cry from his flavor of the week. When you've had my backlist of dating disasters, it's hard to believe that anyone would be interested in you, especially an extremely hot actor who can have anyone he wants.

"I don't like guys like him. You know this."

"Babes? You don't like babes? Because Alyssa, he is such a babe."

"Such a babe," I repeat, shaking my head. I hadn't heard that term in a long time. "He's a babe. Fine," I admit and then something glowers in my heart. "But he reminds me too much of my father. And some exes I've had. I know his type. I know what they do to women. What my father did to my mom. They aren't faithful. They aren't reliable. They're never in it for the long run."

Tiffany's expression softens. "Oh." She smiles up at the cook who's cutting off a slice of roast beef and then lowers her voice. "You've never mentioned your father before."

I sigh. "It's nothing." Nothing I want to get into here and now.

"But aren't all your sisters married with children?"

My sigh deepens. "Yes. That doesn't mean all their marriages are amazing either. Anyway, we probably shouldn't be talking about this at a wedding of all places, especially not Jackie and Will's."

"Well, we both know their happily-ever-after is for real," Tiffany says.

But when we get back to our table, my eyes go to Emmett as he continues to get his food, this time getting extra portions of roast beef. Damn he gives good back.

"You could just sleep with him?" Tiffany muses, stabbing a vegetable with a fork as if it had done something to her. "Forget marrying or dating the guy. Just have a one-night stand. Who says he would want anything more anyway."

Ouch. But good point.

"I need more wine," I tell her, reaching for the bottle. "Let's talk about something else."

It's always a trip when you let Tiffany dictate the conversation. She launches into a tirade about people who dress their dogs in tiny raincoats.

But as dinner goes on, I continue to stuff my face with food as if that will bury the swirling emotions inside and when I'm bloated and ever-so thankful that my dress has an empire waist, I continue with the wine.

Looking around the tables at all the happy couples, I'm getting pulled down into that desperation spiral, the hopeless (and predictable) "what's wrong with me?" phase of the evening that happens at every wedding. And it's not even that everyone here is paired off, of course there are some single people. I see Casey, a guy I work with who would be okay if he wasn't such an inappropriate creeper and if he didn't look like Joaquin Phoenix during his hobo phase. I'm pretty sure he's single for good reason though.

There's a few other single guys and girls from work, then of course all the other people. I know being single isn't a disease or a tragedy by any means and I would way rather live by myself forever than settle for someone who isn't right for me. But at the same time, you start to worry if you'll ever really find that one who gets you for you. I know I'm a handful—what are the odds that I'll find a man that I love who wants to put up with all that?

"How are you holding up?" Jackie asks as she sits down next to me to take off her wedding shoes and slip on a pair of white flip-flops. I've been watching her dance with Will and her father but when it came time for everyone else to dance, I conveniently disappeared to the washroom.

"How are *you* holding up?" I ask her. "You still look beautiful, by the way."

She smiles shyly. "That's good. I'm good. I just feel so bad, so many people want to talk to me, they're practically standing in line. I feel like a cast member at Disneyland. Meanwhile I just want to pull a Ty and go pass out in the coatroom."

I laugh. "He's got the right idea. Will you think it's cute when I do it later?"

She looks me over. "You don't seem that drunk yet."

"Oh, just watch me," I warn her.

A tall presence looms behind me. Both Jackie and I twist in our seats to look up at Emmett as he grins down at us.

47

"Jackie," he says to her. "I was wondering if I could steal your maid of honor for a dance."

Jackie tries not to smile as she looks at me. "Are you sure? I think she needs a few more drinks before she's remotely enjoyable."

"Then I'll make our first stop the bar," Emmett says, holding out his hand for me.

I stare at it for a moment. It's a nice hand. Large, tanned. Slightly weathered, as if he's outside a lot building cars or something in his spare time.

I should probably refuse but Jackie looks way too happy at the thought of me dancing with Emmett, so I give him a polite smile and put my hand in his. He brings me to my feet with ease.

"How are you doing, blondie?" he asks me as we skirt around the edges of the dance floor. I notice that he hasn't let go of my hand yet, which is kind of nice and kind of not.

"Obviously I'm not drunk enough," I tell him, though when we stop at the bar I realize I'm a few drinks away from being too drunk. It's a fine line to tread.

"We'll fix that. What will you have?" he asks.

"Surprise me," I tell him.

"You'll let me order for you? That's a bold move."

"I'm a bold gal," I tell him, meeting his eyes.

They crinkle at the corners when he smiles and when he smiles I feel the air leave my lungs.

It's a famous smile and its impact in person is pretty remarkable.

Tiffany was right.

What a fucking babe.

He turns to the bartender. "I'll get two Manhattans."

"Manhattan," I remark when he looks back to me, leaning casually against the bar. "No wonder you're friends with Will. He orders Old-Fashioneds all the time. I actually have a minibar in my office specifically for Ted and Will's daily drinks."

Emmett laughs which shoots all sorts of lightning down my spine. "That doesn't surprise me. I was wondering what it would be like to work for those two."

"They're a barrel of monkeys," I tell him. "They at least keep you on your toes, even if they make running things harder sometimes."

"They said the place would fall apart without you," he says. "You must be pretty important."

I shrug. The fact is, as nice as it is to hear that second hand from them, I don't feel important at my job. I'm an office manager and have been for a long time now. I know I shouldn't complain about my job when it's a pretty good one. Easy. Reliable. But sometimes I lie awake at night thinking about where it could all go. I don't really have an interest in visual effects or animation so it's not like there's any advancement for me in those areas. It's like job-wise I've peaked and I know that most people are happy having a dependable job that pays well and they don't hate but sometimes I...well, I have to wonder if this is it? Is this really the rest of my life?

The fact is, I have dreams. Small dreams that fester in the depths of my heart, dreams I push aside. But my dreams require money and a lot of risk and I just can't spare any of those at the moment. I'm not sure when I ever will be able to.

"I'm pretty good at keeping people in line," I finally admit.

"I can see that," Emmett says, looking me up and down. "How can someone be so soft and prickly at the same time?"

I glare at him. "I assure you I have no soft spots."

His mouth quirks up, his eyes dancing with a heat that's hard to ignore. "I can see plenty of soft spots right now."

My eyes narrow even more. "I realize you're talking about my breasts now."

"Breasts, ass, thighs," he says casually. "All places I'd like to sink my teeth into."

Oh my god.

Did he really just say that?

"What's wrong with you?" I ask him, feeling flushed all over.

But he doesn't look ashamed at all. Just flashes me that panty-dropping smile again. Luckily, I didn't wear panties today, so it doesn't work on me.

"Oh, blondie, there is plenty wrong with me," he says, taking the drinks from the bartender as he passes them over. He hands me mine which I reluctantly take while he shoves a fifty-dollar bill into the tip jar. "There's a reason they warned me to stay away from you, remember?"

"Right. The corruptible part. I'm starting to think they were right."

Then he grabs my hand again and leads me to the corner of the room where the wedding presents are piled. "And I'm starting to think that you aren't easily corrupted."

"Does being this sleazy usually work for you?" I ask.

He looks at me in surprise and for a moment he almost looks hurt. Then it fades into a cunning smile again. "Yes. It does."

"The perks of being a famous actor," I tell him just as he takes out his phone and glances at it, frowning. "Popular, too," I nod at his phone. "Is it your girlfriend of the week?"

He gives me a loaded stare. "My publicist," he says after a moment. "Who, no, isn't my girlfriend."

"What does she want?" I shouldn't pry but I'm so curious.

He sighs, putting his phone away and having a large swallow of his drink. I can't help but stare at his tanned throat as he does so. "You don't follow any gossip sites?"

"Sometimes. I like Perez now that he's not so bitchy anymore."

Emmett nods. "I got into trouble last night."

"Oh really." I swear he looks ashamed for a moment. "And what did you do this time?"

"Some fuckhead was filming me on his Instagram, harassing me, goading me to do something crazy."

"And did you?" For all that I've heard about Emmett recently, crazy could be a number of things. I really hope that he didn't punch anyone in the face though, because I'm not too fond of brutish violence.

"I took his phone and smashed it," he admits, looking down into his drink as if he's consulting the Manhattan as to whether he made the right choice or not. I'm not sure what the drink whispers back because then he nods and says, "He completely deserved it. I don't feel bad in the slightest."

"Fair enough," I comment. "Though you'd think you'd learn to control your temper at this point."

He stiffens and his eyes blaze darkly as he looks at me. I've touched a nerve. "Control my temper?" he repeats, then shakes his head and looks over my head at the dance floor. "You have no idea."

"Try me," I tell him. "Half the people here at this wedding work with me. Take a good look. Most are potheads and drunks and I have to handle them. Have you ever had to answer questions like 'how do I make a copy?' and 'why isn't my internet working?' day after day? Believe me. I don't have the patience of a saint but I have to control myself. For my job."

"If I didn't know any better, I'd say you were lecturing me," he says, his words sharp. "Do you have any idea what it's like to be me?"

I roll my eyes. "Oh woe is me, huh? I bet having all that money is a fair enough trade for being tabloid fodder. There's nothing worse than a privileged celebrity complaining about this kind of shit. Do you ever stop for a moment and realize the rest of the world would kill to have your problems, especially when you're bringing all of this on yourself?"

Emmett's eyes never leave mine as he finishes the rest of his drink. Totally. Intense.

"You're not as nice as I thought you were."

"Because I'm telling you the truth and people hate that. Believe me. Especially men who think they have their shit together."

He raises his brows. "Wow. Is the alcohol making you worse or better? I can't really tell."

I give him a quick smile. "I'm always like this. Prickly, remember?"

"I think I'd rather focus on the soft bits again. Finish your drink." He nods at it. "Let's dance."

I don't like being told what to do. And though I love dancing, I'm not a fan of slow dancing, especially with someone I don't really know.

But there's a dare in his eyes. He thinks I won't do it.

I drink the rest back and place it on a high table. "Fine."

He breaks into that grin of his, the one he's famous for, that makes him look absolutely boyish.

Fuckin' babe.

Wish it didn't cause that ache between my legs but fuck, I'm pretty sure he knows it.

He grabs my hand, squeezing it tight as he leads me to the dance floor then pulls me close to him, wrapping his arms around me.

Holy crow. It's like being held against a brick wall. We're dancing way too close to each other than we should be and yet even if I felt like putting distance between us I don't think I could. That iron grip from earlier is back but this time it's holding every part of me.

And just as I suspected, the man can dance. His movements are fluid, graceful. We don't just rock back and forth like kids in a high school gym, we glide.

I close my eyes briefly and can't help but breathe him in. He smells delicious.

"Have a good whiff?"

I open my eyes and look up, our faces inches apart as he gazes down at me, lips twitching in amusement.

"It's okay," he goes on, his breath smelling cherry sweet, "I'm used to fans trying to smell me."

I don't give him the satisfaction of acting embarrassed. "I'm not a fan of yours. Believe me."

"You say that," he says, lowering his mouth to my ear. He whispers. "But I bet if you give me two minutes, I can change your mind."

I try to ignore the wave of shivers rushing down my spine. "Do I dare ask how you plan to do that?" I ask but my voice is uneven.

"I think you know," he murmurs, one of his large hands slowly slipping down the small of my back and over my ass where he gives me a subtle grab.

My eyes widen and I look around, wondering if anyone is watching us.

Actually someone is.

Fucking Casey. He's dancing with a woman called Mona, staring at us openly as he does so. His forehead is lined in surprise. I glare at him until he looks away.

"I'm more of a show, don't tell, kinda guy," Emmett adds.

"You're so full of yourself," I manage to say, bringing my attention back to him.

"With good reason," he says, his voice becoming husky as lips brush against my neck. "Just what I thought. You taste sweet. Only your attitude is sour."

"Excuse me?" I say to him, pulling back to glare at him.

"It's okay, I'm starting to like it."

"You're earning it."

"You're earning this," he says, pressing himself against my hip. My god. He has a fucking erection. "Earning every single inch."

Part of me is horrified. I mean, who the hell does he think he is? What makes him think he can just shove his cock against me and I'll be okay with it? If he does this all the time, it's no wonder he gets in fights with people. Cocks aren't hugs you can just go around handing out.

But then the other part of me is insanely curious and, yeah, turned-on. Because he feels fucking divine. Even just like this, I can feel his entire hard length and it's beyond impressive. And the fact that it's because of me is something I'm having a hard time wrapping my head around.

"You still want to take that bet?" he asks. "Two minutes to change your mind about me."

I swallow hard and give him a pointed look. "Two minutes isn't very long."

"I'm a realist," he says, glancing over my shoulder. "I've got my boat right down there."

"No thanks," I tell him quickly before I can be tempted. I've had my fair share of one-night stands and hook-ups and lord knows I need to get laid by someone who knows what he's doing and with his cock and his strength and the way he moves, I have no doubt he'd be a sure bet. But sleeping with Emmett would be a mistake and one I'd probably hate myself for tomorrow.

Even though he would, no doubt, be the most gorgeous man I'd ever be with.

Luckily, the song ends and I manage to pull myself away from him. "I think I need another drink."

I take off toward the bar, hoping I leave Emmett behind me.

CHAPTER 4

EMMETT

*S*hit. Alyssa is stubborn as hell.

And I'm standing in the middle of the dance floor, watching her fine ass as it goes to the bar.

I breathe in deep through my nose and adjust my pants while flashing a smile at the tiny senior couple dancing next to me as the next song starts up.

She can't lose me that fast, though.

I stride over to the bar and just as she's about to put her order in to the bartender, I place my hand on her shoulder and intercept.

"Two Manhattans," I tell him smoothly, "and hold the liquor."

The bartender gives us a look and then shrugs.

"I don't get you," Alyssa says to me. "One minute you're trying to get me drunk, the next you're ordering me a non-alcoholic drink."

"It's not a real Manhattan unless it's made with Crown Royal. Which this bar doesn't have." I grin at the bartender. "No offense, of course. I'm sure the groom made sure to stock all of his favorites."

"And you snuck your own booze into a wedding?" she asks me.

"You've never been here before, have you?"

She shakes her head. "Does it look like I get wined and dined by the yachtie set?"

"Hey *I'm* the yachtie set."

"You're something all right."

Fuck. I can't stop staring at her lips. I could watch her throw sass my way all night.

When the bartender hands me our drinks, I take both and motion with my head for Alyssa to follow me. "Come on."

She doesn't move. "Where are you going?"

"To get the booze. Come on."

"Alyssa," Tiffany says, seeming to appear out of nowhere. She's drunk again, stumbling a bit but smiling. "Where have you been?"

"Hey hot non-blonde," I tell her which makes Tiffany's eyes light up. "How did you get drunk so fast? Again?"

"She can't hold her liquor," Alyssa explains.

"The Asian curse," Tiffany says with a laugh.

"Not a curse, a blessing," I tell her. "Your friend would be a lot easier to seduce if she was a lightweight."

Alyssa smacks me across the arm. "Shut up. You're the one who just ordered me a Manhattan with no booze."

"Oh Alyssa is super easy to seduce," Tiffany says. "You should see how many guys she sleeps with."

A ragged gasp falls from Alyssa's mouth and I laugh.

"Tiffany!" she exclaims.

"What?" says Tiffany, oblivious. "I only know this because you tell me every single detail from your dates. You always said there's no shame in just getting fucking laid when you need it. So you should probably take Emmett up on his offer so I can hear about it."

"Two minutes," I playfully remind Alyssa, wagging my brows.

"Fuck you," she says to me, and then looks at Tiffany. "And fuck you too."

Then she storms off.

I look at Tiffany in surprise. "Man, she is hard to read."

Tiffany shrugs. "She's simple when you get to know her. You must not be used to women giving you the brush off."

Considering the amount of wedding guests who've approached me for an autograph tonight, she's right.

"It happens," I say taking a sip of my drink and then feeling severely disappointed when I remember there's no booze in it.

Since I have no idea where Alyssa has gone, I tell Tiffany, "If you see Alyssa, tell her to find me."

"You think she listens to me?"

"I'm feeling lucky."

Then I leave the ballroom and head down the plush-carpeted hall, past the walls lined with charts and nautical flags, all the way to the locker room. It's a long-standing tradition here for each member to have their own locker. Their purpose is solely to house bottles of booze. That way when you're dining at the yacht club you can just drink from your own stash.

The locker room is long, filled from top to bottom with narrow wooden lockers and mine is located around the corner near the end. I bring out my tiny key from my jacket pocket and unlock it, sliding out a half-empty bottle of Crown Royal. I haven't been at the club all that much since *Boomerang* got started but I make a mental note to take the boat out one free Sunday.

I pour the Crown in both drinks, unsure if I'll actually see Alyssa again and lean against the lockers, enjoying the quiet.

I'm not sure what it is about Alyssa that has me so

intrigued. It's probably a lot to do with being given the brush-off, even though I know that she likes me. Or, maybe she doesn't like me per se, but she wants me. And the fact that I can tell she wants me, that I've seen her checking me out, the lust in her eyes, makes me want her even more. It's her brain that's holding her back. I have to find a way to shut that off.

I sigh and swirl around the glass before taking a gulp. The silence here is good. As much as I love Will and am happy for him, events like this take a lot out of me, especially when I've been working non-stop. I need solitude more and more lately, the more that people want me, the more I need to pull away. The only problem is finding the balance. While I crave alone time when I'm being spread thin, I can't handle too much of it. Loneliness has found me many times before, always the wolf lurking outside.

My phone vibrates again. I don't even bother looking. I know it's Autumn because she's been texting and calling for the last two hours. Guess she did find a pocket of cell reception in the middle of the mountains. You'd think that all that fresh air would have calmed her down a bit but when I talked to her earlier, she sounded angrier than I've ever heard. Of course, being as that I pay her for her services, you'd think she'd still have a level of decorum with me but that ship has sailed. Now it's like I have a full-time babysitter.

Honestly, I don't see why it's a big deal.

Okay, I guess I can see why she's freaking out. Kept telling me that I was getting in dangerous territory and that this could even jeopardize my contract with *Boomerang* or any other work in the future. No one wants to be uninsurable. Just look at Lindsay Lohan.

That's not what I want. Fuck. Half the time I don't know what I want.

I close my eyes and lean my head back again.

"Here you are."

I must be dreaming. I open my eyes to see Alyssa standing among the lockers. Her hip juts out to the side, one hand on it, full of fucking sass.

"And here you are," I tell her, unable to keep the grin off my face.

"Double fisting?" She nods at the drinks in my hand.

"Only for you," I tell her, holding hers out to her.

She hesitates, her eyes jetting from the drink and back to my face. "What is this place, anyway? The seducing room?"

I chuckle, looking away briefly. "It's where the club members keep their booze. The locker room."

She steps toward me, running her fingers over the wood walls. "Such a fucking rich guy thing, isn't it? Don't you all have booze on your fancy ass boats?"

"We do," I tell her. "But sometimes we're lazy." I pause, watching her carefully. "I'd be more than happy to take you to the boat though, show you around."

"Not interested."

"And yet here you are in the seducing room, looking for me."

"I was looking for my drink," she says breezily. She stops in front of me and takes the drink from my hands. I hang onto the glass for a few seconds too long, staring intently into her eyes before I let go.

She holds it in her hands, stares down at the liquid. Before my eyes, a wash of vulnerability comes over her, softening her features. She's almost delicate.

It makes my dick ridiculously hard. Then again, what doesn't.

"I just wanted to apologize for earlier," she says quietly, avoiding my gaze.

"For what?"

"For telling you to fuck off. Not a very nice thing to say to a stranger."

"I thought it was hot."

She rolls her eyes. "You would."

I shrug. "I think everything you do is hot. Just standing here right now with that pouty lip and your soft eyes and your gorgeous tits. I'm getting fucking hard as cement."

Shocked, she meets my eyes and for a moment it really looks like she's going to throw the drink in my face. I'm almost flinching. Second nature, I suppose.

I gesture to it. "Drink up, sunshine."

"You're unbelievable," she says, shaking her head in disdain. But the annoyance is short-lived. She doesn't throw the drink in my face, she doesn't turn and walk away. Instead she stays and has a sip of the Manhattan.

That tells me I can push this as far as it can go.

I take a step toward her until she's backed up against the wall and with one arm above her head I lean against the lockers, nearly fencing her in. "How is it?" I ask, keeping my voice low, my face closer to hers.

She swallows and I swear she purposely licks her lips. "It's very good." She glances up at me through her long lashes. "You were right about that one."

"I'm right about most things," I tell her. "I bet you're absolutely gorgeous when you come."

Even though I know she's getting used to me, she still startles when I say that, unable to keep from reacting. Of course she'd be gorgeous when she comes, she's gorgeous when she looks totally blindsided.

"You have quite the mouth on you, you know that?" she manages to ask smoothly.

I nod and slowly reach out, brushing her silky strands over her shoulder, my eyes fixated on the creamy slope of her neck. "I know. My mouth would love to take you down to the boat, spread your legs wide and bury my lips against you. I'll lick and suck your sweet pussy for hours before I fuck you hard with my tongue."

She stills, her eyes shimmering with want and shock and a million other things and I know I've got her.

I reach down and wrap my fingers around hers on the glass and lift it up to her lips. "Finish your drink. Then I'll fuck you whichever way you want."

Her eyes narrow and I can feel the heat from her gaze. I can't tell if it's sexual or anger based but either way, I think I finally crossed a line.

"Does that work on every girl you try and sleep with?" Her voice is raw.

"Normally other women don't make me work so hard."

She laughs dryly. "Oh my god. Emmett. You're insane. Can your ego get any bigger?"

"No and my dick definitely can't either," I tell her, grabbing her hand and placing it against my crotch where I'm straining against the tuxedo pants.

She gasps but her hand still grips me, hard enough that my eyes fall closed, wanting, needing more of that delicious friction.

"You see what you're doing to me?" I whisper to her. "Why I have to work so hard?"

She clears her throat as I close the tiny gap between us. "You call spouting off lines from erotica as working hard? Please, I eat romance novels for breakfast, you're no different from the vapid dirty-talking alphas I read. I wouldn't be surprised if you had a Kindle highlighted with all the best lines to try."

If I wasn't so turned on and determined, I'd be laughing at that.

"Except that I'm real and I'm here, right now. Don't you think it's time you got fucked by someone who knows how?"

She couldn't look more unimpressed. "Why the hell do you think I'm not getting properly laid? That's mighty presumptuous of you."

"I can just tell."

"Oh yeah? Can you tell I'm about to walk away and leave you to deal with your massive erection on your own?"

And at that, she turns on her heel and starts walking away.

Damn. She wasn't joking.

Without thinking, I reach out and grab her arm, pulling her back and into me. One hand goes behind her head, the other around the small of her waist.

She looks at me with big blue eyes.

She knows what's about to happen.

The risk is if she likes it or not.

A risk worth taking.

I kiss her, hard enough that she gasps, breathless, my lips pressed flushed against hers until she yields, her mouth opening. She moans into me, my tongue sliding in sweet. God, she tastes like sugar and spice, better than I imagined.

My hand buries into her hair, tilting her head so I can kiss her with everything I have. I know I've been watching her all night, wanting her, wanting this, but I've never felt such a primal need until this moment. The urge to be inside her, deep, fucking deep, is all I can think about.

I hear the glass drop from her hand, bouncing on the carpet, while my tongue and lips work feverishly against her mouth, a searing, rhythmic kiss. I brush my hand over her breast until I feel her nipple harden underneath the material.

A groan escapes her lips which only deepens my drive. I pull the edge of the fabric aside until her breast pops out, her nipple rosy and stiff. I lower my head and suck it gently into my mouth before giving it a gentle bite.

"Oh god," she whimpers, her hands sinking into my hair and holding tight.

I smile against her tit then take my other hand and reach down her thigh until I'm gathering up the fabric until it's at her waist.

"I bet your pussy is just as wet as your mouth," I murmur to her, my breath hitching as I slide my hand between her soft thighs.

She makes a greedy little sound of surprise that deepens just as my fingers skirt over her pussy.

No underwear.

Wet as sin.

Christ, I think I've found heaven.

"You're ready to go," I tell her, as I quickly reach back into my pocket and pull out a condom. While I tear it open with my teeth, my other hand keeps rubbing her mercilessly before slipping two fingers deep inside her.

"Oh god," she says again, opening her eyes to look straight into mine. They're lazy with lust, sparking with fire. I'm going to make this so good for her.

Deftly, I take my cock out of my pants and slip the condom on just as she wraps her legs around my waist, digging her heels in.

Fuck, fuck, fuck.

This already feels too good.

I'm about to go into a frenzy.

I quickly push into her with one quick, brutal thrust that wrings all the air from my lungs.

She gasps, my mouth biting at her neck, my hand yanking at her neckline again, taking her nipple back in my mouth until she's writhing, moaning.

"Fuck," I groan, slamming her back against the lockers, my pumps becoming faster and faster, like I'm trying to impale her on the spot. We kiss and it's messy, teeth clacking against each other, lips and tongues trying in wild desperation to win.

"Emmett," she gasps and I think maybe I'm fucking her too hard. Her head is starting to slam back against the lockers, her nails are digging into my suit jacket.

But when I look at her, she gives me a look that ignites me.

Her wet mouth open, her blue eyes languid with lust.

"Fuck me harder," she says. Her voice is all sex.

"Jesus," I swear. She's a wild one. I start grunting into her neck as my pace picks up, sweat dripping from my brow and onto her chest. The fact that anyone could walk around the corner and see us only heightens the sensations, makes me extra aware of her sexy little gasps as I slide my fingers over her clit, the hot feel of her skin.

"I'm coming," she moans, eyes closing, head rolling to the side.

For a moment I think she'll stifle her cries–she knows there's a wedding reception just around the corner. But she doesn't. She lets it all go.

"Fuck, fuck!" she yells hoarsely, her fingers holding tighter and tighter as she pulses and jerks around me. "Oh, god, *Emmett.*"

I can only grunt in response as I watch her. I was right. She is gorgeous when she comes.

Then my orgasm sneaks up on me, a total force of nature.

It rips through me, fast, violent, uncontrollable.

Unbelievable.

"Fucking hell, woman," I groan into her as I feel myself empty into the condom. She's getting every last drop out of me.

I collapse against her, sweat dripping off my brow and over my nose. I can hardly breathe but I don't care. I'm shuddering on the inside, completely unraveled.

This sexy stranger, this prickly thing. She might just be the best lay I've ever had.

I can't even think straight.

"Are you going to let me down?" she asks after a moment, wrapping her hands behind my neck for support.

"Maybe," I tell her even though I grab her waist and she unhooks her legs from around me. I pull out, grabbing the condom by the end, then pull it off and tie it.

Meanwhile she smooths out her dress, puts her tits back in place. "Well, that was…"

"A long time coming," I tell her as I put the condom in the trash and pull my pants back up.

She laughs dryly. "You have a strange concept of time."

"Hey, I wanted you all night, sunshine. Looked like my dreams weren't going to come true for a while there."

She rolls her eyes and bends over to pick up the glass she had dropped.

"Well, now that the sexual tension is all out of the way," she says with a smirk, "how about we go back to getting drunk."

"Who said it was out of the way?" I ask her, pulling her into me and giving her a long, deep kiss. Fuck. She's a great kisser. If she gave me another five minutes or so, I could go again.

She smiles against my lips and then playfully pushes me back. "Come on, you made all these promises. Fill 'er up."

Dutifully, I do as I'm told. I fill up her glass with Crown Royal, fill up mine and the two of us sit down on the carpet, leaning against the lockers, drinking the liquor straight.

"Cheers," I tell her, clinking my glass against hers. "To Will and Jackie."

"To Will and Jackie."

"And the best two minutes of your life?"

She bursts out laughing. "And to that too."

CHAPTER 5

ALYSSA

There's a landslide inside my brain.

Deafening.

Giant slabs of stone slicing off the mountains and tumbling to the ground in a cloud of dust.

Boom. Boom. Boom.

Each impact makes me jolt, brings an array of sharpened knives into my grey matter.

What the fuck is going on?

Boom. Boom. Boom.

It gradually turns into knock, knock, knock.

As in someone at my door.

Carla.

"Go away," I mumble, my mouth desert dry. I try and open my eyes but I think my fake eyelashes are glued to each other. Did I not take off my makeup? Am I even in my bedroom?

Oh my god, please don't tell me I'm still in my clothes.

I feel down my sides, my hands skirting over voluminous silk.

There is no worse feeling in the world than waking up

the next morning in the clothes you wore out drinking. In this case, my bridesmaid's dress. It's a sign that you totally failed and got beyond trashtastic. Not washing off your makeup before bed? That's bearable. But not even managing to get undressed? That's close to getting your adulting card revoked.

And then I'm hit with a memory.

The feel of Emmett inside me as he slammed me against the locker walls, the hoarse grunts from his throat as he came.

OH MY GOD.

And then Carla opens the door.

"I had to make sure you weren't dead," she says. I don't even have to open my eyes to know the look she has on her face: totally unimpressed. You know, my normal expression when I'm not waking up the morning after a wedding. There's a reason we get on so well as roommates. Plus, there's the fact that she's a stoner and extremely low maintenance.

"And?" I croak, blinking at the light that's coming in my window. Vile, horrible light. "Am I dead?"

"You look like you died in the middle of your prom. Please tell me you at least got laid."

I can't help but grin. In fact, I'm not just grinning up at the ceiling like I'm high, I'm laughing.

"Oh boy," Carla says. "I've got pickle juice ready if you want a quick fix."

Even though a hit of pickle juice is essential to any hangover recovery methods, I'm still laughing. Because, OH MY GOD.

I totally got fucked by Emmett Hill last night.

Cruiser McGill.

Bruiser NoChill.

Doctor Death.

And whatever else name he has.

And even though I know I should be deeply ashamed by all of this, I'm not.

I mean, he was good.

He was really fucking good.

Best fucking cock I've got in a very, very long time.

Maybe ever.

I'd be sad about it if the endorphins weren't still running through me, faint but present.

"Should I call a doctor?" Carla asks, approaching the bed warily.

I shake my head and then stop immediately. The pain makes me wince and yet I'm still smiling. "I'm fine, I'm fine."

"Then what's so funny? Usually you're moping around for a few days after a wedding and eating all my chocolate. In fact, I bought a few extra bars because I expected your wallowing."

"No moping, just…" I slowly ease myself up and give her a lazy grin.

"You *did* get laid," Carla says, patting my leg. "Good for you. With who?"

"You wouldn't believe it if I told you."

"You know I'm gullible," she says, sitting on the edge of the bed. "Do I need to get a coffee for this? Popcorn? Pot cookies?"

I bite my lip, buying time while I figure out what I should say. There are no secrets between Carla and I. It's hard for there to be when you're both like-minded people sharing a 600 square foot apartment. Whenever we come home from our dates or hook-ups, we give each other the play-by-play.

But this time it feels a bit different. Not because I don't want to jinx it or anything. Honestly, I'm not planning on seeing Emmett again. Hell, we didn't even exchange phone numbers and I was completely okay with that.

It's just that…Emmett isn't anonymous and I'm not a star fucker. I mean, I'm anti all that shit (not that this opportunity has ever come up in my life before). Carla knows that too, which is why it all feels so weird.

Plus, there's the fact that he totally screwed me in public. I'm obviously not shy when it comes to sex and one-night stands but I've never had sex in public like that. A locker room in the yacht club where any drunken sailor–or wedding guest–could come in and see us with my legs wrapped around his ass, his thick cock driven deep inside me.

Fuck. I'm throbbing between my legs just thinking about it. I have a feeling once I start moving I'm going to be sore, like his body has made its mark on me.

"Alyssa," Carla says slowly, studying my face in such a way, like a detective, that I know there's no point in lying.

"Okay but promise you won't tell anyone."

She rolls her eyes, throwing up her hands. "Who am I going to tell? Don't take this the wrong way, but my friends don't care about my roommate's sex life."

I tilt my head. "Well, they might."

Carla just stares. "Spill the beans or no pickle juice for you."

"Jeez, hard bargain." I take in a deep breath and try to say it as normally as possible. "Did you ever watch Degrassi?"

She's totally puzzled. "Yes…wait, the new or the old one?"

"The new one."

"Then yes…why? Why?! Did you sleep with Drake?!"

I have never seen her look so excited before.

I shake my head. "You know that stupid superhero show, Boomerang?"

"With the hot Aussie? Yes. Alyssa…what are you…"

And then she starts to put it all together, her brow furrowing, her mouth gaping slightly.

"Oh my god. You didn't…you didn't sleep with that other guy, did you? What's his name? Cruiser McGill!"

I shrug. "Less sleep, more straight-up fucking."

"Noooo," Carla says in disbelief. "You didn't."

I raise my hand, dip my head. "Guilty."

"What's his name again? Emerson?"

"Emmett."

"How did that happen? I mean…he was at the wedding?"

"One of the groomsmen. Will's best friend, other than Ted of course."

"Hold up," she says, pulling out her phone and Googling his name. "This guy."

Of course it's a pic of Emmett from *Degrassi*, when he was all fresh-faced and floppy-haired. It was almost impossible to picture him as the man that fucked my brains out last night. The man from last night knew exactly what to do with my body, playing it like a fine-tuned instrument, even if we only had a few minutes with each other.

"He's all grown-up, Carla," I remind her. "And he is packing heat."

She gives a giddy squeal and starts pulling up more photos. One of them is from a recent photoshoot where he's shirtless. I'd felt those muscles under my hands last night, how hard and big and toned he was. Though he was clothed with me, the picture of him here doesn't even encompass everything he is.

Watch yourself, a loud voice in my head sounds off. *You're starting to sound like you're crushing.* I make an attempt to rein myself in.

"So where did it happen?"

"In this room with all these tiny wood lockers where rich yachtsman keep their liquor bottles." I go on to tell her how persistent he was all night with me, not to mention the stuff that kept coming from his lips. I have never in my life been around someone more forward. In fact, it was borderline off-putting.

Okay, it should have been off-putting. Maybe that's why this thing bothers me a little bit. It's not that I slept with Emmett Hill, it's that I slept with a guy who knew he could get me into bed and had no problems acting like it. I don't mind honesty in people but in some ways I wish I hadn't succumbed to someone so outright cocky.

When I'm done describing the night, Carla lets out a low whistle. Only she can't whistle so it comes out as a high-pitched squeak. "I'm not exactly up-to-date with celebrity rumors but I guess what I've heard is kind of true."

"Which is?"

"Manwhore about town."

I sigh. "Yeah. Well…obviously I'm one of his victims."

"Oh come on," she says, getting off the bed. "You needed a good romp and you got it. You came right?"

"Hell yes." My voice is blissful. "Haven't come that hard in forever."

"TMI," Carla says. "Didn't need the details. But seriously, who cares if he's a manwhore? You got your fun. You're not going to date him, right? Now you have a fun story to tell and you got the dick you needed."

I guess the real problem here is, it is a fun story but one I wouldn't repeat. If I had slept with like, I don't know, Chris Evans, I'm sure it wouldn't stay a secret. It would feel beyond special. But Emmett Hill? He's probably with someone else tonight, maybe even right now.

"Wow," Carla says as she stares down at her screen, scrolling around. "He broke someone's phone last night. A fan or something was trying to take his picture."

"Actually it wasn't a fan, it was a dickhead who was stalking him and putting it on his Instagram, live video, trying to trip him up." I'm strangely defensive.

"Oh okay, that sucks," she says, reading something. Then suddenly her eyes bug out. "Oh my god!" she exclaims.

"What?"

"Oh my god, Alyssa! Look!" She shoves the phone in my face. "Am I that high, or is this *you*?"

It takes me a moment to adjust, my eyes tired. What at first looks like a random couple kissing comes into focus and I realize it's not a random couple at all.

It's me.

And it's Emmett.

At the wedding, when we were hanging out in the hallway after we had sex. That limbo period where we drank the rest of his Crown Royal and just acted like...well, like a couple.

At the time I had remembered that it was strange to go from hooking up to kissing and hanging onto each other like we knew each other well. Strange because it was both a foreign feeling and something that somehow felt right.

But whatever it felt like didn't fucking matter because holy crow, there are pictures of us kissing.

I snatch the phone from her hands and start violently scrolling down. There are pictures of us holding hands, me leaning into him, another with his arm around me and he's laughing. It looks far more intimate than it was. I just remember being drunk and laughing a lot. That's it.

Hell! And the pictures are on Perez Hilton of all things.

"Alyssa," Carla says.

"I know, I know, what the hell." My voice is shaking, my heart racing. I'm sure some people dream about making Perez's radar but I certainly don't. Thankfully as I read the short article, Perez calls me a mystery blonde.

Then he goes on to mention that it's nice for Emmett to find a girl who is, and I quote, "a nice, curvy, normal looking girl, not those gorgeous, young actresses he's always with."

I'm stewing over that too much to even realize that Perez is painting the scene about us as if I'm Emmett's girlfriend instead of a hookup. Right. Because Emmett would never just have sex with someone as big and "normal" as me.

"This isn't good," I tell her, my hand starting to shake.

"I wonder who took the photo?" Carla says. "Whoever did it probably got a lot of money for it. Was there paparazzi at the wedding?"

I shake my head, trying to think but the pounding in my brain is back with a vengeance. "No. I don't think so. Maybe? I mean, I didn't recognize everyone. Will has a hell of a lot of contacts and many are in the film business, so it could have been anyone."

"You should find out. And then set the record straight. Email Perez and tell him you're the mystery girl."

"Why would I do that?"

"I dunno. Because Perez Hilton, like, the most popular celeb gossip blogger in the world, is implying you're a couple and you're not a couple. Unless you want to keep up the charade..."

"God no," I tell her quickly, trying to imagine what my sisters would say. God, I would never hear the end of it. We don't keep in touch much but they would surely reach out over this shit. And then there's everyone at work. And Jackie and Will.

Oh my god, Jackie and Will.

I have to tell them. They have to hear it from me before anyone else. They have to know the truth, especially after they specifically warned Emmett to stay away from me.

If only he listened. I knew I was showing too much cleavage last night. I practically lured him between my legs.

I put my head in my hands, tossing the phone on the bed. "Aaaaargh," I moan. "I don't know how to deal with this shit. Usually my sex life stays pretty damn private."

"Hey, at least there isn't a picture of you actually having sex," she points out. She picks up her phone and starts going through it again for a minute while my brain stutters, trying to figure out what to do. "Just Jared is reporting it. And so is TMZ. They're following Perez's lead and saying you're, well…anyway, a new girl and it could be something serious."

"Oh my god!" I exclaim. "How are they getting that info? We hooked up. End of story!"

"They're spinning stuff, this is what they do. Everything that gets reported in the tabloids and shit are half-truths."

"Well what is this half-truth?"

"It's not like it's not what it looks like. You did sleep with him right and did all this cuddly shit after. That's the half-truth. They're just stretching and speculating. You know most people don't believe everything they read."

I wish that was true but it's only getting worse these days.

"Anyway, what's the worst that can happen?" Carla asks.

"You just said I needed to set the record straight," I remind her, exasperated.

"Just trying to figure this out. If you look at it from another angle, it's actually pretty cool. Or at least funny."

"How is it either of those things?"

"Because you're on all the gossip sites because you had sex with Hollywood's current bad boy and now everyone in the world thinks you're his girlfriend. It's pretty fucking funny."

But I'm not even amused in the slightest. Carla decides to make me breakfast to wake me up and help me cope and while she does that, I frantically try to get a hold of Jackie or Will. But of course they're on their honeymoon to Mexico and are probably in the air.

"Maybe no one will notice," Carla says as she watches me shovel bacon into my mouth. "And it will all blow over. I mean, do you even remember the names of the girls that

Emmett's been with before? No. There's always someone else. I'm sure in a few days there will be some other girl he'll be caught sucking face with and it will all be over. Plus, they don't have your name. So there's that."

I think about that for a moment. It doesn't necessarily sting. I knew that it was a one-night stand but again it makes me feel utterly disposable. And I'm starting to think that there's a good chance they could get my name. Obviously whoever was at the party and took the photos could find that out pretty quick.

Shit. What if it's someone I actually know. Like, personally.

As in, someone I work with.

Casey. Fucking hell, it's probably Casey. Casey who seemed way too interested in us on the dance floor. If he found that part interesting, I'm sure he'd do the same if he caught us kissing.

Then again, I have to be sure before I make any accusations. As much as I don't really like Casey, especially as I've been brushing off his sleazy advances as of late, and as much as I feel like firing blame at the first person I can think of, I know I have to hold off until I know for sure.

"So you don't have Emmett's number or anything?" Carla asks me, reaching over to pour me a cup of coffee. Usually she's not this doting, it's like I'm sick or something.

It's not far off. My hangover is still lingering and I'm sick to my stomach over the fact that there are secret photos of me circulating the entire world.

"No we didn't exchange numbers," I tell her. "What was the point? It was what it was."

"And apparently a hell of a lot more to the rest of the world."

"We'll see," I say with a sigh just as my phone beeps. It's a text from Tiffany.

All caps.

OMG YOU'RE FAMOUS! DID YOU SEE?!

And then she sends a million links and screenshots of the infamous pictures.

When it stops I text: *Old news Tiffy. Now I need you to find out who took those fucking pictures! Do you know who it could have been?*

NO IDEA! She replies. *BUT LET ME PUT ON MY THINKING CAP.*

Tiffany's thinking cap isn't always screwed on properly, so I'm staring at the phone for a few moments, waiting for her to reply and come up with something when there's a buzz at the door.

I glance at Carla. "Are you expecting someone?"

She shakes her head and goes over to the console on the wall, pressing the button. "Who is it?"

"Is this Alyssa Martin?" A raspy voice says.

The same raspy voice that told me I was gorgeous when I came. Who told me he wanted to fuck me hard with his tongue.

Oh. No.

"No this is Carla, who is this?" Carla says, obviously not recognizing Emmett's voice like I do.

"Does Alyssa live there?"

"Who is asking?" she volleys back.

Meanwhile I'm staring at her with wide eyes, not sure what the hell I'm going to do. I'm at least out of my brides-maid dress but I haven't showered, I'm in just a baggy t-shirt and shorts and my hair and leftover makeup is a greasy gross mess. I am not the girl from last night, not by a long shot.

"It's Emmett. A friend of hers."

Carla lets go of the button and gasps. "Oh my god, Alyssa!"

"I know!" I yell right back. "We aren't friends! What do I do?"

"You let him up!"

"Why?!"

"Because you need to figure this shit out with him. You're in it together."

"But–" I start to protest but she's jabbing the button forcefully.

"Come on up!" she yells into it then whirls around, clapping her hands together. "This is going to be fun."

"You're worse than Tiffany," I tell her with a groan.

"For shame," Carla says. "I'm just glad that things will be sorted out. I didn't sign up for a famous roommate. By the way, you should probably change."

I glance down at my wanton bralessness and know I look like a hot mess. I know I want to go change, make myself look presentable, then I remember I shouldn't care what Emmett thinks.

And there's also not enough time. Our apartment is on the ground floor and now Emmett is knocking at the door.

Carla goes to answer it but I quickly brush past her. I don't even know if I want Emmett in the apartment not with everything that's going on, and Carla would probably sit him down and start cooking him breakfast too, telling him my entire life story and especially all the embarrassing bits.

With my hand on the knob, I take in a deep breath and open the door.

And there he is.

I hoped, hoped, hoped that it was the excess alcohol and the sappiness of the wedding that skewed my memory of him, making him more attractive in my head.

But that is not the case at all.

Here, today, in the sobering light of the hallway, he's tall and deliciously broad-shouldered, in a faded charcoal t-shirt and dark jeans that look as fantastic on him as the suit did. Maybe even more so because now I can make out the hard lines of his chest, the bulge of those huge biceps and thick forearms, the very arms that held me up last night like I weighed nothing at all.

And then there's his face. It's absolutely boyish with that wide, cheeky smile of his, his blue eyes twinkling. My stomach shouldn't be doing flips at the sight of it and *he* certainly shouldn't be smiling given the circumstances, but this is what's at my doorstep today.

To think I didn't want to open the door.

"Hey blondie," he says. "Can I speak to you for a second?" And before I can say anything he looks me up and down. "Rough night?"

"Why are you here?" I manage to say, ignoring his comment. "How did you find me?"

"You really don't know why I'm here?"

"How did you find me?" I repeat.

"I have ways," he says, his eyes flitting over my shoulder to Carla. "Hello," he says to her cordially.

"Hey," she responds in a voice that tells me she's trying hard to play it cool.

"So can I come in?" he asks, looking back to me, brows raised, creating lines across his forehead. Somehow it makes him look even more adorable.

I know I have to let him in. That we have to talk about what happened, especially since he went out of his way to find me. But still, I don't move for a few seconds, the two of us locked in some kind of staring contest.

Finally, Carla clears her throat, breaking the tension. "So, thou shalt not pass or what?"

I give Emmett a slight nod of approval and step out of the way, letting him into our place. As he passes by me I get a whiff of his smell. God, it's like an instant aphrodisiac, a lightning bolt of lust straight between my legs. Flashbacks from last night crowd behind my eyes.

"So this is where you live," he says, looking around. He crosses his arms across his chest as he does so, which causes his shirt to rise a little. It draws my eyes like bees to honey and I see out of my peripheral Carla has the same staring problem. Hot damn. He has the stomach you just want to lick right up.

"Cute place," he adds.

"Yeah, sorry you're slumming it at the moment," I tell him sharply.

I can feel Carla giving me a look at that. I'm not sure why I feel the need to take jabs at him.

Except, you know, he's part of the reason of the current mess we're in.

"Anyway," Emmett says, sliding over that with ease and flashing me a reassuring smile. Really wish he would stop doing that. "I'm assuming you know the reason why I'm here."

"Do tell," I say, playing dumb.

He doesn't buy it. "Look, I guess I should have discussed with Will if there were going to be guests at the wedding who wouldn't be respectful with privacy. I wasn't thinking, really, that anyone would be there who would want to take and sell pictures of me."

"It also would have helped if you two didn't screw each other in public," Carla says.

Emmett gives her a questioning look, one with a hint of coldness in his eyes.

"Carla," I admonish her. Then I nod at my bedroom. "Perhaps we should discuss this in my bedroom. And no, it's not an invitation."

The coldness in Emmett's eyes disappears and the grin is back. "Whatever you say."

With a long exhale, I head toward my door and open it, ushering Emmett inside.

Once I close the door behind me though, I'm starting to rethink this as being a good idea. With him in my room, alone with me, suddenly everything seems very small. Everything but him. His presence is taking over.

I lean back against the door, keeping my distance just in case he starts talking dirty again or I catch another whiff of whatever crazy ass pheromone made me jump his bones last night.

"So…" I say.

"So," he says, rubbing the back of his neck and looking mildly sheepish for once. "Look…last night…" he pauses, searching for words, "I didn't think anything of it."

I give him the evil eye of all evil eyes. "Thanks."

"What I mean is…I had a lot of fun with you. You kept me on my toes the whole fucking night. I don't know the last time that happened."

"Well hurray for me then. Glad I could keep you on your toes and our picture all over the damn internet."

"Once I find out who took that picture, you know I'll fucking kill them. You didn't sign up for any of that and I should have been more…aware of the situation. I guess I just…I don't know. I'm not used to this, you know? That people give a shit and give a shit about the wrong thing." He looks off, his eyes absently searching the walls. "I know the last thing you want to hear is the woe is me celebrity thing, I got that from you last night, but the honest truth is I forget that my life has changed and in some ways is no longer my life, no matter how hard I try to keep some things private."

I can't help but laugh. "What do you keep private? I don't even keep up with this pop culture and yet I know that you've hooked up with a shitload of girls, that you're getting in fights, that you're causing trouble on set. What else could you possibly keep under wraps? If the world feels like they know you and own you, it's because *you* let them."

He stares at me blankly for a few moments as if he didn't hear what I said. Then he scoffs. "Forget about keeping me on my toes. Sometimes I think you want to knock me right down."

I shrug. "Just calling it as I see it. As an outsider. Although I guess I'm not really that anymore, am I?"

"No, you're not." He looks serious for once. "And that's why I had to talk to you. You see…I know that this is all new and strange for you and you probably don't appreciate having your photo splashed across the internet, even though they are very lovely photos, of course. You look fucking fantastic."

I don't even bother mentioning the way the sites are humoring the way I look and how different I am from his usual arm candy.

He goes on. "So I can see why this is a shock to you and an invasion of privacy of sorts. But…I don't think this is the end of the world."

I frown at him, crossing my arms. "Come again."

He takes a step toward me, his broad hands raised. "This is going to sound all sorts of crazy but just hear me out, okay?" A beat passes, his mouth quirks up into a half smile. "I have a proposition for you."

CHAPTER 6

*A*lyssa is immediately suspicious. I don't blame her. I mean I just showed up at her apartment when she never told me where she lived and now I have a proposition for her. And I know she's going to get even more wary once she hears what it is.

Not that I mind. She's fucking adorable when she's confused, her cute nose is all scrunched, her mouth is pursed and pouty, all ready to fire some kind of insult or comeback at me.

Fucking hell. I could easily kiss her all over again, get lost in it. And I love how relaxed and messy and real she's looking right now, totally your girl next door except she's a girl next door that turned me into a total savage last night.

But whatever vibes she was giving me last night she's sure not giving them to me today. She's pissed. At me, at the situation. And I totally get it. No one likes their privacy violated.

Which makes what I'm about to propose to her all that much trickier.

To be fair, it was my publicist's idea.

I'm still not even sure it will work.

But I got the message loud and clear.

I don't have much choice.

I rub my lips together as Alyssa stares at me impatiently, waiting for the shoe to drop.

"Autumn, my publicist, thinks that you are just what I need."

She cocks her head at me, taken aback. "Huh?"

"You see, they say all publicity is good publicity and that's not exactly true. Good publicity is good publicity and if you have too much of the bad, you need the good to balance it out. Like anything in life, right. So I've been pretty fucking bad as of late. Now it's time to turn it over."

Alyssa shakes her head. "I don't understand. What does this have to do with me?"

I know I have to tread delicately and wish Autumn was here with me to do this the right way. I'm not exactly known for my tact and Alyssa is especially prickly. Plus, there's a part of me that seems to like pissing her off.

"Don't ask me why or how. I don't understand how the fucking industry works, the tabloids and the gossip sites. I don't know why certain things get hits or seem to attract the public. But the fact is, people are really...*enamored* with those photos. The idea of me with, well, someone like you."

She looks like I just slapped her. I didn't mean for it to come out that way. "Sorry," I say quickly, "I mean–"

"Oh, I get it," she snipes with fire in her eyes. "People think you're all humble now because you're with a fat chick."

Now I feel like I've been slapped. "Fat? What the fuck are you talking about? You're gorgeous. You're perfect."

"I'm ten times the size of whatever girl you're usually with. I'm curvy, I'm soft, I have a cute face. I'm not all angles and bones and fake boobs and long legs and–"

I raise my hand. "Whoa, whoa, whoa. Alyssa. Let's not get crazy here. You're all those wonderful things and people like that. They think it's a good change of pace for me. All of them, all of the comments, they want this to be a *thing*. For the mystery girl to actually mean something to me and not be just some random screw."

"So what?"

"So the fact is, I want to keep up appearances. I want the world to believe that you and I are serious."

Her face is blank. "But we aren't."

"I know."

"We had sex."

"I know."

"That was it. Right?"

Normally I would be careful here because every single time I've been with a girl who seemed okay with a one-night stand or a purely physical relationship, it turned out they always hoped for more or expected more. But with Alyssa, I'm pretty sure she might just hate me, so...

"Right. I honestly never expected to see you again," I admit.

She doesn't flinch. "Same."

"But here I am."

"And you're talking nonsense. What did your publicist say exactly?"

"Autumn. You'd like her. Really. She said that if you were my girlfriend that it would make me a lot more palatable for people right now. The bad boy image apparently doesn't work when you're thirty-eight."

Alyssa stares at me for an eternity, eyes flickering with something I can't read while a million thoughts seem to wage a war inside.

"Your publicist thinks we should date?" she repeats. "How is that even a PR strategy?"

"I assure you she's good. She's been in the business a long time, deals with actors here and in LA all the time. She's got contacts. She's got ways. She was able to get me your address, after all. If she suggests this, I believe her."

She shakes her head, rubbing her hand down her face with a sigh. "It's just…stupid. Why would you even entertain this? Just get your shit together and stop acting like a douche. Is it so hard?"

Ouch. "I'm working on it but this will help. And what will it hurt?"

"You? Nothing. It won't hurt at all. But what about me? Name a single fucking thing I would have to gain by pretending to be your girlfriend? I'm not a famewhore. I like my privacy. I like being anonymous. This sounds like absolute hell."

I frown. "I'm not that bad."

"I think you might just be."

I didn't want to bring up this next part. The part that makes it seem a bit sketchy. But here it goes.

"I would make it worth your while."

She laughs bitterly. "Oh my god. You think fucking me is a selling point?"

"This has nothing to do with sex," I tell her quickly. "You don't have to touch me ever again."

"Good."

"Great," I fire back, eyes narrowing. "This is just for show. We do it for the photos, for the publicity. You'll just be arm candy, someone who's with me in public. You don't need to sleep with me, or sleep over or visa versa or anything like that." I pause. "And I would make it worth your while because I'll be paying you."

Her head jerks back. "You'd pay me to be your fake girlfriend?"

Man, it sounds asinine when she puts it that way. "Yes."

Heavy silence looms over us like a cloud.

Then.

"How much?"

I tilt my head at her curiously. I'm actually surprised she asked. "Whatever you want."

She watches me carefully and comes away from the door, slowly walking toward me. I keep my eyes trained to her face and not her breasts which are swaying seductively under her thin t-shirt. "You're telling me that you'll give me however much I want for this?"

I nod, wondering just how crazy negotiations might get. "Money, privilege, access. However much you want, whatever you want."

"You know I want this in writing, in an actual contract," she says cautiously.

"Of course. Autumn can have the lawyers draw one up tomorrow. So wait, are you actually seriously considering it?"

"I'm considering it," she says. "I'm not saying yes."

"But you're not saying no."

A wry smile plays across her lips as she appraises me coolly. "I wonder how many times you've had to say that."

"You know I'm persistent."

"Like a fucking mosquito."

It's in this moment that I have to take a minute and wonder if this really is the right thing. Because as hot as I find her, as much as she turns me on, I know that being around Alyssa might not always be a pleasant thing. There's a chance I can win her over but there's also the chance that... well, it's the chance I face with most women when they get to know me. If she gets to know me, the real me, she'll run for the fucking hills.

If Alyssa does agree to be my fake girlfriend, she might just make my life a living hell.

"Look," I tell her. "Have dinner with me tonight, with Autumn. You can hear the whole thing from someone else.

86

We'll talk about the contract, about everything. You can just do this for three months, tops."

"That's still a long time," she says. "And it means I can't date during that time. And neither can you."

I hadn't thought about that. "Well, I'll manage," I tell her.

"Whatever you need managing, it won't be me doing it."

I come closer, feeling a flame in my chest. "Did I do something to you to make you hate me this much? You seemed to like me a lot better last night. Don't pretend you didn't, there's photographic proof now."

Her eyes go up to the ceiling. "Just because I let you fuck me, doesn't mean I like you."

"Let me?" I reply, aghast. Fuck that. "You didn't let me. You wanted me just as badly as I wanted you. Explain how your pussy got so fucking wet from just my kiss."

Her nostrils flare and she looks away and I can tell, somewhere inside her, she wants it all over again.

I can't pretend I don't either.

I take another step toward her. With Alyssa, I just need to push. I need to piss her off. I'm starting to think it's what really gets her going. "You fucking want me right now. You want me to strip you naked, throw you on the bed, lick up between your thighs until you're screaming my name again." I lean in close, daring her to meet my eyes. Pure heat thrums through my veins. "You've been dreaming about it all morning. I bet you can still feel my cock inside you. That you're a little raw from being fucked so thoroughly."

She slowly meets my eyes, swallowing audibly. "If I sign this contract," she says, her voice husky. "That means this can't happen."

"What is this?" There's barely any space between us now.

She puts her hand on my chest, holding me back. "You coming on to me. If you're going to pay me to be your girlfriend, I can't sleep with you. I'll feel like a whore."

I didn't think about that. "So let's pretend you don't sign the contract. Would you fuck me anyway?"

"If I didn't sign the contract, I'd have no reason to see you again. So no." She closes her eyes. "I just...I made a mistake last night with you. I can't do it again."

Fuck. A mistake. That's not at all what I've been considering it. And yet I can't blame her for feeling that way, even if it makes me feel a bit fragile.

"Are you saying there's no way you can resist my advances?" I ask her with a grin.

Her lips press together in a thin line as she stares right into my eyes. "The last thing I want in this world is to add to your ridiculous ego but...you make it very, very hard." Pause. Hint of a smile. "Pun intended."

Smarten up, I tell myself quickly. *This might work if you can just back off.*

I nod and straighten, creating distance between us. I need to put on the gentleman act and just fucking behave for once.

"Okay," I tell her, trying to seem as harmless as possible. "I'll keep that in mind. So what do you say? Dinner tonight? If you don't want to do it, then fine. No harm, no foul. But if you do...I promise your life will change. For the better."

"Right. Because being Emmett Hill's girlfriend is that amazing."

"No. Because I'll treat you like a fucking queen, the way no one else has, the way you deserve to be treated. I'll take you to every fine restaurant you want, I'll shower you with gifts and jewels, I'll pay your rent, I'll take you anywhere in the world. And you'll be living a life you've only dreamed of for three months. I promise you I'll make them the best months of your life."

She doesn't believe me. I can tell.

But I can also tell she's up for the challenge.

Just like I am.

"Okay," she says. Reluctant. "Dinner. But this better just be a dinner. I'm not down for threesomes unless they're the male male variety." She taps her fingers along her chin. "Then again, you did say I could have whatever I wanted."

"Let's save the negotiations for later," I tell her. There's an awkward moment where I'm not sure if I should kiss her cheek or shake her hand so instead I just dig my business card out of my jeans and hand it to her. "Now you have my number. Call me if there are any changes but I'll be by at six-thirty."

Then I pat her on the shoulder and leave her room, striding past her roommate on the way to the front door. She was hovering around nearby, obviously trying to listen and not caring if I knew.

"Hopefully I'll be seeing you a lot," I tell her and then I'm out of the apartment.

When I get to my Audi on the street, I take a moment to breathe. I'm having second thoughts again. I mean, I have money but I have no idea what Alyssa wants. I'm curious, of course, because whatever she wants will reveal a lot about her but at the same time, well, I've done my share of gay scenes before in acting but a real life threesome like that isn't exactly up for negotiation. Thankfully, I don't think she's serious.

Then there's the fact that our real relationship–if you can call it that–is a lot messier than it should be for people who have to pretend to be something else. There are a million things that could go wrong, one of them being that if I need to get laid by someone in the next three months, I'll have to be especially sly about it or I'm going to cause an even worse publicity problem. If people don't like destructive, playboy Emmett, they'll *hate* cheating Emmett.

But if Autumn really thinks this will help, and could possibly get me future jobs, then it's a risk I have to take.

All I have to do is keep it in my pants and put up with Alyssa.

Sounds easier said than done.

Regardless, I text Autumn: *She's on for dinner tonight. Sounds interested.*

And then I set off for home.

But once I get to my house, everything seems cold and empty. I have to admit, sometimes the beautiful things feel the most hollow. Even though Alyssa's apartment was tiny and messy, it was full of life and energy. It reminded me of the way I used to live, especially when I was in London and doing theatre. I was often alone, but never really felt it. Being around Alyssa in her space...even for a short amount of time, it felt strangely comforting.

Guilt comes for me again, as it often does when I look at everything I have.

I remember where I came from.

I remember everything I'm still looking for.

It's time to pay Jimmy a visit.

CHAPTER 7

"Are you sure you're okay?" Jackie asks me for the millionth time.

I sigh into the phone, cradling it between my chin and my shoulder while I wash the dishes in the sink. "I'm okay. Really. Go back to having sex with your husband."

Jackie laughs. "You know we were having plenty of sex before we got married. The whole purpose of sex on the honeymoon is to produce a baby and guess what, we've got a bun in the oven."

"And how is that bun making the oven feel?"

"Tired, actually. Plus, the traveling has taken it out of me. And I'm totally showing now, I'm just not huge, so when I walk around in a bikini, people can't tell if I'm pregnant or just extra fat."

"You look extra beautiful and you know it. You better go enjoy that sunshine. And I better not drop this phone in the sink."

"Okay," she says warily. "But text me. I know this whole thing is so fucking bizarre and I really hope no one gives you shit at work tomorrow. If they do, tell them they're fired. On behalf of Will."

"Jackie," I can hear Will playfully chastising her in the background.

"Ha, will do," I tell her. "Talk to you later."

It takes me a moment to dry my hands before I hang up the phone. Normally it's Carla's job to do the dishes but today I needed something to do.

I've cleaned the entire apartment.

Anything to keep my mind off of Emmett.

I even tried to listen to an audiobook while vacuuming but the dirty talk that the hero was spouting reminded me way too much of Emmett. Fucking hell, he's like a book boyfriend come to life.

And I might be his girlfriend.

Fake one, that is.

Ever since this morning when my entire world was flipped upside down, I've been faced with a dilemma unlike any I've ever faced before. Basically, Emmett asked me to not only be okay with those photos, but to actually do more of them. Staged of course, but still. I'll be purposely thrust into the sleazy limelight.

To my credit, my first reaction was no fucking way. I mean, I figured he had practically stalked me and came over to tell me that he was filing a lawsuit against Perez Hilton or something and was going to find out who took the photograph and beat his fucking ass down. But then he opened his stupid mouth and came up with a proposition only an immoral fool would consider. And while I may be loose with my morals sometimes, this was something that really shook the ground I stood on.

But then I started to think about it. Obviously this whole thing would benefit Emmett and I really couldn't give a shit if I help his image or not. He seems to think there's some conspiracy against him, like it's totally unfair that the media is painting him a certain way when he is, in fact, a certain way. They're just reflecting the truth.

Then he said it would benefit me. Money, plus anything else.

And honestly, I could use the money. My savings account is nonexistent, I'm tired of scrambling from paycheck to paycheck. I'm twenty-eight and I feel like I have miles to go before I'm an adult. I want something to fall back on, a sense of security in a life that increasingly feels insecure. Plus, I have dreams that are probably fruitless and futile but money could at least give me a shot at them.

Of course there's also the curiosity factor. The excitement. I'm not really sure what else Emmett could give me and I wouldn't feel right asking for it but when he told me I would be treated like a queen with him, a little thrill ran through me. Every woman dreams about being swept off their feet but the way things have aligned in my life, I'm not sure that's ever going to happen. I've just had a string of dates and short-term boyfriends who never really looked at me as more than just another person taking up space.

Does that make me epically shallow, the fact that I'm considering all of this just to feel special and doted on? Maybe. But for the first time in years, I'm actually excited about *something*.

I sigh and look around the apartment. It's spotless. When Carla gets home from her shift, the place will be fit for a queen.

It's not long before six-thirty rolls around. I've spent a good hour getting ready, spending way too much time on the dress, hair and makeup, trying to look just right. I keep telling myself it's because I want to look good for his publicist—who knows why—and that I rarely go on fancy dinner

93

dates. I tell myself everything in order to pretend I'm not looking good for him.

See, I'm an expert at faking it already. And especially to myself.

When the buzzer goes off, I practically jump out of my skin. I grab my purse and hurry over to the intercom.

"Hello?" I say into it, hoping I don't sound nervous.

"Hey sunshine." God, even through a crackly speaker, his voice sounds sexy. I swear, I'm getting a little wet just hearing it, like it's some sort of automatic reaction.

I clear my throat, ignoring the heat between my legs. "I'll be right down," I tell him. Then I take a moment to compose myself and get my hormones under control. I swear to god, earlier today I was so close to pushing him back on my bed and taking off his pants. It was so bad, I could barely look at him. Every time I met his eyes I was hit with a pang of desire, like a punch to the chest.

Not that looking elsewhere helped. His body in that shirt was just...there are no words. All I wanted was to grab hold of his arms and shoulders and climb him like a monkey. Then there was all the lewd and crude dirty talk coming out of his mouth and I was practically melting on the spot. There was a war inside me, a bitter battle between my brain and my vagina and I know next time my vagina might be the victor. I can already see the victory dance. Very similar to a touchdown but it results in an orgasm.

Ugh. I should have just had sex with him. Gotten it out of my system...again. Now if I actually end up going through with this crazy plan, sleeping with him has to be taken out of the equation. It's one thing to be paid to be someone's girlfriend. But when sex enters the question...no thanks. That going into pretty dicey territory.

You haven't agreed to anything yet, I remind myself. *Just go out for dinner and make your decision later.*

I nod at my internal pep talk and go out the door.

Emmett is waiting outside the lobby. Of course he looks amazing, slightly more dressed up now. Jeans, a white button down shirt, skate shoes. Casual and completely fuckable all at once.

Shut up vagina.

"You look beautiful," he says to me and for once his eyes don't leer at my breasts.

"Thank you," I say, taking the compliment as coolly as possible. Just because he said I look beautiful, doesn't mean I need to swoon.

"Trying to impress me?" he asks as he starts toward an Audi, its silver sheen gleaming under the sun.

"I knew you were going to say that," I tell him. "I was tempted to show up in what I wore this morning, just to prove a point."

"Go braless? Best decision you ever made. If I didn't know any better, I'd say you did that for me too."

"I didn't even know you were coming over. You're the crazy person who stalked me and showed up at my door."

"Persistent as a mosquito," he says as he opens the passenger door for me. "After you, sunshine."

I snort and slide on in. Obviously my nickname is an ironic one.

"So where is this Autumn?" I ask him as I casually glance around the car. It's really fucking nice. All black leather interior, walnut trim. But I can't let him know I think that.

"At the restaurant already," he says, starting the engine. It purrs like a dream. When he starts driving down the street, I've got that thrill going through me again like a rogue wave. I'm nervous and I'm excited. Just to be in a car like this, with a guy the world is talking about, off to some fancy restaurant. Maybe being his pretend girlfriend wouldn't be the worst thing in the world. Maybe it would just be a lot like this.

As if he can hear my thoughts, he turns to me. "Can I ask you a question?"

"Sure," I say, my eyes fixated on his hand on the gear shift, his tanned, muscular forearm, the white shirt sleeves shoved up to his elbows.

"Why did the concept of money make you change your mind?"

I swallow, feeling a tad uncomfortable, even though I shouldn't. It's why I'm here. "Money talks, doesn't it? Didn't it buy you this car?"

"So that's what you want? Cars? Designer clothes? Expensive shoes?"

I shake my head. "No, actually. I mean, those are all nice, though I doubt I fit into any designer clothes."

"Baby, you have got to rethink your body issues."

I give him a sharp look. "You just called me baby."

"I did," he says, grabbing a pair of aviator sunglasses from the center console and slipping them on. "You have a problem with that?"

He flashes me that stupidly handsome grin of his.

So of course, no, I don't have a problem with it.

"Back to my question," he goes on. "What do you need right now?"

"What do I need?"

"What will money buy you? This money. What are you looking for? We all have needs, we're all looking for something. What do you think all of this will solve?"

I frown as I study him, wondering why he's getting all philosophical.

"Is this some kind of test? Find out if I'm spending it on drugs or something?"

I expect him to laugh but he doesn't. "I'm being serious."

Well okay then. "I don't know," I say after a beat. "I'm working paycheck to paycheck. I have nothing in my savings. I feel like I'm just...surviving. Not living. I want to have enough money, or just some money, so that I can live for a while."

"You mean not work?"

"No...I want to work. I just..."

"You don't want the job you have anymore. You want to do something else."

What is he, a mind reader? I rub my lips together. Definitely need some more lip gloss.

"You can tell me, you know," he says. "Will is my friend but whatever you tell me, I'll keep to myself. I know you don't believe me but I don't kiss and tell."

Yeah right!

He reads the look on my face. "Okay, so sometimes I do. But whatever is between us, I'll keep between us. You have my word, Alyssa. It's good for something."

I sigh, not willing to trust him yet. "I just need money."

I can tell he's not satisfied with that answer but he lets it go. "Well, don't we all. But we haven't even started negotiating yet. What if it's not enough? What if it's more than enough?"

"We'll find out soon then, won't we."

The drive from my apartment in East Van to the restaurant is long, especially during rush hour. I wish I could say it was easy and comfortable between Emmett and I but I would be lying. All I could think about was his hands on the steering wheel and how they felt to grip me—strong, assertive and yet desperate. His fresh, herbal scent didn't help either, it just added to the growing sexual tension between us. How on earth was this even going to work? I mean, really. What the hell was I doing?

But once we arrive at the seafood restaurant, things get down to business.

Emmett takes my arm like a gentleman—even though I know he's anything but—and leads me toward the entrance where a tall, slim woman is waiting near the hostess desk.

Once she sees us together, she gets up, a big smile on her face.

Fuck. This must be Autumn.

She is absolutely gorgeous. Dressed in a short white shift dress that shows off her bronzed limbs and gleaming golden hair. Teeth as white and straight as a toothpaste commercial (gotta be veneers). Minimal makeup and a scattering of freckles across her nose. A fuchsia, velvet Gucci tucked under her arm.

In my flowy black maxi with flutter sleeves, my cheap sandals and straw clutch, I feel frumpy as hell. Any progress I thought I made earlier with my makeup and hair has suddenly evaporated next to this Giselle Bündchen clone.

They've got to be screwing. In fact, as I see them both together, they look like a match-made in heaven, the Canadian version of Brangelina, pre-crazy break-up.

"Autumn, this is Alyssa," Emmett says to her.

"So nice to meet you!" she exclaims and damn it, she has that throaty sex voice too.

"Likewise," I lie. Okay, I'm already being unfair about this woman and I just met her. I have to remind myself to give her a chance.

The hostess takes us over to a table, situated in a low-lit corner by the windows overlooking the water. The place isn't overly swanky but from the fact that I recognize a hockey player and a news anchor, I know it's got to be expensive.

Both Autumn and Emmett sit across from me at the table and suddenly I feel like I'm being inspected like a prize cow.

While Emmett takes care of the ordering, getting a bottle of wine for the table and some kind of tataki appetizers, Autumn studies me with bright eyes. I can just tell this whole idea is some form of entertainment for her, that Emmett and I are puppets on a string.

"So, Alyssa," she says, folding her hands in front of her. Long slender fingers adorned with sparkling rings. "I'm sure you have many questions for us about the whole deal and we're here to answer them all to help you make the best decision possible."

I glance at Emmett while she's saying this. He's watching me, rather warily I might add, and I realize he has no real idea what I might say or do.

"Okay. I've only heard it from Emmett so let's hear it from you," I tell her. I was prepared for her to give me a speech but instead I just barrel on and throw questions at her. "How the hell do you think him dating me is going help his career? Do you really think people care that much about who he dates, enough that it influences the work that he does? He's a grown man...well, a grown man-child," Emmett frowns, "and I would think his own personal life should have no bearing on his professional one. I guess I just don't get any of this. How is it so important that you'd be willing to spend money on someone like me?"

Autumn laughs and I detect a hint of nervousness in her voice. Good. She should be prepared to answer this shit. "Wow, you are thorough. But that's good. It's great. And I totally hear you on this, which is why we're all here right now. This doesn't have to be so complicated. But let me just tell you, I've been working in this business for ten years. My father was a PR man and he took me under his wing. He was in charge of Bryan Adams, among others."

I roll my eyes.

"You don't like Bryan Adams?" Autumn asks in a hush, as

if saying it out loud will result in us getting kicked out of the restaurant.

"Have you heard the lyrics to Run to You?" I ask her.

Emmett laughs out loud. I wish he didn't have such a nice laugh, it makes my heart positively buoyant.

I push the feeling away. There's no place for feelings here.

"Fair enough," she says. "I guess in some ways he's like Emmett here. The country thinks he's a good boy when he's got that bad boy side to him."

"Are you seriously comparing this guy," I point at Emmett, "to Bryan Adams?"

"Hey," Emmett says, his blue eyes flashing. "I can sing, I'll have you know. You can't survive in London theatre without being able to."

I can tell my comment bothered him and I'm just petty enough that it makes me happy. The man's ego can definitely use a few rounds in the ring, that's for sure, and there's something rather appealing about pissing him off. Like, if I actually do become his fake girlfriend, I foresee three months of getting under his skin. That alone might be worth it.

"Anyway," Autumn says, glancing between the two of us like she's just realizing what she's dealing with, "my point is that I've got experience and I know the ins and outs of the industry as well as how it plays into public image. And I know this might surprise you, but the way an actor is perceived in public definitely has an impact on how his career goes."

"I don't know, Sean Penn has a terrible attitude and he's done just fine."

"But Sean Penn is established. He's won awards. He has a lifetime of work behind him and more in the future. And when he was going through his worst, he was with Madonna...she was an easy scapegoat for the blame. Simply put, Sean Penn is well-respected, no matter his past behaviour."

"And I'm not?" Emmett questions gruffly, twisting in his seat to give her a steady look.

Just then the waiter appears with the wine, distracting us all. I'm watching Emmett closely though. Again, I'm seeing his sore spots. He brings up the London theatre because he feels it gives him credibility even if not fame. But the fame he gets is from playing a dweeb on one of Canada's cheesiest shows (and that says a lot) and a superhero villain. Not exactly respectable material. It's like there are two sides of him, one that wants the respect, the other that wants the fame. And so far he's been unable to have both at the same time.

I think I'm starting to understand this man a little bit more. Even though I probably shouldn't.

When the wine has been tasted and poured, Autumn raises her glass to me. "Let's make this toast to Alyssa. Thank you for being gracious enough to hear us out."

I shrug and clink my glasses against theirs, noticing that Emmett avoided my eyes. I think both of them are now realizing that what they're proposing isn't exactly as enticing as they first thought.

Autumn takes a sip and clears her throat delicately. "So, what I'm saying, is that Emmett's career is rocky at the moment."

"Rocky?" he asks, his forehead lined with worry.

"Not rocky," she says smoothly as she flashes him a placating smile, "fragile. I mean, instable. Like, resting on the edge of a precipitous cliff."

"Oh yeah, that's way better."

"Well it's the truth," she says and now anger is creeping into her voice. "And if you would just play the game right, we wouldn't be in this mess."

He rolls his eyes, leaning back in his chair. "Oh that's right, be a good sweet boy, suck it up. Don't be a fucking human being, lest the world turn on you."

"But it's true. This is your comeback, you don't get a chance to mess it up."

I can't help but make a snorting sound. Both of them look to me sharply.

"What?" Emmett asks tiredly.

I swirl the wine around the glass, wondering how he's going to take this. "I don't know. This doesn't seem like much of a comeback, does it?"

Emmett is shooting me daggers. He's practically smoldering in his seat.

"Look, he had faded into obscurity," she says. "Doing theatre in London is great and all but no one really gives a shit. It's a has-been move."

"It's not a has-been move," I tell her. "It's not even a move at all. It's something to do because you love to act. You love the art and the craft of it. It's a place where you really learn the extent of your talents, where you're able to do something you love for a living. Maybe it doesn't make you rich, maybe people don't remember who you are but you're making art every single day."

Emmett frowns, totally puzzled as to why I'm standing up for him. The thing is, I'm not standing up for him at all. It's just she touched on something dear to me. Not that I would admit it.

"Fine," Autumn says. Then she composes herself and flashes me those pearly whites again. "But you can't say this isn't a comeback. He was big when he was on Degrassi, or at least known. He went away to London. Now he's back, better than ever. He's sexy now. Age has only been his friend."

"Sexy or not," I say, knowing his ego is probably soaking up that one, "a real comeback is one when you're proud of the work you're doing. Emmett isn't proud. He's just working. He's working on his comeback. That will still happen."

I'm making all the assumptions in the world, I know this, and yet I get the feeling off of him that he probably agrees with me.

"But only if he smartens up," Autumn says, as if she's his school teacher. "And that's where you come in."

I sigh before taking a large gulp of wine. Jeez, I could go for a martini or something. "So you think that by the public thinking that we're dating, they'll look more favorably upon him and then he'll get more popular? I mean, what if it doesn't work like that? Or what if he does something stupid again?"

"You know I'd really appreciate it if the two of you would stop talking like I'm not here."

Autumn waves him away with her hand. "If he does something stupid, then I'm not representing him anymore. Don't worry, he knows that. We've discussed it. I can only do so much and it doesn't look favorably on me and my services if I have a client who is consistently out of line."

"Consistently," he mutters to himself, shaking his head.

"And if he's a good boy and, well, you're a good girl, and the public buys into it and it still doesn't help, well, no harm done. It's just three months."

"But he'll be out of money," I tell her. "And he has to put up with me for three months and I'll have to put up with him."

She shrugs, pressing her hands into the table. "It's a hard bargain, I know. So now that you've brought up the money part of the negotiations, how much are you wanting?"

I raise my brow. "Isn't it dangerous to ask me that?"

"I can tell you're not easily convinced, so it's better to just see what we can do to make it happen."

I rub my lips together, thinking. I came up with a number

earlier and I have no idea if it's fair or not. But we all know this isn't going to be a walk in the park. And I know this is the one chance I have to finally give my dreams a go. I'll never have another one.

"Do you have a pen?" I ask Autumn. "Because I have terms."

She pulls out her phone and shows me her notepad app. "Go."

I take in a deep breath. "I still have a personal life that I want to keep personal. I don't want to do any interviews with anyone. I don't want paparazzi banging on my door, so I don't want anyone to know where I live. Or work. I want to keep my life as normal as possible. If anyone says anything rude or slanderous about me, especially regarding my appearance, I want you to handle it and I don't want to see or hear about it. I want to keep whatever dignity and respect I have during this whole thing. I want at least three nights a week to myself. I want my family kept out of it. I want Emmett to stop hitting on me," I give him a loaded look, to which I swear his cheeks go red. Autumn, who has been furiously taking notes on her phone, pauses, narrowing her eyes. "And on top of it all, I want fifty thousand dollars."

"Fifty thousand dollars?" Emmett repeats with wide eyes.

"Forty thousand dollars," I quickly amend myself. I knew I was pushing it. "Deposited into my bank account tomorrow."

"Whoa, whoa, whoa," Emmett says, leaning across the table. "You a mob boss all of a sudden? You're not getting a dime until three months is over. How do I know you won't up and leave right away?"

"He's right," Autumn says. "We have to make sure that this runs smoothly. Remember, neither of you can date or hook-up with anyone else. It's not worth the risk. That will be in your contract too."

"Fine," I grumble.

"And giving you the money upfront is a dangerous move. I mean, you could just leave town, couldn't you?"

Maybe that's the plan, I think to myself.

"Emmett will be taking you out for dinner, mini-trips, buying you whatever your heart desires, so don't forget that part too. In exchange, you'll need to pretend to be his girlfriend in your personal life and public one. This means, you can't tell your friends and family that this is a set-up. Not even your closest ones. Not even the ones whose wedding you were at. You can't trust any of them."

I nod, even though I already told Jackie everything this morning. Luckily I know she and Will can keep a secret. I exchange a glance with Emmett and wonder if he's told Will anything at all. Men can be so damn secretive, it wouldn't surprise me.

"Now," Autumn says, "that everything has been laid out, is this something you'd be willing to do Alyssa?"

I take a moment to think about it, even though I've already made up my mind. I suppose if I were downright evil instead of slightly evil, I could tell them no and then threaten to tell the gossip sites everything they just told me, unless they gave me the money to shut me up.

But the truth is, even though I still think the whole idea is ridiculous and the next three months are going to turn my life upside down in ways I can't imagine, I wouldn't do that to Emmett. For all his many faults, I can tell he's got a good heart somewhere underneath his manwhore façade. His honesty and sincerity can be endearing and maybe it's pure ego that's putting himself up to this risk, thinking nothing could possibly go wrong, but he's got just as much to lose as I do. Actually, he has a hell of a lot more. Both of our dreams are at stake but at least his are realized and apparently hang in the balance.

I give them a quick smile. "If all terms are held to…yes. This is something I can do."

Autumn grins at me. "Fantastic! I'll get the lawyers to draw up the contacts tomorrow and have them sent to your work."

"You know where I work?"

"I know everything about you Alyssa," she says. If she wasn't so pretty I'd think that was the creepiest thing I'd ever heard.

"Well, just make sure the rest of the world doesn't know it too," I remind her.

After the meal is over (though delicious, I barely ate since my nerves were doing a conga line), the three of us step outside of the restaurant to the flash of a camera blub. There's just one photographer but he's already here and already capturing us together.

"What's your name sweetheart?" he yells at me and for a moment I don't know what to do, I just stare blindly at the camera and hope my makeup still looks presentable.

"Emmett needs his privacy," Autumn says to the photographer. "This is a very new relationship."

And then she whisks the two of us away to his car, getting me in the passenger seat. Before I know what's going on, Emmett is driving the two of us away, leaving Autumn and the photographer behind.

"Holy crow," I say, turning in my seat to watch as we drive off. "That started fast. How the hell did they know you were even there?"

"All the best restaurants have spies," he says with a sigh. "They place a call and then the paparazzi show up. I think they must get paid out for it."

"Well then it was pretty dangerous to have the meeting there, wasn't it? I mean, I still haven't signed the contract."

"Yeah, well," he says. In the passing orange street lights I can see his hands kneading the steering wheel. "Autumn thinks more highly of me than you do. She assumed you were someone who actually liked me."

"Oh," I say quietly. In the car, in the fading evening light, everything seems more intimate. Being at dinner with Autumn put a nice distance between us, a distance that helped me analyze everything from a business point of view. But being alone with him is already changing that and the three months have barely started.

As silence slides in, I feel forced to explain. "It's not that I don't like you."

"Alyssa, it's fine."

"No seriously. I'll admit I don't know you at all. I just don't like your type."

"My type?" He glances at me and something hot flashes behind his eyes.

"Yeah. You know. A womanizer. You sleep around."

"So? You do too."

"I do not."

"And I don't care if you do. If you go and get laid most nights of the week, have one-night stands. You do you. I'm not here to judge. But it's not exactly fair that you judge me."

"I don't just sleep with men and discard them. I date them. And yeah, maybe the date ends with sex but I'm not using people."

"Who says I'm using people? Do you think I used you the other night?"

"No…"

"I got you off, didn't I?"

I roll my eyes. "Yes. You don't need to remind me. Remember, that's something that can't happen again."

"Regardless, I didn't use you. We both got what wanted. There's nothing wrong with that."

"It's dirty."

At that he grins, even though there's a hint of coldness in his eyes. "Dirty? I admit I like it dirty, but I'm clean. I always use protection. Don't you?"

"Yeah, but…"

"But nothing. What's really the deal here? You can sleep around and have sex with as many guys as you want and it's empowering or something. Because you're a woman. And that's fine. But don't give me the double standard."

"Women have been getting the double standard all our lives!" I exclaim.

"I agree. I know they have. But no one should be judged for the way they operate their sex lives, men or women. If they're being careful and not hurting anyone, I just don't see why it's anyone's business."

I know I should keep it to myself. That my personal life doesn't belong in something that's fake. But I can't help it. Verbal diarrhea strikes at the worst times.

"My father was like that," I blurt out. "He was a gambler, a drunk. Always getting into trouble. He was cheating on my mother all the time for as long as I can remember and finally left her high and dry, all alone to take care of me and my four sisters. I don't know where he went. Back to England maybe. Who knows. Really, who cares. But when he wasn't a supreme asshole, he was nice and charming and constantly trying to win her back, win us all over. And then he would fuck up all over again until he disappeared one day with just a single note. So yeah, I've seen the damage that kind of thinking can do. I've seen the truth about *that* type."

More silence envelopes us. The engine hums, the dashboard lights making everything glow with an eerie quality. I can't believe I just unloaded all of that on him.

After a few long, agonizing beats, Emmett clears his throat. "I'm really sorry your dad was an asshole. To leave your mother and you like that, well, he's no fucking man, that's for sure. But this isn't even something you need to worry about with me. We're not actually dating, remember? It's all for show. You don't have to worry about getting hurt when there's nothing at stake."

I stare at him curiously. What's odd about all that is that he's not promising he's not like my father. He's just reminding me that it's irrelevant. Does that mean if we were actually dating, his faithfulness would come into question?

I guess that shouldn't surprise me if it's true. And in the end he's right. It doesn't matter.

"Tell me something," he says to me. "Did you mean what you said earlier, when you were talking about the theatre?"

I nod, looking out the window as the city flies past. It's getting darker earlier now, a sign that summer is coming to a close. I always get painfully sad as July turns to August, mourning the end of summer before it's actually over.

"You just..." he pauses. "You said everything I was thinking. Or that I've been trying to tell myself."

"Well it's true," I tell him. "I know it feels like all or nothing sometimes in life, but there's nothing wrong with living in the space in-between."

"Very astute," he says. "You're smarter than you look."

I twist my head to give him a dirty look. "Hey."

He shrugs, biting his lip momentarily. His eyes are back to being playful, mischievous, the same kind of eyes that lured me into having sex with him. Now, more than ever, I have to stay vigilant. "Just being honest. You're blonde, you've got gorgeous tits, a sweet ass. Skin like cream. Fuck me eyes." His smile broadens. "Or fuck you eyes, depending on your mood."

"What's my mood telling you now?" Man, the nerve of this guy.

"Oh, you're definitely giving me the finger," he says with a laugh.

"Do you really think we're going to survive three months of this?" I ask him. Point-blank. No beating around the bush.

"I've had to survive a lot worse than you, sunshine," he says to me. "I know you're going to get on my nerves and push my buttons and tease me with those lips of yours. But I'm always up for a challenge. Surviving is just another word for adapting. I'll adapt to you. You'll adapt to me. We'll survive each other. Got it?"

"Got it," I tell him. If he's this game for it, then so am I.

We're almost at my apartment when he lowers his voice and asks, "So, forty thousand dollars. Can I ask again what you're planning to with that money?"

I should just tell him. I know he might even help me. Or maybe that's why I don't.

"It's nothing," I say. "Besides, we're going to be spending a lot of time together. Might as well have something left to talk about."

I thought he would press me more but instead he says, "Fair enough."

When he pulls up alongside the apartment building, he turns in his seat toward me and puts his arm behind my seat, leaning in as if he's going to kiss me.

"What are you doing?" I ask him, jerking my head back.

"Giving you a kiss goodnight," he says, as if I'm clueless.

"Can you not?"

He laughs but doesn't move. "Hey, you better get used to it."

"I told you I'm not sleeping with you."

His mouth quirks up into a half-smile. "I know you did and I shall cry myself to sleep about it every night. But when we're together, in public, well…we're going to make out and I'm going to feel you up. Feel free to do the same to me." He sighs as he reads the shock on my face. "Alyssa, that's what couples do. They show affection with each other in public. If we don't, people will talk."

"But we're in your car. There's no one around to even see us right now," I point out.

Emmett stares at me and I can almost see him trying to form an argument. Then he looks down and smiles, shaking his head. "All right, so I was just trying to get a head start."

Shit. He's actually being adorable right now.

I think it's time for me to escape.

I put my hand on the door handle and push it open a few inches. "Thank you for dinner. I guess I'll sign the papers tomorrow and we'll take it from there."

"Dinner tomorrow night?" he asks.

"Already?"

"I don't have to be on set until Wednesday. Might as well take advantage of my days off while we can."

Just as long as you don't think you can take advantage of me.

"All right. I don't get off work until five so I don't think I'll be ready earlier than seven."

"Seven it is. See you tomorrow, sunshine."

CHAPTER 8

ALYSSA

I've been working at Mad Men Studios for six years now. Started as receptionist and then worked my way up to office manager. And when I say worked my way up, I mean about a year into the job, I had a meeting with Ted and asked if I could do something more challenging. He agreed. Office managing it was.

I have to admit, I'm not the most organized person when it comes to my own personal life, but I seem to have it down when it comes to business. Maybe it's because I've been doing it for so long, the same damn thing day-in and day-out, that it's become as natural as breathing.

Today though, has been the first day that's really thrown me for a loop.

Usually I'm at work about ten minutes early. I like to take my time to look around the office, get a cup of coffee and slowly settle into the day before anyone can bug me about something. The quiet and peacefulness really helps set the tone for the day.

Today I was a few minutes late, having overslept. I don't think I finally closed my eyes until three in the morning, my brain was just stewing over Emmett and the situation, my heart racing like crazy. So of course when I finally did pass out, I slept through my first alarm.

The moment I walked into the building, I saw Tiffany at reception staring at me with an expression I couldn't read. It was like she was bursting at the seams to tell me something and having to hold it back made her face red and sweat profusely.

When I went into the main office though, then I got it.

Everyone erupted into applause.

All these years at my job and I barely get a thank you from some colleagues.

But become Emmett Hill's girlfriend and front page news for gossip sites and suddenly that's something worth congratulating me on.

Needless to say, it was beyond embarrassing and I couldn't even disappear into my office because now all anyone wants to ask me about is Emmett. To think that all these people were at the wedding on Saturday, not even paying attention to what was really going on, and now they all think they're part of some clandestine love affair or some start-up they got in on from the ground floor.

Speaking of, I try and look around for Casey but I don't see him in his office. I need to ask him straight up if it was him that took and sold the pictures. He'd lie, of course, but I'm pretty good at telling when people are lying. And if it was him, I would take great pleasure in whipping his ass with my handbag (and not in some kinky sexual way).

Thankfully, things start quieting down, even though every time someone walks past my office they do this sly kind of head nod or wink. Have we all resorted to being in high school or what? What's next, someone is going to pass me a note asking if we've gotten to second base?

By the time lunch time rolls around, I need someone to

talk to. It's only then that I realize I can't talk to Tiffany about it. While I did tell Jackie the truth, she can keep a secret. Tiffany cannot. She means well but she's prone to bursting out the wrong thing at the wrong moment, like the time she told Casey to give me the last donut because I was having an extremely heavy period and therefore deserved it.

It doesn't matter anyway. Ted just called me into his office.

I take in a deep breath and smooth my flowy blouse over my hips before I go inside. I can only imagine how this is going to go.

"Alyssa," Ted says to me with a big smile. He's sitting at his desk, leaning back in his chair and sipping from a mug that I doubt contains coffee. "Shut the door, have a seat."

Hmmm. Usually Ted does all business with the door open, unless he's on a conference call.

I cautiously take my seat, trying to keep cool even though my heart is starting to skip. "Everything okay?" I ask him.

"Yes, of course. I'm fine. Perfectly fine. Right as rain. I know you expect me to be crying in my boots because my daughter is gone, perhaps forever, run off with my best friend. That I'm overwhelmed by the bills of the wedding, let alone the fact that there's going to be another grandchild popping up in eight months or so." He says this so deadpan that I can't tell if he's joking or not. "I'm fine. Absolutely fine. Business as usual."

He takes a sip of his coffee and a waft of whisky assaults my nose. Figures.

"Well, you look young for a grandfather," I say lamely, not sure what to say.

He squints at me. "You know, I do want to talk to you about Emmett. I really, really do. But first, must I remind you that you called this meeting? Last week? Said you wanted to talk to me?"

Oh right. That. Funny how important it all seemed a few days ago and now it's like everything has changed.

"No, I haven't forgotten," I say, not missing a beat. "It was just regarding my job…and my future here."

Ted gives me an exaggerated frown. "Jesus Murphy. Please don't tell me you're quitting. You're one of a kind and you know it." He pauses. "And please don't tell me you want a raise because we just can't afford it right now, so sorry."

I exhale but keep the smile pasted on my face. "A raise would be nice. But I know it's all dependent on Warner Brothers and if they sign the next films to us, so I'm not going to be greedy. I've seen our books, I know what goes in and out. It's just…I would like to be challenged more."

He cocks a grey brow. "You want more responsibility?"

"I want *different* responsibility."

"You mean you don't want to be an office manager anymore."

"I just want to know what else is available for me here."

He nods, sucking on his teeth and looking away. "Okay," he says after a moment. "I can appreciate that. It's just that things are constantly changing here. Each film is something new."

"For you," I point out. "For me it's always the same. I need to know I'm working toward something."

"Okay. So what do you want to do?"

"I don't know," I tell him. And that's a lie. Because what I want has nothing to do with this job whatsoever and never will. But even so, if there's no place for me to go in this company…what am I doing?

"We could transfer you to marketing, with Casey."

I scrunch up my nose, wincing internally. "No thank you." I pause, taking the plunge. "What if you transfer me to the LA office?"

"It would be no different than here."

"That's where you would be wrong. It would be LA. Every single thing would be different."

Oh please, please, please.

If he could transfer me there, then maybe I wouldn't even have to do this thing with Emmett after all.

But he shakes his head. "Wish I could, but it's not as easy as it sounds. Will was easy because his ex-wife was American but they're getting pretty strict these days. You can go and visit, of course, and go to meetings, just like I do, but getting you a permanent position wouldn't be justifiable when there are so many qualified people there already."

"You could sponsor me."

"It's just not worth it for us, Alyssa."

Fuck. I'm sure as hell glad I had this conversation now after Emmett's proposal. Suddenly the deal, and the money, looks like my only way out.

"I'm sorry," Ted says, reading my face. "How about when Will gets back from his honeymoon, the three of us put our heads together. I'm sure we can find a way for you to feel more challenged at the office."

I nod politely but the truth is I'm already imagining my escape route.

"Now, onto other business. What in sweet hell is going on with you and Emmett Hill?"

"Why, what does it look like?" I ask innocently.

He points his finger at me. "I warned him to stay away from you."

"I think that only spurred him on."

"Alyssa. Are you serious about him? The last two days I've been reading about it everywhere. You even went to dinner with him last night. I saw the photos."

I give him a small smile, finding it easier than I thought it would be to play this part. "A real lady doesn't kiss and tell." I get to my feet. "And I'm not about to give you the inside scoop. For all I know, you're the one who took the pictures at the wedding and sold it to Perez, since you have such a boner for him."

"I do not have a…" he cries out and then gives me a stern look. "That is not an appropriate way to talk to your boss."

"Good thing I don't have an appropriate boss. Can we drop it now?"

"Fine," he says in a huff, like a child who hasn't gotten his way. "But seriously, Alyssa. You're a bright, smart, pretty young girl. Please don't expect anything serious with Emmett. I've got to know him well enough over the years and while I like him, the man has some serious issues."

"You can say that again," I say under my breath as I head to the door.

"I mean it," Ted says and when I glance at him, he's morphed into dad mode. "If you expect anything serious from him, you're just going to get hurt. And I don't want to have to come into work to find you crying at your desk, day after day. Okay?"

"I'm a big girl, Mr. Phillips," I tell him and open the door with sassy flourish. "I can take care of myself."

If only he knew the truth about the two of us. A one-night stand turned into a lie of epic proportions.

* * *

I DON'T KNOW how I got through the rest of the day but somehow time still passed and placed me back at home, frantically tearing through my closet, looking for something to wear. I mean, now I have to think like a celebrity and I can't get caught wearing the same outfit twice.

Or maybe I can because I'm just a normal girl and that's why the media is running with this, because I am the type of person—you know, normal—who would wear a repeat outfit.

Argh. I can't decide. I've literally tried on everything I own and everything comes across as either too revealing or too dowdy. Plus, it's growing hotter as the day goes on, which is effectively ruining my makeup job, going from looking like I'm not making an effort (but really am) to just looking like I'm not making an effort. There's a big difference between the glow of a highlighter and an oil slick of sweat.

I can't even borrow Carla's clothes because she's two sizes smaller than me and even after I lost some weight, my hips remain their stubborn size. Stupid bones. Forget child-bearing hips, mine can birth a whole heifer.

In the end, I decide to slip on a red sundress and sandals. The color is flashy but I know it suits me and the neckline is fairly modest. The only dilemma now is whether I should wear my shorts or not. Yes, shorts. Not just for unexpected breezes but to protect against chub rub. My thighs are gapless and if there's a lot of walking, they can create enough friction to start a fire.

Normally, I wouldn't wear them on a date, particularly if I was feeling lucky. They don't seem to have the Bridget Jones' granny panty effect, wherein wearing them increases my chances of having sex. Instead, they just turn into awkward conversation when you're trying to get naked. You know, let me take off my sexy bra and also these shorts that I have to wear so that my ample thighs don't incinerate me on the spot. Yeah, super sexy.

But Emmett is texting me that he's waiting outside, so I opt to wear them, thinking it will remind me to not have sex with him, no matter what happens.

It isn't until I'm stepping out into the kitchen that I remember Bridget Jones wore her granny panties for the exact same reason. And look what happened. She slept with sleazy Hugh Grant and her whole life got turned upside down.

I suppose it's a little too late for that.

"You look hot," Carla says as she stands by the oven, munching on a cookie. "Hot with a W. Like *hawt*. Which means really hot. Speaking of hot, it's really hot today. Or maybe it's this oven. Hey, want a cookie?"

I eye her and the cookies. I've learned my lesson with her baking many times before.

"What kind of cookies are they?" I ask suspiciously.

"Pot cookies," she says, a few crumbs falling from her mouth. She covers her smile with her hand.

"And how many of them have you had?"

"I've only had one before. If you include this, it's two. But it hasn't been digested yet, so I'm not sure."

"It's okay, I'm good."

"So you're actually seeing this guy now, huh."

I shrug. Carla is another person I can't quite tell the truth to. I've been passing it off like this is just something fun for now and not going into too much detail, which thankfully she hasn't been pushing with me. I think the fact that she's stoned most of the time helps.

"I thought I'd give him a chance," I tell her. "Not everyone gets to go out with Cruiser McGill."

"I thought it was Bruiser NoChill," she says. Then she starts laughing. "The Bruiser and the Blonde. Bruiser and Blondie. I like that. Hey, do you think if I call up TMZ and tell them about your nickname, they'll pay me?"

"You can give it a shot," I tell her, knowing full well she'll forget this idea in a minute. "But if you get rich off of it, you owe me."

"Deal. Have fun, okay?"

"I will," I lie.

Because honestly, I don't see how any of this is going to be fun. It's going to be weird, that's what it is. And sometimes weird is all fun and good but going on a date with your fake boyfriend whom you find ridiculously attractive and also really dislike at the same time pushes weird to a whole other level.

Maybe I should have grabbed a pot cookie after all. Really shake this shit up.

The sun is still shining and right into my eyes when I step out of the apartment building. I don't see Emmett's Audi anywhere but I do see a giant black Suburban with a smartly dressed man, I'm guessing the driver, standing by the back door.

"After you, ma'am," he says to me as I approach, opening the door for me.

"Uh, thanks, person I don't know." I peek inside and see Emmett in a slick suit, sitting in the backseat, grinning at me. "Come on in, beautiful," he says to me and he says it with so much feeling and sincerity that my stomach does a couple of backflips.

Damn it. That actually felt nice.

Smiling like all kinds of awkward, I slide into the backseat as the driver shuts the door.

I barely have time to settle and take in the scene when Emmett is cupping my face in his broad hands and pulling me into him.

His lips crash against mine, soft and gentle and warm and I'm so shocked at what's happening, I can't even move. But then my lips know what to do and my mouth yields to him as I'm sucked into a long, sweet kiss. A current runs through me when his tongue touches mine; I feel it all the way to my toes which I know are curling in my sandals.

Everything inside me is coming alive, not with a cold slap but with a slow, luxurious build, just this kiss that deepens with each second, a long, languid pull that stirs me around inside, sugar dissolving.

I'm barely aware of where we are, what we are, when the driver's door slams shut, shaking the car.

It's then that Emmett pulls back and stares at me so intensely that I feel everything inside me light on fire and melt.

"I have missed you *so much*," he says to me, his voice low, raspy and completely earnest as he searches my eyes.

My jaw would be on the floor if his strong hands weren't securely holding my face.

Holy shit.

Does he mean this?

And then...

He winks at me. Subtle, but it's a wink.

And then reality comes along.

I pull back slightly, trying to catch my breath, to calm my heart. God damn it, I swear I'm throbbing between my legs just from that simple kiss.

And it was all for show.

None of that was real.

That was just for the driver, that was the first performance of our fake relationship.

I had no fucking idea he was *that* good of an actor. No wonder he sleeps with his co-workers, how can they tell the difference between acting and reality?

I should be impressed but actually I'm a little ashamed of myself for falling for it for a split second. I'm going to need to keep my guard up.

"Did you miss *me*?" he asks in deliberation, coaxing me to respond.

Right. That. "Uh yeah. I missed you," I tell him. Damn it, I don't sound convincing at all. "Like, real bad. Baby."

Emmett is trying not to laugh at how absolutely lame I sound. He manages to cover it up. "Alyssa, I'd like you to meet our driver, Alfonso. He'll be taking us to dinner tonight."

I straighten in my seat and glance at the rearview mirror to see Alfonso staring back at me and nodding.

I guess there really is no privacy for him. If people in restaurants are spies, who is to say that private drivers aren't either. Which makes me realize, unless we're completely alone somewhere, we'll always have to be *on*.

On the plus side, that means I'll be kissed like that more often.

Negative side, it means I'll be kissed like that more often.

You can only be kissed like that, looked at like that, talked to like that, so many times before you either, A) screw him silly or B) start believing it.

God, I hope there's an option C.

I manage to momentarily get myself together as we pull away from the curb, inching away from Emmett and trying to smooth out my dress over my thighs so my shorts aren't showing, all while trying to calm my heart.

But Emmett isn't having any of it. He keeps close to me, his hand goes right on my thigh while his other arm goes around my shoulder. I can feel the heat transfer from his clothes to my skin, smell the product he used in his hair, the scent of his cologne. I have to close my eyes briefly, caught between wanting to revel in the feel of him like this, and trying to push it away.

In the end, I can't win. Everything about him is overpowering, overwhelming. I can't stop feeling his palm against my thigh, the way he plays with my hair, how his eyes keep skirting over my face and body in awe, like he's seeing me for the first time.

"How are you?" he asks me, his mouth close to my ear, blowing hot air over me. I can't help but shiver in response and he grins at that, which only worsens the problem. "Cold?"

"I'm good," I say in a small voice. "A bit tired, I think."

"Tough day at work?"

I nod, keeping my eyes forward and focusing on the road ahead. "You could say that."

"Did your co-workers say anything about us?"

Now I glance at him. I shouldn't have. I'd forgotten somehow how mesmerizing his eyes are at this non-distance. "They did, actually."

"Good things?"

I bite my lip, thinking it over. "It depends. I got a standing ovation over you."

"No kidding. And that's bad?"

I guess in these circumstances it can't be.

"No, it was wonderful."

Lie, lie, lie, I tell myself. Then again, it was kind of nice for once to feel special among my peers. But I wouldn't admit that to Emmett.

"And did you sign that contract we were talking about?"

I nod. "I did."

Even though the courier dropped it off at my desk and I signed the simple documents alone under fluorescent lights, I felt like I might as well have been in a dungeon, by candle-light, and signing it with my own blood.

"Did you find out who took the photographs? Anyone from your work?"

"The guy who I suspect was out sick so I couldn't ask him," I tell him.

"That's convenient…"

"Right?"

Our conversation changes to easy topics after that, though the entire drive he keeps his hands all over me. I keep going from wanting him to touch me and enjoying it

123

to hating the fact that I'm enjoying it because none of it is real.

By the time we get to the restaurant, Rodney's Oyster House in Yaletown, I need a drink or twenty. Especially as the driver lets us off a few blocks away and we have to walk there, holding hands, past people who stop and take pictures. Luckily it's only a few people who actually recognize Emmett but it's still enough to make me feel awkward and question why I'm doing this again.

Forty grand, forty grand. It's a mantra I'm repeating in my head.

"You're doing so well," Emmett whispers to me at the restaurant while the hostess walks us toward our table. He gives my hand a reassuring squeeze and instinctively I squeeze his hand right back. That part I know was real and it gives me a dash of courage.

We're lucky that even though we're on display, the booth where we're seated is out of earshot of everyone else in the restaurant so we don't have to carry on a fake conversation. After the waitress leaves with our orders for drinks and a dozen oysters, Emmett gives me a sweet smile.

"How are you holding up?" he asks, tilting his head as he inspects me. I'm assuming I must look absolutely shell-shocked.

Well, I am.

"I'm...okay," I tell him. I take in a deep breath and try to smile. "This is just really...weird."

"I know."

"I mean it has to be weird for you, too."

"It is," he says, still smiling.

"Why are you smiling like that then?"

"Because if you were my girlfriend and we were on this date, this is how I'd be looking at you."

Oh.

He frowns. "Don't tell me the guys you date aren't drooling all over themselves when they talk to you."

I let out a dry laugh. "Yeah right."

"You're either exceedingly modest or just plain oblivious."

"I'm neither of those things," I tell him. "It's just the truth. The guys here in this city, they're constantly looking over my shoulder for someone better."

"And where are you finding these guys?"

I swallow. "Dating apps." I don't know why I suddenly find it so embarrassing when that's how everyone is doing it these days.

"That's what you get for using those."

"Easy for you to say, you're Cruiser McGill and Doctor Death. You don't need them, you can just snap your fingers and girls will appear in front of you. Naked, probably."

He smiles and looks off, running his hand over his jaw. When he looks back to me, his eyes are dancing like he has a secret. "You want to know something? Before I got the role of the Doctor, I was using dating apps too."

I blink at him in surprise. "Really?"

He nods slowly. "Yes. And you know what I discovered? That the women in this city were constantly looking over *my* shoulder for someone better. It goes both ways, you know."

"Then it's too bad we didn't end up on a date with each other."

"It is too bad," he says this almost wistfully. "I would have liked that."

The way he's staring at me is causing all sorts of raucous inside. I clear my throat, not sure what to do with his sincerity. Is it acting or is it real?

"But you're not really a city girl, are you?" he asks me. "You're from Penticton."

I shouldn't be surprised he knows that. Autumn probably did his homework.

"Yep."

"Did you like growing up there?"

I nod. "I love it out there. I miss it, actually. Cold winters, hot summers, none of this doom and gloom. I love how dry it is, like a desert. I miss the smell of the sagebrush in the morning, the calm of the lake. The vineyards and the big, big sky."

Shit. All this talk is making me want to take a quick trip to visit my mother now. I wonder if I can get away with doing that without having Emmett come along. I feel like my mother would pick him apart.

"So why did you move to Vancouver?" he asks.

Here it comes. I try and play it off. "Why does everyone move to Vancouver? Opportunity. A taste of the city life."

"But why did *you* move here? What brought Alyssa Martin out further west? What did this place promise you?"

The way he's staring at me is like he's looking right through me and if I don't tell him the truth, he won't be satisfied. He knows something is there, even if he doesn't know what it is.

"Honestly?" I say slowly. "I wanted to be an actress."

He stares at me with a blank expression. "Are you serious?"

"Yup," I tell him and smile at the waitress as she approaches. The oysters look good but my dirty martini looks even better. Emmett, of course, is having a Manhattan.

When she's gone, he's back to grilling me.

"I had no idea," he says, watching as I drink. "What happened?"

I swallow a mouthful, feeling the delicious burn. "What happens to most people. The dream didn't work out. I couldn't afford it."

"But it's not that expensive," he says, then trails off.

"Did you just say Vancouver isn't that expensive? When

double-income couples who have no debt and make over two hundred grand a year still can't afford to buy a home here?"

"I mean that acting shouldn't cost that much. Just head-shots, maybe some classes."

"And time. Time is money, especially when you live here. I went to auditions and took classes all while working wait-ressing jobs. But it wasn't going anywhere and I wasn't making enough money, so after a while I realized I needed to smarten up. I put it on hold, promising myself that I'd give myself another shot at it later. But I needed a proper job. My mom couldn't support me, we barely had any money growing up. My sisters are all scattered around the world, even then, and I'm the youngest so I was on my own. I got a real job, administration for an engineering firm, and then life just...got in the way."

"How come I didn't know this about you?"

I smirk at him over my drink. "Because this is all fake and we don't know a thing about each other." I take another sip and give him a steadying gaze. "I know you must hear this all the time, but you're one of the lucky ones, Emmett. You had a dream, you went for it, and you got it. You didn't have the struggle."

At that he bursts out laughing, head thrown back. "Struggle? Baby, all I did was struggle."

"Didn't you have a rich aunt or something that helped fund you when you first started?" I'm trying to remember the Wikipedia page on him but judging by the look on his face, I'm not sure how accurate it is.

"I didn't have anything like that," he says soberly. "You're right though. We don't know a thing about each other."

We lapse into a strange silence. Both of us almost sound bitter at that fact.

"So tell me," he says, after we've started to tuck into the

oysters. "Does this forty grand you've wanted have anything to do with your original dream?"

"Yeah."

"How come you didn't want to tell me?"

I bite my lip, considering it while I watch him swallow the oyster downs. God, he even makes eating oysters look sexy.

"I guess I just felt…like a fame chaser or something."

"A fame chaser." He lets out a wry chuckle. "Is that similar to a star fucker? Those are all the things you don't like about me. Though perhaps the real reason you don't like me is because I'm a working actor and you aren't."

"Ouch," I tell him with a frown. "Naturally you would assume I'm jealous of you."

"I didn't say jealous," he says. "But slighted."

"Well I'm not slighted," I say, busying myself by finishing off the rest of the martini. But as I drink, I'm starting to wonder if he's right. Maybe one of the many reasons why I have such an aversion to him is because he's an actor who has been working a long time. Forget the fact that he's on a TV show, he was doing theatre in London, which is pretty much my idea of the dream. But that dream wasn't enough for him.

I shake the feelings off. It doesn't really matter and it's useless to compare us. After all, I'm the one who gave her dream a half-hearted approach and gave up when the going got rough. Whether he struggled or not, he didn't give up. And that's why he's here right now.

"Actually," I tell him, though I'm already starting to regret the words that are about to come out of my mouth, "I admire you."

A cautious smile tilts his lips. "You admire me?"

"Let me rephrase that. I admire that you went for what you wanted and you didn't give up."

He seems to let that sink in, nodding slowly. "Well, then I suppose I have one admiral quality about me. That's good to know." He pushes the tray of oysters toward me. "I've had my share. These are all yours. Eat up, baby."

I love, love, love oysters. But there's something insanely sexual about them and it's not that they're supposed aphrodisiacs. Or maybe it's that being around Emmett, everything turns sexual after a while. Either way, I hesitate before I pick one up.

After sprinkling some horseradish and vinegar on the oyster, I slide it off the shell and let it sink down my throat. Like I figured, Emmett is watching me the entire time, his gaze growing heated.

"God," he practically growls, his voice low, "I can imagine you swallowing my cum in the same way."

I nearly choke on it. In fact, I start coughing harshly, the vinegar catching in my throat and immediately grab my glass of water, gulping it down.

When my coughing fit has subsided and I can breathe again, I shoot him a glare. "What did I say about hitting on me?"

"Oh, sunshine, I wasn't hitting on you. I was just thinking out loud."

"Then how about you keep your thoughts to yourself."

He raises his drink to his lips and smiles at me over it. "No promises."

To his credit, for the rest of the date he doesn't say anything else lewd and crude. Sometimes I wonder how much he actually means the dirty things he says and how much of it is just to shock me. He does seem to get more of a kick out of my reaction.

Then again, this man has been inside me. He's made me crazy with just a kiss. I have a feeling that when it comes down to it, he means every single filthy word that leaves his lips.

And, truth be told...I think I'm starting to like it.

We've just finished our desert when he reaches across the table and grabs my hand.

"Kiss me," he says, giving my hand a squeeze.

"What?"

He smiles that gorgeous grin, and I feel my resolve slowly melting inside. "Kiss me. Trust me, it will look good."

Ah hell. I'm tempted to look around the restaurant to see who is watching but I have a feeling if no one is now, they will be in a second.

Kiss him, I tell myself. *This is part of the deal.*

It's not even the kiss that I mind so much, it's that I have to do it in public, in front of everyone, and there's a good chance that someone is going to take a picture of this moment.

Still, I give him a smile, trying to look at him like I'm in love with him, and then I lean across the table and he leans across the table and I kiss him. *Good Will Hunting*, eat your heart out.

I mean it to be short and sweet, nothing more than a press of the lips. But just like what happened in the car, the moment our mouths touch, there's a magnetic pull between us, our lips immediately wanting, no, *demanding*, more of each other.

Before my brain can catch up with what's going on, we are full on Frenching in front of the entire restaurant like a pair of horny teenagers.

And the moment we pull back, I see something in his eyes, a wild sort of tenderness, that I can only hope is true. The fact that there are a million eyes and even the flash of a camera on us doesn't seem to matter. When we kiss, it becomes the only thing that's real.

I give him a shy smile and sit back down. I'm not embarrassed at having done that in public but once again I'm chiding myself for letting me read into something that's just an act.

Don't catch feelings. You might not be as immune as you think.

"Thank you," he says to me. "I almost believed that."

I give him a puzzling look just as the waitress comes by with the bill. Then I put back on my happy girlfriend face, which slides in place with ease. Maybe I'm a natural born faker.

After dinner, while the heads in the restaurant swivel our way as we leave, we get into the waiting Suburban.

I expect Emmett to start touching me wildly like he was doing earlier, but he just stares out the window, deep in thought. The silence isn't uncomfortable for once, so I close my eyes and nearly doze off in my seat, only waking up once the car comes to a stop outside my apartment.

"Let me walk you to your door," he says to me, taking my arm and leading up the path toward the building. He stops, grabbing both of my hands.

"You survived your first date with me," he says, eyes shining with quiet amusement. "Congratulations. How does it feel?"

"Strange," I admit. I can't help but smile. "But actually it was a lot more fun than I thought it would be."

"You know how we can make it even more fun," he says, taking a step toward me, closing in the inches. One of his hands disappears into my hair and I try not to sink into this feeling, the easy way he touches me. "Invite me in."

"Emmett," I whisper, trying to find my nerve. I need to be hard and prickly to stand up to him, to turn him down, and yet the more he touches me, his fingers now trailing down the back of my neck, the softer I get. "I don't think this is a good idea." But my words come out in a squeak.

He leans in closer and I swear he's coming into kiss me again and if he does, fuck, there's no way in hell that I'll be able to resist this time. I'll be dragging him up to my bedroom in a hot second and riding him ragged.

But he closes his eyes and presses his forehead against mine, taking in a deep breath.

"I know you don't always like it when I speak what's on my mind," he murmurs, my skin igniting just from the raw lust I hear in his voice. "But it's taking everything I have to not try and persuade you." He bites his lip and glances up at me through his long lashes. "For you, though, I'll be the gentleman you need me to be."

Then he pulls back to press his lips into my cheek, shivers cascading down my back, and straightens up.

"I'll call you tomorrow," he says to me with that easy smile of his and then he turns and walks away, calling over his shoulder. "Sleep well, sunshine."

And then I'm left in front of my apartment building, turned on and bereft. I was this close to having a wild night of hot, sweaty sex with him and then he had to suddenly turn into a gentleman and leave me be.

I watch as the Suburban drives off and shake my head as I go into the building. I love a gentleman as much as the next girl, but damn it, Emmett sure has a knack for making me appreciate a scoundrel.

CHAPTER 9

EMMETT

"So, how's the new Sheila treating you?" Julian asks me while the hair, makeup and wardrobe team flits around us, adjusting us under the lights. I can tell they're listening as they always do.

I give Julian a look. "You know, I've been to Australia and I never heard a single Aussie use the term Sheila. Nor were there any shrimp tossed on any barbies, either."

Julian shrugs and gives me a sheepish grin. "Sorry mate. I know the ladies here love it, ain't that right girls?"

On cue, all of them give him a placating smile, just to keep him happy. The fact is, I might have a bad reputation for being a bit, well, to borrow from Alyssa, *prickly* on set, but Julian Crane is an outright douchebag. But he's the star of *Boomerang* and the one with the permanent contract, so it doesn't seem to matter what he gets up to, he's staying put.

As for me, well, I have to say the crew is treating me a bit differently today. Pretty sure it's all because of Alyssa. They aren't exactly falling over themselves to talk to me or be extra nice, but I've seen a few more smiles tossed my way than what I normally get.

Knowing I have a captive audience who might go report this down the entertainment grapevine, I say, "It's actually going really well. It's still really early of course, I met her at a mutual friend's wedding. But she's really quite special."

"She's very pretty," Tina, my makeup artist says, as she presses powder onto my forehead. "So natural looking."

"Yeah, she definitely doesn't seem very LA," Julian says. "Except for her tits, am I right mate? They have to be real."

For some reason it bothers me to hear him talk about Alyssa that way.

Remember, you're her supposed boyfriend. You should be bothered.

"That's none of your business," I tell him. "But yes, everything about her is real."

Well, everything except our relationship.

"So refreshing to see a man like you find a nice, normal girl," Yvonne, our wardrobe girl says as she adjusts the tie on the black suit I'm wearing for the scene. "Gives the rest of us hope."

"Yeah," Tina says with a dreamy sigh. "And to think you met at a wedding. It's just so romantic. She must feel like she's in a fairy-tale dating you."

Or a nightmare. It's hard to tell with her sometimes.

When the scene is over, fifty million takes later and all Julian's fault, not mine, I get in my car and leave the studios. It's too late to go and find Alyssa and I feel like she was pretty serious about having her three nights a week to herself, so I head downtown.

But I don't go to Gastown or Coal Harbor or Yaletown for a drink or a bite to eat. Instead, I park my car in a secure parking garage off Hastings, grab the plastic bag beside me, put a baseball cap on my head, and head out onto the street.

If you've never been to Vancouver's downtown east side, consider yourself lucky. And maybe a bit naïve. The city is known around the world as being one of the best places to live thanks to the gorgeous scenery and healthy living and it being Canada, of course. But aside from the outrageous expense, Vancouver has a dark and dirty secret that most citizens turn a blind eye to.

Homelessness and drug addiction rules the east side of downtown, so much that you can't walk down those streets without seeing something horrible. Hundreds of junkies wander about, sleep outside doorways, try and sell DVDs, yell and scream at nothing or shoot heroin right in front of you. The police can't handle it, the province and their non-existent health care sources can't handle it. So it's just this lawless town where people are dead and dying, a sort of limbo leaning towards Hell.

I grew up down here. I lived at the top floor of a flea-ridden apartment, the hallways filled with addicts trying to find shelter for the night. My mother did the best she could for me even as her addiction worsened. By the time I was ten, I was pretty much fending for myself while she tried to wean herself off her medicine.

I was ten years old when she just took too much. She became another statistic, one of the hundreds of souls who die each and every month on these streets, alone and undoc-umented. If it wasn't for me, no one would have even noticed or known her name.

But for my shitty upbringing, one I try so hard to bury, one that's impossible to escape, I harbor no hard feelings toward my mother. Despite her addiction, she did everything she could to provide the best life she could for me. I never went hungry, I always had a bed. I was able to go to school with other kids who had lives just like me. On her best and brightest days we would escape the east side and walk just a few blocks over to where the scenery changes and China-town begins. We'd explore strange shops and she'd pretend she spoke Cantonese. I could never quite figure out if the merchants understood her or not.

And through it all, my mother always had a back-up plan. I think she knew, deep down, that she'd die from the drugs one day, which is why she arranged for her estranged-sister to be my guardian. She needed to know that I would be okay in the end.

Little did she know that I had actually preferred living with my comatose but loving mother in the zombie-like slums compared to the cold, Christian prison of my aunt. But life isn't something you can plan. You can only hope for the best.

"Hey man, can you spare a quarter?" a toothless man asks me. His face is caved in, covered in sores. Maybe meth, maybe carfentanil or whatever opioid of the month is killing people in the alleyways. Either way, though his voice sounds young, his face is halfway to dying and I have no idea his age.

I reach into the plastic bag and pull out an energy bar I had gotten from craft services on set. "I can spare you this."

"Nah man, I need a *quarter*," he says and when he sees I'm not budging, he takes the bar. I watch him, curious, and see him shuffle down the street before trying to sell it to another junkie for a dollar.

I'm not surprised. I never give them money because they only want it for one thing and as often as I do bring food from the set, occasionally buying someone in need a burger from McDonalds down the road, it can be hard to find people who are seriously hungry. Usually their only hunger is for drugs.

But there's always Jimmy. Jimmy's been part of my life for as long as I can remember and by some kind of luck, he's never been addicted to the hard stuff. That's not to say he's perfect. He's a drunk, through and through. But he's a good man and even as he's pushing into his seventies, he's still living in the same apartment in my old building, with a job working at the homeless shelter and soup kitchen.

I tuck down the brim of my baseball cap by habit, even though no one would ever recognize me here, and then head into the apartment. I step over a man passed out on the stairs, cover my mouth with my sleeve to block out the smells of urine, vomit and shit, and head up to Jimmy's apartment.

I knock on his door, even though it's partially open, and wait a long minute before I step inside.

This is the moment I fear. The idea that I might step in here and find him dead. It only gets worse as time goes on, that I'll have to deal with the same situation I found my mother in.

But this time, Jimmy is snoring loudly on the sagging couch in the living room. I take the moment to put the plastic bag on the counter and put some of the food away before slipping on a pair of rubber gloves and cleaning his apartment the best I can.

I do this about once every two weeks, more if I can get away from work. I know it sounds strange but there are times when I look up to Jimmy as if he's my father. My actual father left when I was two years old, which then turned my mom onto drugs, but growing up Jimmy was really the only face that was always around. Sometimes it feels like he's my only real friend. That's not to say Will isn't. But even though Will knows bits and pieces of my childhood, he doesn't really understand. How could he? How could anyone know what it's like to grow up in a true house of horrors, surrounded by the stench of death and depravity at every turn.

But Jimmy knows. He understands. And he doesn't judge. With him, I can just be me. I can let it all out, all the hurt and the fear and the anger that still lingers in me. The kind of stuff that even my therapist couldn't coax out.

"Hey, Tetty," Jimmy says, stirring from the couch. "What time is it, Tetty?"

Tetty has always been my nickname. He wouldn't call me Em because he says it sounded too much like my mother's name (Emily), so Tetty it was.

"It's late," I tell him. "You can go back to sleep, I'm almost done."

"You love me and leave me, don't you boy?" he says and after a feeble attempt to get off the couch, he lies back down again. "You didn't happen to bring me anything to drink, did ya?"

From the way he's slurring his words, I can tell he's been on another bender. He normally isn't so bold as to ask me, either. I'm not an enabler.

"Just fruit juice," I tell him. "And food. Please tell me that you're still keeping your job." I know he doesn't actually need the job to survive. The government only gives him a couple of hundred a month for welfare but I've secretly been paying his rent here for the last fifteen years. If it weren't for me, he would have been homeless a long time ago.

And yet, that's the extent of what I can do for him. I can bring him food, give him shelter, but I can't get him to stop drinking. I can't make him go to work. I can't make sure he's brushing his teeth and eating right and taking care of himself. Which makes me both direly needed and absolutely useless.

"Fruit juice?" he says, grumbling. "Ah hell, I guess it will mix well."

I close my eyes and lean against the counter, taking in a deep breath that smells mercifully like the bleach I just used to clean his place. "Jimmy, promise me that you're going to pick yourself back up tomorrow and go to work. They need you there."

"Bah," he says, turning over on the couch so his face is in

the cushions. "No one needs me and I don't need them. I don't need you either, Tetty, so get your fancy suit out of here and leave."

I glance down at my dirty jeans and t-shirt and Timberland boots and nod. When he gets abrasive like this, there's no reasoning with him. "I'll come back soon," I tell him. "Might even pop in at your work and see you there."

He mumbles something in response and as I turn toward the door, he starts snoring.

I leave his place feeling dirtier than when I came in, with the same damn thoughts as ever bouncing around in my head.

I tried.

But it's never enough.

* * *

IT'S SATURDAY MORNING, bright and early, when I swing by Alyssa's to pick her up. I saw her briefly on Thursday night when I took her for a quick dinner at Gotham steakhouse, but today we have the whole day together and Autumn said that some fun outdoor date would really help my image. I guess too many nights spent at the bar paint a different picture.

When Alyssa emerges from her apartment I can't help but smile.

Fucking hell. In the week that I've known Alyssa, I've seen the overly-done bridesmaids version, the hungover in her pajamas version, the dressy summer version, the date night version, but I think my favorite version of her is this one: working out Alyssa.

She's dressed in purple running tights, bright pink running shoes, and a tight yellow top that puts her breasts front and center. I guess to the average person, her outfit might totally clash but I love the colors on her. They're a perfect representation of who she is, bold, fun and sexy as hell.

She slides in the passenger seat and glances at me over her shades.

"You know, I didn't think we were actually going for a run," she says slowly. She eyes me up and down, her nose crinkling in disdain. I'm in a wife-beater, mid-thigh running shorts, sneakers, set up for a run just as she is.

"I'm actually more of a trail runner," I admit. "Have you done that before?"

She laughs. "Trail running? My god. I walk on trails, Emmett. I don't run on them. I don't even run on pavement. Or treadmills. I only run to the bar when they're giving last call."

"Well, I hate to break it to you but we're going to be going around Stanley Park today." I wait until she's buckled in before I drive off.

"You've got to be kidding me, that's like...ten kilometers."

"We can walk most of it."

"It's still ten K! I don't know what kind of girls you're used to dating but I do not go on jogging dates and I certainly don't spend hours walking. In a circle, mind you."

"And yet here you are, dressed like you do it all the time." While we pause at a light, I lean in closer to inspect her clothing. They do look brand new. "In fact, I have a feeling you just bought all this just to impress me."

"Phhfff," she says, waving me away. "You think everything revolves around you. I'm trying to impress the damn paparazzi."

"By wearing the most-mismatched outfit in the city?"

She shrugs. "Why not? Damned if you do, damned if you don't. Might as well go all out." Her eyes trail over my arms and chest. "Besides, you're doing the same. Yeah right you would normally go running in that."

"This old thing?" I ask, pulling at the wife-beater.

"Yeah. Also brand new. You're just trying to show off your muscles."

She's got me on that one. "Hey, I have a lady here I'm trying hard to impress. Problem is, even if she was impressed, she'd never tell me."

"She sounds prickly. You better tread carefully with her."

"The only time I can get any sort of reaction out of her is when I'm kissing her. Then it's like she forgets how to breathe, she can only moan my name in response."

That gets her attention. Even though I can't see her eyes beneath her glasses, I can feel them burn. "Maybe she's as good of an actor as you are."

In this instance, I hope that's not true.

Still, I flash her a smile. "Maybe."

It takes a long time to find a free parking spot in downtown's West End, closest to the park, and by the time we get out and are ready to go, Alyssa is already complaining about shin splints.

"But we've been jogging for one minute," I tell her as we negotiate the crowded path along the seawall.

"For the last time," she says with a scowl, her blonde ponytail swinging in her face in time with her steps, "I don't run. I don't jog. And if this keeps up, I'm going to have a coronary." She puts her hand at her heart for added effect.

I bite back a laugh. "Fine. Let's just go around Lost Lagoon then and come back."

Lost Lagoon is a small lake situated just outside of downtown and one of the more popular places to take a stroll. With a fountain in the middle, weeping willows that hang over the water with swans that glide to and fro and the glass high-rises of the city rising into the sky behind it all, it's an urban oasis.

It's also the perfect place to be seen if that's what you're looking for, the path filled with tourists and locals alike. Every now and then as we jog past, Alyssa huffing and puffing beside me, someone takes our picture or records us.

When we complete the loop around the lake, we decide to explore some of the trails leading off of it until Alyssa insists on having a break.

"Are you okay?" I ask her, hand on her back as she's leaning over and breathing hard. Luckily we're in a forested nook by the lagoon with plenty of privacy, if you don't count the rustling in the bushes. I'm assuming it's from raccoons and not the paps.

She looks up at me, sweaty and red-faced and nods. "Yes. Just. Trying. To. Survive."

"I can't believe I didn't bring any water, I don't know what I was thinking," I tell her. I'm fit as fuck thanks to my role, which has me working out harder than anyone should, but even so I rarely go trail-running without at least a Camel-Pak. "We'll just walk from now on."

"How about you just drag me along, that's much better," she says, taking in a deep breath and straightening up. "Jeez. I have extra admiration for those muscles of yours now." She gestures to them half-heartedly. "How many times did you almost die in order to get them?"

"Enough," I tell her. "But I was on the swim team in high school, so it's kind of ingrained in me."

A lazy smile teases her lips. "A swimmer. I can tell. No one can naturally have that chest and those shoulders."

I can't help but grin at the compliments. "How rare it is for you to say something nice. I must take you jogging more often, you're totally delirious."

She laughs. "Yeah, well, I call it as I see it. Your face and body are as gorgeous as they get. Too bad your personality doesn't match."

"Ha, ha," I say dryly. "Are you feeling better? On second thought, I'm not sure I should be in the woods with you at all, you might just off me when you catch your breath."

She shakes her head, smiling, and looks away. Then her face freezes in shock.

I turn to see what she's looking at.

It's a raccoon.

A three-legged raccoon to be more specific, looking up at us from the edge of the bush with big eyes.

"Oh my god," she says in a panicked whisper. "We should go. Now."

"Why? It's just Cyril Sneer."

She looks at me in confusion, her face scrunched comically. "*Who?*"

I gesture to the raccoon. "Cyril Sneer. You're not a real Canadian unless you've seen the cartoon The Raccoons. Actually, you're probably too young."

She takes a step closer to me, her eyes fixed on the raccoon again. "I've seen the show. But Cyril Sneer isn't a raccoon."

"Sure he is," I tell her. "And this is Cyril. He's the three-legged raccoon of Lost Lagoon. Hey. That rhymes."

"Uh huh. So you personally know this raccoon?"

I crouch down so that I'm at eye-level with him. Cyril takes a few awkward steps closer and tilts his head, eying me. "Sure do. He's friendly. I always feed him."

I stick my hand into shorts and bring out a small piece of beef jerky I was eating in the car earlier. I'm about to give it to him, knowing he'll come over and take it from me with his little human-like paws when I stick my hand up and give it to Alyssa.

"What is this?" she asks, peering at it.

"Beef jerky. He'll love it. Give it to him."

She raises her arm, about to throw it.

"No, feed him by hand."

She shakes her head. "I've had bad experiences with raccoons."

"But you've never met Cyril Sneer before."

"Emmett, for the last time, Cyril Sneer isn't a raccoon," she says, not breaking focus with the animal. "He was a pink aardvark on the show, and the raccoons' enemy. If you're going to name a three-legged raccoon after an iconic cartoon character, at least get the character right."

I'm trying to think if she's right or not. I remember the show's villain being a pink animal...

But as I'm pondering the names of the raccoons on the cartoon, Cyril is coming towards Alyssa.

"Give him the food," I tell her.

But Alyssa just grasps the jerky to her chest, totally frozen on the spot.

And Cyril is picking up speed, wobbling on three legs toward her, a crazy bloodlust in his eyes.

"Alyssa, throw it!"

"Ahhhhh," she yells as Cyril somehow leaps up into the air and starts clawing up Alyssa's body.

"Holy shit!" I jump up to my feet as Cyril claws at her bare arms and chest, trying to get to the jerky. What the fuck do I do?

"Ahhhhhhh!' she keeps screaming, trying to turn around. "Get it off, get if off, get it off!"

I look around for the nearest branch even though hitting a three-legged raccoon seems kind of cruel. Then again, I can't just let it mob her like this, what kind of man would I be?

In the end I reach over and grab the racoon by the scruff

of its neck and yank him off her before throwing him to the bushes where he lands on his three feet.

Alyssa is still trying to spin around, flailing her arms. As she does, the piece of jerky goes flying to the ground, which Cyril scoops up with his hand before running into the brush.

"It's okay," I tell her, trying to calm her down while I grab her by the shoulders. "It's gone. It's gone."

"I told you Cyril Sneer was the enemy!" she yells at me, almost in tears.

"Hey, hey, it's okay," I repeat. "Let's get a look at you."

She's fairly scratched up on her arms and there's a swipe across her chest, but there doesn't seem to be any puncture wounds or bites. "Minor scratches," I tell her. "But we'll still get you to the hospital to get a rabies shot just in case."

"No, no I'm fine," she says, taking a step back from me and trying to compose herself. "I'm fine."

"He could have rabies," I tell her.

She inspects her arms briefly and then looks at me squarely. "I've had worse."

"What do you mean you've had worse?"

"I've already had a rabies shot."

"What? When?"

"Last year."

"Last year? Why?"

"This isn't the first time this has happened."

I cock my head, trying to form words but the only thing that comes out is, "Huh?"

"I said this has happened before. I told you I've had bad experiences."

As she's saying this, I recall something that Tiffany had said at the wedding.

"Bad luck with animals?" I ask.

She shrugs and brushes a strand of hair from her face. "I love them but they don't seem to love me."

"Maybe they love you too much," I tell her.

She laughs. "Yeah. Maybe."

I grab her by the hand and give it a squeeze. "Hey. Let's get out of here before the squirrels turn on us." She visibly shudders when I say that, which makes me think it's happened before too. "We'll go back to my house and I'll get you fixed right up."

"I'm okay," she says feebly.

But after the long walk back to the car, she's too weary to put up any sort of argument.

I take her home.

CHAPTER 10

*B*y the time we're pulling up to my place, Alyssa is practically asleep in her seat, yawning as we walk toward the house.

"This is where you live?" she asks as we enter the front courtyard.

"My humble abode."

She snorts. "Good lord, to have this type of money."

"Hey, this is my Degrassi money. I invested and I saved."

"I'm not saying you don't deserve it," she says, giving me a quick smile. "I'm just saying…you're lucky."

In some ways, I think to myself. But the last thing I want to do is bring up the whole "money doesn't buy you happiness" argument to someone who agreed to fake date me in order to get money. Alyssa doesn't have time for my douchebag thoughts, she'd call me on it right away.

Which is one thing I like about her.

I open the door and we step inside.

My house is fairly simple. The best part is the open kitchen, living and dining area, with the massive patio over the ocean. Otherwise it's a pretty small two-bedroom. I'm mainly paying for the view of the water, the city, the mountains.

"I'd give you the tour but there isn't much to see except the view," I tell her as I start looking through my cupboards for a first aid kit. Finally, I find it in one of the kitchen drawers as Alyssa slowly wanders along the white tile floor.

"Take a seat," I tell her, gesturing to the couch.

She eases herself down, her eyes taking in everything. "All white. Don't you find it so hard to clean?"

I drop to a crouch in front of her and fish out the iodine and cotton pads, then pull her arm out so the scratches are facing me. "To be honest, I'm just here to sleep. I'm on set most of the time or I'm out."

"Out where?" she asks and winces as I press the yellow liquid into her.

"Sorry," I apologize for the pain. "Out with you."

"But we're a new thing. So, you were out with other girls before me?"

I try and shrug it off as I dab it along her arm. "Yeah. I guess."

"And Will."

I nod. "Sometimes Will."

"Who else do you hang out with?"

I pause, lick my lips. "I have a friend, Jimmy. Known him all my life."

"Will I ever meet this Jimmy?"

I glance up at her face, her big eyes earnest and questioning. Despite the fact that she's injured and I'm fixing her up, she looks so fucking sweet right now it makes my heart ache.

"Maybe," I tell her. No one I know has ever met Jimmy and I can't imagine how she would react. Then again, something tells me that maybe she might be one to understand.

I push the thoughts away, to dwell on for another time.

"Does this hurt?" I ask her, gently working on the other arm.

She shakes her head. "Not really," she says softly, watching me as I work. Then she nods to the corner of the room where I have a few plants. "I like your cactus."

I grin. "Thanks. I just got it. Named it after you."

She laughs. "You did *not*."

"I did. Alyssa the cactus. She's a prickly one."

"Oh come on," she says. "You are too much, you know that."

Too much and not enough all at once.

I ignore that sobering thought. "I thought when I start missing you, I'd have something just like you to talk to."

She just laughs and I feel this strange warmth spreading in my chest, something I haven't felt in a very long time. I like her. A lot. And I like being with her. A lot.

Maybe she can read the expression on my face or pick up on the vibe I'm giving, because she then lowers her voice and says, "Do you ever get lonely?"

I pause and meet her eyes. "That's a bold question."

"I know," she says and see that she's completely serious. Her questions are coming from a soft, kind place though.

I run my tongue over my teeth as I think. "Yes. Very much so," I admit.

She nods slowly. "So why don't you ever settle down?"

"You're asking the thirty-eight-year-old man-child why he doesn't settle down?"

"Yeah. I am. There's a reason. What is it?"

I exhale, taking a moment to get a new cotton ball out. "Honestly? I just…I don't think it's in the cards for me."

"Because you haven't met the right person. Have you ever had a serious relationship?"

"Of course. I was even engaged."

She jerks her head back in surprise. "Really? Who? What happened?"

"It's a long story. Not very interesting. She was in wardrobe. We met on our play in London. I fell in love, or in something I thought was love. So did she. I moved back here and convinced her to come. She left it all behind. And then I realized...she didn't really know the real me. And I couldn't pretend anymore. So I broke it off." The dark sticky swirls of the memory attempt to drag me down but I brush them off. "Poor girl. I felt horrible. Honestly, I still do. She gave it all up to be with me, moved her life all the way over here, and I left her in the end. I guess that's just the type of person I am."

I briefly meet Alyssa's eyes but instead of seeing disappointment in them, I see compassion. "But that's life," she says after a moment. "People take chances and get their hearts broken and break up. It's the chance every single one of us have to take if we ever really want to get anywhere. And in the end, it means she just wasn't the right person for you."

I shake my head. "I can't even imagine who the right person could possibly be."

But that's a lie. You can imagine. She might be right in front of you.

Scratch that. I don't *want* to imagine.

"I'm complicated," I go on. "And complicated people need other complicated people to work. Otherwise, you don't fit."

"That's a load of crap," she says, eyes fiery. "The right person might be complicated or simple or both. The right person will find a way to fit into your cracks until you're flush."

Alyssa is taking me by surprise here. For someone so dry and cynical as she seems to be, she's doling out the advice like it's her job. I'm starting to think there's something much softer hidden under her armor. Whoever gets to see that secret part of her is a lucky man.

150

"I'm not an easy person to love," I admit and the words crash around us like a demolition.

Fuck.

I can't believe I just said that. That's the kind of thing you tell your therapist, not your date.

Then it's good you aren't actually dating her.

Nothing to lose.

"That was a brave thing to say," Alyssa says softly, seeming as surprised as I am. "But if that's true, then it just means the right person needs to work a little harder, that's all."

"Love shouldn't be work." I pour more iodine on the pad and lean in closer, patting it on her chest.

"Sometimes it is though," she says. "But it's worth it."

I bite my lip and nod, trying to pay attention to the scratches on her chest and not look into her eyes. The last thing I want is to believe that I might be worth it.

Deep down, I know I'm not.

I screw the cap back on the iodine bottle and finish up on her chest, even though it's pretty obvious now that she's cleaned up enough and I'm just touching her for the sake of touching her.

"Thank you," she says in a whisper.

I take in a deep breath through my nose and look up at her. "For what?" My throat feels dry, my words come out slow.

"For patching me up," she says, giving me a wane smile that puts a dimple in her left cheek. "It feels nice to be taken care of."

In this moment, she looks absolutely vulnerable. She looks like her armor is starting to slip, that I might be getting a glimpse of the beautiful pink heart underneath.

Before I can stop myself, I'm reaching up to cup her face, pulling her face toward mine until our lips are crashing against each other. She lets out a moan I feel all the way to my toes as our tongues stroke each other into an inferno.

"Emmett," she says softly–fuck, does my name sound good right now–and her hand disappears into my hair, taking a hold and tugging.

I unleash myself on her neck, licking and sucking just the way she liked it before, until she seems to yield, her body running hot, her moans so sweet and desperate and hungry for more.

Fuck I'll give her more. So much more.

While she sits there, all flushed and bothered on the couch, I get undressed to my briefs in a flash, her eyes taking in my body before she's joining in and ripping her shirt over her head, her breasts bouncing free. I drop to my knees and take off her running shoes, then pull down her tights. My hands slowly work their way back up her thighs.

My fingers find her underwear, the silky material wet with her desire.

"God, you're so wet for me," I whisper to her, my voice catching in my throat. "Can I make you wetter?" I move her panties to the side and slip my finger along her sweet pussy, the sensation making me delirious with lust. She lets out a lengthy moan, her hands tighter in my hair. "I want my cock to slide into you, just like this." I add an extra finger and move them in together. "In and out, in and out," I whisper as my fingers go along. "You want it harder, deeper?"

She groans and I look up to see her arch back, her breasts pointed forward, her sweet, pink nipples tight and hard.

What a fucking sight, her pale skin glowing against my white couch, like an angel waiting to be fucked.

I can scarcely believe what's happening but all thoughts in my head are slowly shutting down, drowned out by the pounding of my heart, the raw, hot tension running through me. How easy this is to touch her here, to coax these perfect sounds out of her, to say all the dirty things I want to say.

"Do you want my cock?" I ask softly. "My tongue? How would you like me to fuck you?"

"Anything, anything," she says through another moan as I drive my fingers even deeper.

I hunch down and press my face in, my tongue snaking out and licking up to her clit.

Heaven. This angel tastes like heaven.

"You taste so good," I murmur into her and she shudders from the vibrations. "I could feast on you for hours. Would you like that? Tell me what you like, what you want."

"More, I want more." She's practically whimpering.

I suck her clit into my mouth, wet, warm, and she gives a sharp cry, calling out my name in such a way that it will be my undoing if she keeps this up.

My tongue and fingers work her harder and from the way she bucks her hips into me, I know she can take more. But I don't want it all to end here.

I pull away and get to my feet. Her eyes are half-closed, dazed, mouth open. Lust and sex just oozes out of her. God, I'm a lucky son-of-a-bitch.

I step out of my briefs, my cock popping out. I lazily stroke myself, my eyes never leaving hers. "Is this what you want?"

She swallows loudly, her eyes pleading. "God, yes."

I grin. I fucking love how she isn't afraid of my mouth. She's got quite the dirty one herself.

"Flip over," I tell her.

She bites her lip and grins and then slowly turns over so she's on all fours.

"Just a second," I tell her, grabbing a condom from my bedroom and coming right back. I roll it over my shaft, my cock hot and inflexible in my hands. "Can you move yourself up a bit?"

She pulls herself forward so that she's in the middle of the couch and I climb behind her, my thighs on either side of hers, tanned skin against pale, straddling her just below her ass.

And what an ass. I can't help myself, I quickly lean over and sink my teeth into her perfect skin.

She lets out a yelp.

"Sorry," I tell her, my finger trailing down the middle of it. It's so soft and plump that I instinctively give it a smack with my palm.

She yelps again, though this time it's choked and wanting.

I wait a moment, watching for her reaction. Her ass rises a little higher, wanting more, teasing me, daring me.

I smack it again, hard–*crack*–the sound filling the room. My handprint blooms on her pale skin like a cherry blossom.

"You like that too?" I murmur and the moment she nods, I spank her again, this time getting both cheeks.

"And this?" I ask, bringing my finger back to her crack and trailing it down until it settles deep into her pussy. She's slippery, warm, completely intoxicating. The sounds coming out of her mouth are growing deeper, more primal and raw, causing my skin to feel tight and hot, the blood to pound wildly in my head.

Fucking hell. This woman feels so good, my cock is jealous of my finger. But as much as I want to be inside her, I could literally spend hours just exploring every single crevice of her plush body, finding what she likes, what she wants. I don't think I could ever get enough of her, ever get my fill.

These are dangerous thoughts, especially when we probably shouldn't be having sex in the first place. But fuck, does this ever feel right. Just me straddling her, the tip of my cock rutting against her ass, her skin still red from my hands—it's the tip of the iceberg.

She wiggles her hips, trying to push my finger in deeper, crazy for more.

"Don't be so greedy," I admonish her but it's futile. I grab my cock at the base and steadily push it in between her legs, into her as deep as I can go.

I groan as she envelops me, a tight velvet fist. The fact that her legs are close together means I have the added friction from her thighs.

Fuck. I'm not sure how long I'm going to last.

Everything is hot and electric. My heart pounds inside my chest.

This woman, this woman...

She grips me from the inside out and I push in further, my breath shuddering.

I press my hand down on her shoulder for leverage, slowly pulling myself out, then back in, trying to find the rhythm without crushing her. My thighs are doing most of the work, shaking slightly, the muscles popping as I move faster and faster, my cock disappearing entirely inside her, the base shiny from her desire.

My hips circle and I shorten my thrusts so I don't slip out. She's wet down to the middle of her thighs and I want to stay inside her deep like this, tightly packed. It's such a fucking squeeze that a sweat is breaking out at my temples, my muscles wound too tight.

Alyssa is moaning something deep and desperate which only makes me more desperate in return.

"Do you want to come, sunshine?" I whisper hoarsely. "Will you come on my cock? Make my cock so fucking wet."

She's groaning, whimpering.

"I'm going to make you come," I say. Breathless. Rough.

"I'm going to make you come so fucking hard you won't be able to move for days."

I move one hand down to her waist and grip her while the other reaches under her until I reach her clit. It's soaked and my finger slides over it with ease.

That's all it takes.

Her body tenses and then starts to quake beneath me. She pulses around my cock, her clit throbbing under my finger. A sharp cry leaves her lips, then fades off into breathless little moans.

I come immediately after. There's a rush along my spine until something at the base of me explodes. I grunt like an animal, thrusting deeper and deeper, the couch shaking while the cum shoots hard into the condom.

I exhale loudly, my breath elsewhere, my heart thudding to a marching beat inside my head. I lean back on my thighs, absently run my hands over her ass while I remember how to breathe. Then, when it doesn't feel like I'm having a heart attack, when the sweat stops rolling off my brow, I gently pull out.

Leaning forward, I put my lips to her ear. "Did you like that, sunshine?"

She turns her head, her eyes closed and makes a noise that I think means *yes.*

I brush the hair off her face and kiss her cheek. Then place tiny, soft kisses on her neck, shoulder, down her spine, until I finally get off of her.

After I dispose of the condom, I toss her leggings and tank top onto the couch and then put my briefs back on.

"I don't know about you," I say as I pull on my shirt. "But that was a hell of a lot better cardio than the running was."

She gives me a sheepish look as she gets to her feet, totally naked, totally beautiful.

"What?" I ask.

She nods at the couch before she starts getting dressed. "The iodine. Your couch."

I look over. It's no longer pristine white. The iodine from her scratches has left stains.

I shrug. "Worth it."

"I bet," she says with a smirk and I'm almost bereft when she's fully clothed again. I could have stared at her body for hours. "I have a feeling your house is so white and clean because you like the taboo of dirtying it up."

"Only with you, my prickly one," I tell her.

She glares at me, sticking out her tongue.

"Careful," I warn her. "You go around showing off your tongue like that, I may have to put it to a better use."

She shakes her head. "Don't tell me you can go again."

"I can do a lot of things. I think with you, sunshine, I might just be able to go for days."

"Well don't get any wrong ideas," she says, her mouth turning down. "That wasn't really supposed to happen."

"What? The me fucking you senseless on my couch or you getting attacked by a three-legged raccoon?"

"Both."

I fold my arms across my chest and grin at her. "Hey, I can't promise neither of those things won't happen again. You might have just as bad luck with me as you do with animals."

She watches me for a moment, trying to suss me out. I'm not sure what kind of conclusion she comes to though because she just brushes her hair off her face, her cheeks still pink and flushed, and gives me a small smile. "I guess you should probably take me home. It's been a *day*."

I probably shouldn't feel all that disappointed, especially after what just happened. I mean, I'm used to loving them and leaving them and if this is what Alyssa is doing, I need to just take it in stride. I'm no better.

And yet I find myself wishing there was something I could do to entice her to stay. Funnily enough, there is. I almost open my mouth and tell her she's contractually obligated to have dinner with me.

But I can't do that. No matter what our arrangement is, in the end, I want to do what she wants, what makes her happy. If she wants to go home, I'm taking her home.

It isn't until after I drop her off that I realize that our fake little relationship is starting to feel more real than it probably should.

CHAPTER 11

ALYSSA

"*P*ot cookie?" Carla asks me as she appears in my bedroom doorway, holding out a tray. As usual, she's biting into one. I don't know how she survives from day-to-day, just eating cookies and being high all the time.

And normally I would be turning her down unless we were spending the whole day together just hanging out in the apartment or day-drinking in the park or something. I tend to get quite paranoid if I'm around people.

But it's been a stressful week and I haven't been able to shake it.

First of all, there was the fact that I had crazy mad sex with Emmett at his house last weekend after I was molested by a three-legged raccoon. As mind-blowing as it was, it wasn't smart, especially considering it started up a case of the feels right after, the feels that I spent the next few days after trying to overcome and ignore.

Second of all, there was the fact that I went out with Emmett three times after that, three whole times where I had to give the feels the middle finger and remind myself that everything we're doing is a lie. Even if the sex was real, it just complicates everything else.

And I had to remind myself of this while we went out to another fancy restaurant and he wore a slick suit that he looked absolutely delicious in. Then when we played mini golf together and he wore a tight white t-shirt that showed off every beautiful muscle on his body, muscles I knew intimately. Then when we went to the beach to play Frisbee, which he did while wearing just a small pair of shorts.

Totally unfair. I almost didn't survive. Not just the playing Frisbee part, because I got whacked in the head a million times by the villainous flying disc (some of which made for delightful photographs on the gossip sites), but having to act like his girlfriend and touch him when he's nearly naked really did a fucking number on me. I mean, the only way to prevent the feels is to keep my distance but I can't keep my distance because it's my job to be as close to him as possible.

Third of all, work this week just plain sucked. I don't know if it's because I can't wait to get out of there so everything is extra slow and boring, or that Will's still gone on the honeymoon so Ted was extra stressed, or that I tried to get it out of Casey that he was the one who took the photos and I actually believe him when he said it wasn't him.

Needless to say, now that Carla is waving the cookies in front of me, I'm almost considering having one.

She can see I'm hesitant. "They're very mild," she says. "And they have walnuts."

I grab a cookie from her and slide it into my purse. "I'll save it for an emergency," I tell her.

"What kind of emergency? You're going sailing. If you're drowning, a pot cookie is not an acceptable substitute for a rescue ring."

She's right. And I am going sailing. It's Sunday afternoon

and Emmett is supposed to be swinging by at any moment to pick me up and take me on his boat, Sick Buoy. It's a gorgeous day too, with sunshine and light winds, but to be honest I'm a bit apprehensive about the whole thing. It's nothing to do with sailing or being on the water. It's just that all week long, our interactions together have been very public-oriented and we've managed to part ways each night without falling back into bed with each other.

But out on his boat...I mean, I know he's doing it for some sort of photo opportunity as we sail around but otherwise, a sailboat is pretty much a giant floating sex pad, isn't it?

I need to keep my head engaged and my heart and vagina as distant as possible.

"So how is everything going?" Carla asks. "You seem even more nervous now than you were on your first date. Are you doing things backwards?"

In a way...

"What can I say, the man keeps me on my toes." I look down at my outfit just as my phone beeps. Emmett is outside. Like clockwork, my thighs clench together, and my heart picks up the pace. I hate that he's starting to have this effect on me. I give Carla a pitiful look. "Do I look okay?"

Just like I was trying too hard with the running outfit last week, I'm going all out on my sailing one. Sperry Topsiders, white Bermuda shorts, a navy-blue tank top and a baseball cap with a yachty-looking emblem on it.

"If I was a captain who needed crew, I'd hire you in a second," she says.

Not exactly what I wanted to hear but it will do.

I sigh and head out of the apartment.

The silver Audi is outside waiting and I feel a thrum of electricity run through me.

Just fucking great. Even the sight of his car is starting to get me going.

I exhale again and head towards him.

"Morning, sunshine," he says to me as I open the door, flashing that gorgeous smile beneath a pair of super reflective aviators. I catch my reflection in them and I really do look like I'm about to go work on boat somewhere.

"Hey," I say, sliding in and buckling my seat belt.

As soon as it's clicked in, Emmett is leaning over and pulling me into a long, tender kiss.

I respond because I have no choice. My body molds to him, adapts to him, like magnets you can't keep apart.

And god, does it ever feel good. To kiss this man. To be kissed by him. I could literally do it for hours, the slow, teasing give and take of our bodies.

When he slowly pulls away, he runs his thumb over my lips and looks like he's about to say something. But he just gives me a closed-lipped smile as his eyes skirt over my mouth, nose, as if he's in on some inside joke, and then he pulls away.

I should probably let it go and let a kiss be a kiss. But still...

"What was that for?" I ask him as he starts the car.

"The kiss? I always kiss you."

"Not when we're outside my apartment and no one is around."

He shrugs with one shoulder and smiles. "You look beautiful. I wanted to kiss you. And so I did."

I should let it go. I really should. But getting annoyed is the only way to keep things professional and put some distance between us.

"Well I'd rather you didn't."

He glances at me over his glasses. "Bullshit."

Fuck.

I cross my arms. "I'm serious. This isn't part of the deal. There was no one around, therefore you had no reason to kiss me."

"I know. But I did anyway."

"Because you're a jerk."

His laughter fills the car. "A jerk because I kissed you? That's a new one."

"You know it…it…"

He frowns as he glances at me again. "What? What does it do? Turn you on?"

I press my lips together and look out the window. He's got me there.

"And you do look beautiful, by the way," he says. "You remind me of this movie, Anchors Aweigh? Fred Astaire wore an outfit just like it."

"Shut up."

It's then that I figure there's only one way out of this.

I reach into my purse and start eating the cookie.

"Didn't your kindergarten teacher ever teach you how to share?" he asks me as I pop the last piece in my mouth.

I just smile at him through chocolate chip teeth. There. That'll teach him not to kiss me.

"Sorry, if you're trying to make yourself look less attractive, it's not working," he says matter-of-factly. "Not only do I like things messy, but now I know you taste like chocolate."

I flip him the bird and go back to staring out the window.

When we finally get to the yacht club, I'm starting to feel more relaxed even though I know the cookie probably hasn't kicked in yet. I just hope that Carla was telling the truth about the cookie not being strong, because it also didn't have the walnuts that she promised.

"Have you ever been sailing before?" Emmett asks me as we climb on board the sailboat.

"*Now* you ask me?"

"Well I figured you had, considering it looks like you used to captain a ship in the Caribbean, but still I thought I'd ask."

"Yes, a few times. But don't ask me to do anything complicated."

He nods as he unlocks the door to the cabin and slides the glass back on the top. "So it's true then that blondes can't handle complicated tasks."

"Fuck off," I tell him. "And you were practically blonde when you were on Degrassi."

"Practically but not quite," he says as he heads down the stairs into the cabin. "And you can attest now that the carpet wouldn't have matched the drapes anyway."

I give him an evil grin. "I don't know, it's hard to tell when it's all grey."

He gives me a sharp look.

Now that got him good. How fucking vain. Of course, Emmett's body hair is light brown and well-groomed without a speck of grey hair to be seen but it gets under his skin anyway.

"You watch yourself," he says, shaking his finger at me. "You're more feisty today than you oughta be."

It's true. And as the day goes on it only gets worse.

As do my giggles.

At first I couldn't figure out why everything Emmett was doing was making me laugh.

Then I remembered the cookie.

"All right Miss Giggle Pants," he says to me as we cruise around the bay. He's leaning back on his seat with a beer in his hand and letting autopilot steer the boat, the front sail taut under the breeze which makes the boat heel slightly to the side. "How are you liking sailing so far?"

"It's not so bad," I admit with a grin that won't leave my face. I'm sitting on the opposite side of him, trying to keep upright. "I like how the city looks from here."

He nods and seems to relax visibly as I say that. "Distant. No one can touch you out here."

"I don't know why I'm telling you this," I begin, "but I think I might have been a bit unfair to you when we first met."

"When we first met, or like five minutes ago?"

"I'm being serious."

"Which is strange, since you were just having a laughing fit."

"Emmett."

"Alyssa."

"Look…" I go on. "I guess I just thought you were a spoiled celebrity. Like I assume they all are. Complaining about the hardships of the life when there's so much given in return. But…I get where you're coming from. I've seen it firsthand. I have the same feeling out here that you have. Freedom. Freedom to be yourself, to think your own thoughts, to not worry. And while I know that people will tell you not to care what other people think, the truth is you've been doing that. And you've been punished for it."

I don't know if I'm on the right track with all the shit I'm babbling or if it's hitting home for him because he's not saying anything, but I continue. "I like my privacy. I like being able to be myself. And on a lesser scale, I'm judged for it too. Let's ignore the fact that I've been your girlfriend for two weeks now and that people are talking about me and there are pictures and all that, because that shit is weird. But I mean like, in the life I was living before I met you, I was still judged. I have sisters you know, and they are all married and they all have kids and they all have that life they've always wanted. Even if that life isn't perfect, it's the life society expects them to have. Then there's me, who is in a dead-end job, perpetually single, who likes sex, who isn't skinny. Those things alone represent me right now and those things are harshly judged all the time."

Man. I can't tell if I'm droning on and being philosophical because I'm high or not. I better stop talking. Emmett might get suspicious.

But after a few beats he says, "Go on."

Did it sound like I was supposed to continue?

High. You're so high.

"Anyway, I'm sorry that I didn't get it. I know now why you've acted the way you have, you were trying to stay true to yourself in a world that doesn't want you to. And you'll pay for it." I pause. "Do you have any chips?"

He frowns at me and then nods to the cabin. "I think there are some stale salt and vinegar ones in the galley."

"Yes!" I exclaim, doing a fist pump before I scramble downstairs. When I come back up, Emmett is staring at me quizzically.

"What?" I ask through a mouthful.

He shakes his head. "Nothing. I mean...I guess it's just weird to have someone understand. And even weirder to have someone apologize for judging me. I'm not sure I deserve that. I've done some pretty dickish things."

"Because you're a *scoundrel*," I tell him with a smile. "And one I happen to like very much."

Oh shit. Did I just say that?

"I mean..."

Emmett raises his hand, breaking into a grin. "Nope!" he says loudly. "Too late. You admitted that you like me. Let the council have that written down on record. Alyssa Martin admits she likes Emmett Hill. Very much, I might add."

"I didn't mean it," I protest. "I'm high!"

"Sure you are, sunshine." He chuckles to himself. "Now you'll never be able to pretend you hate me again."

"Unless you totally screw things up," I point out.

His smile falters slightly but he shrugs. "Maybe I won't. First time for everything."

After that, we go around the bay a few more times, both of us seeming to have more appreciation at the sense of freedom out here. No prying eyes, no societal constraints. Just the salt air and the ocean and the sunshine and the gorgeous land around us. Just us. And Emmett opens up to me about his work schedule, how he misses the security and consistency of doing the plays in London, the anonymity of his day-to-day life, how the passion almost eclipsed his need for more recognition. Almost, but not quite.

When we start heading back, I'm pretty sure the pot cookies are starting to wear off so when he asks me if I want to steer, I don't say no.

That said, I'm still pretty hesitant.

"I'll show you," he says, coming behind me as I stand at the wheel, trying to put his arms down either side of mine.

"I'm good," I tell him, trying to shrug him off. "You're too enticing to have so close."

He laughs. "You really are something today. What happened to my prickly Alyssa? I'll have to throw out the cactus and get a sunflower instead."

My prickly Alyssa.

Ignore the prickly part.

He called me *his*.

And the funny thing is, I liked it.

"Just tell me what to do," I tell him. I don't dare look over my shoulder at him because I know he's got that wicked smile on his face.

"Oh really? Anything?"

"Emmett," I warn.

"All right well let me take it off auto-pilot." He lifts off me and pushes a few buttons on a console and suddenly I feel the pull of the wheel. "Just try to aim for that building over there, the sail should hold. Don't make any sudden movements or turn too much in either direction, or we'll lose it."

Seems pretty straight forward. I keep the wheel as straight as possible with an iron grip, even as the wind starts to pick up and I have to fight it a bit.

Emmett, meanwhile, stands by the boom with a beer in hand, grinning at me like a fool.

"Are you enjoying this?" I yell over the wind.

"Sexiest fucking sight I've ever seen," he says to me. "Why don't you show me your tit and make it even better."

I balk. "Fuck you. Let's see your dick then."

He considers it, then nods. "Okay." Starts to unzip his jeans.

"Stop," I tell him. "I was kidding."

"Secretly you weren't," he says, reaching into his boxer briefs.

I should look away, I really should but I'm also curious to see if he's hard or not.

My brain wins at the last minute.

Just as he starts whipping it out, I throw up my hands to shield my eyes.

It all happens in slow motion.

I let go of the wheel.

The wheel starts to violently spin.

The boat begins to turn.

The boom begins to swing.

The boom comes across hard and strikes Emmett in the shoulder and sends him, his dick, and his beer, soaring through the air and right over the side of the boat.

Into the water.

Splash.

Man overboard.

"Emmett!" I scream, my hands grabbing onto the wheel and trying to control the boat as it keeps sailing forward. I look over at my shoulder to see him surfacing and starting to tread water, gasping for air.

"Hold on I'm coming!" I yell at him, trying to turn the boat around but now the boom is swinging the other way. "How do I reverse?!"

"You can't reverse!" he yells from the waves. "You're under sail!"

"How do I turn it off?" I yell back, frantically trying to hit all the buttons with one hand while steering the boat with the other.

"You can't! You're under fucking sail! Jesus Murphy, Alyssa, throw me the ring!"

Right. The ring. I have no choice but to let go of the wheel again until the boat is completely turned around. At least now, the sails are slack and flapping and the boat is slowing down.

I grab the ring off the back of the boat and quickly throw it into the water with all my might. My throw isn't the best–neither is my aim–but at least it's in the water and Emmett is swimming toward it.

Despite the danger and trauma of watching him possibly drown, there's something incredibly sexy about the way he's slicing through the water, doing a front crawl through the waves like he's a fucking tugboat on speed.

Damn. No wonder the man used to be on the swim team.

It's not long before he's reached the ring and slides it over his head. He then grabs the rope and starts pulling himself in after the boat until he's finally at the platform at the back.

"I am so, so sorry!" I cry out to him as I feebly try to help him on board. He's so cold to touch and shivering, his lips looking a shade of blue.

"It's okay," he says, trying to catch his breath as he crawls onto the deck and slowly tries to get to his knees. "It's okay. It was my fault."

"No, I'm an idiot, I shouldn't have let go of the wheel," I tell him, holding onto his wet shirt, afraid to let go in case I lose him again.

"No, it was my fault. I shouldn't have shown you my penis. I know the power it has over you."

He's smiling as he says this but it still doesn't make me feel any better.

"Hold on," I tell him. "I'll get you some blankets, you would have gotten hypothermia if you were in there for one minute longer. Do you think you can steer it back or should I call the Coast Guard?"

"I'll be fine," he says, heading over to the wheel.

I swallow hard, hating the sight of him like this, regardless of how well his wet clothes are sticking to his muscles, and I quickly hurry downstairs to gather up as many blankets as I can. When I get up top, I dump them at my feet and then start pulling his shirt off his head. "Gotta get you out of these first," I tell him. "That's all."

"Sure, sure," he says with a grin, even though he's unable to keep from shivering. "Pants next. But, mind you, the water is cold."

His pants are unzipped anyway, so I pull them down until he's naked and try not to stare at his cock, which truly does look quite different than what he was showing me prior to going overboard. Then again, the man is blessed in that department, so it doesn't look any different from average.

"You don't need to stare at it," he says. "You're making him shy."

I smile at him. "Shy or not, I have to stop and appreciate. I learned my lesson before."

"Never look away from my dick."

"You got that right."

Then I start wrapping the blankets all over him, covering up every wet inch so that by the time we're heading back into

170

the marina, he looks like he's started some kind of blanket-wearing fashion trend. I'm sure Kanye West would try and sell it for a couple grand.

Somehow, we manage to dock the boat and he gives me instructions on how to properly tie it down, fancy knots and all.

Then I come back on board.

"Are you sure we shouldn't take you to the hospital?" I ask him, even though the color is coming back into his lips and his eyes look brighter.

He nods. "I just need to get warm and rest. Come on." He puts his arm around me and ushers me downstairs into the cabin.

Cold and wet (him), high (me) and exhausted (both of us), we crawl into the berth with each other.

And promptly pass out.

CHAPTER 12

ALYSSA

When I wake up it takes me a moment to realize where I am.

It's almost dark, the blue glow of twilight comes through the glass hatch above me. I yawn, feeling as if I could sleep forever, and slowly turn my head to see Emmett beside me.

This is the first time I've seen him sleeping.

I feel like such a creeper.

Because even when he's asleep, he's a fucking babe. His boyish face is almost pretty with his tan skin and long eyelashes. His thick hair is slightly mussed up from the seawater and his stubble seems darker in the dim light.

I could literally stare at him forever.

That's when I'm hit with a curious pang. This side of us, the one rife with intimacy, where we can sleep beside each other, is not part of the deal. This isn't supposed to happen, it just has by silly accident, and now I'm soaking it up as much as I can.

This is the part that feels real.

And this is the part I really want.

I close my eyes and lie my head back on the pillow, letting

out a dramatic sigh.

After a few beats, Emmett murmurs, "Everything okay?"

"You aren't sleeping?"

"Not when I can feel your eyes on me," he says. "Though I do like being admired."

"You would."

He opens his eyes and looks at me. "Kiss me."

"What?"

"Kiss me."

I give him a wary look, even though kissing him really is one of my favorite things. "Why?"

"Because I want you to."

"But no one is here to take a picture of it."

"But I want you to."

I stare at him for a moment, trying to figure him out. "Is this what Emmett Hill wants?"

"I want more than just a kiss, but it will do."

I close my eyes, lean over and leave a soft, sweet kiss on his lips.

I'm about to pull back and ask if that was enough but he reaches up and grabs me by the back of the neck, pulling me further down so my mouth is crushed against his, my breasts pressed against his chest. He moans into my mouth and I feel it all the way through me.

I'm wet in a second. Damn that he has this kind of power over me.

Before I even know what's happening, my clothes are being pulled off and I'm pulling off the blankets he's wrapped in and then the both of us are naked on the berth, our bodies tangled in each other.

"Fuck," he swears, holding my face in his hands and sucking my lower lip into my mouth like it's candy. "You're so fucking beautiful, Alyssa. I can't survive the days anymore without feeling you like this."

173

Jesus. When he says things like that, I don't even stand a chance.

Real or fake?

But it doesn't fucking matter. I want him, I want him so deep inside until I can't breathe. I want to feel just how real he is.

"Lie back," he whispers hoarsely, his eyes burning, lit from within. "Spread your legs. Touch yourself. Show me what you like. Where you want me to put my tongue, my lips. Where I need to take my time tasting you."

I swallow hard. My cheeks are hot, tight, flaming red. There's blushing and then there's me.

I'm not sure I'll ever get used to his dirty talk.

But I know one thing, I never want him to stop.

And so I do as he says. I scoot back onto the bed and, teasingly I might add, I open my legs.

I know we've had sex before but this is the first time he's getting a good long look at me.

It feels extra-long because he's taking his time, staring at me with simmering lust.

"I could feast on you for hours," he murmurs, his eyes briefly meeting mine before settling between my legs again. "What a perfect, wet, pink pussy. You're fucking stunning, baby."

I swallow. My body is absolutely ravenous. I feel put on display but the way he's looking at me only makes me want him more.

"You want me?" he asks gently, coming closer, prowling like a jungle cat.

I nod. "Fuck yes."

"I want to lick every inch of your body," he murmurs as he looms over top of me, his hard chest and tanned skin taking over my world. "Is that all right?" He licks along the rim of my ear, the sensation causing my skin to tingle.

174

"Yes," I say and it sounds like I'm begging.

I *am* begging.

He continues to move his lips and tongue down the length of my body, caressing my collarbone, my breasts, sucking hard at my nipples until I'm dizzy and nearly mad with sensation.

God, this is so good, so good.

My stomach shivers under his tongue and my hips jerk under the tickle of his permanent stubble, the sweep of his full lips.

Finally, his head settles between my legs, already parted wide for him, hungry with want. Just as he did before as he gazed at me, he takes his time. He parts me open, slowly letting the rough pad of his fingertip brush over my sensitive flesh.

I'm already gasping, unable to keep quiet, to contain myself.

Yes, yes, yes. More.

Give me more.

Then his tongue snakes out, sliding along my clit and setting off more fireworks that flame the fire inside me. My breath shakes, unstable, my fingers clawing at the cushions. My hips lift up, wanting more of him.

He obliges, putting his mouth and lips into it. He's watching me. Those icy-blue eyes are watching my every movement as he gives me more and more pleasure, his teeth grazing over my clit, his tongue plunging deep inside. His head between my legs is the world's most beautiful sight.

This feels more real than anything else before.

I can't hold his gaze any longer. I throw my head back and the world becomes hotter, tighter, combustible. The heat inside me grows and grows and grows, this impossible force, like the sun, that gathers every single nerve in my body, winding it over and over again.

The slide of his tongue sets me off.

"Emmett," I cry out, and he murmurs into me, his groans vibrating deep inside and kicking me over the edge. I'm going over, falling over the edge, whistling through the wind, and my body quakes endlessly, until I'm quivering, boneless, spent.

I can barely catch my breath, my chest heaving and covered in sweat. He gets off of me and disappears briefly into the galley. When he comes back, he's got a condom in his hands, sliding it on his cock with ease.

Then he's back on the berth and he's yanking my thighs, positioning himself. He pushes inside, still fucking hard through all of that. I'm so wet that he slides in easily, as huge and thick as he is.

What a man, to have that face, that body and that cock and still know exactly what to do with it.

And that he does.

He shoves himself into me with raw urgency that borders on savage.

I cry out, gripping the cushions again, filled to the brim with too many sensations to understand at once. I am wonderfully, stunningly overwhelmed.

Emmett is merciless and I am at his mercy. He grinds into me, his hips circling as he pistons himself in and out. He grunts hard with each thrust, this rough, animalistic noise that gets louder and louder the closer he gets to coming. It's such a gorgeous, raw noise that causes the heat to build in my core, the beautiful pressure inside rising again.

Faster, harder, deeper. His pace is relentless. It slams me hard into the berth, enough that I'm afraid he might hit his head.

But he has no fear.

Only raw lust.

And it has never felt so good.

I can see him starting to lose control, dipping over the edge. His eyes burn into mine, and then he's in deep, so deep that he's shaking and muttering my name in low, guttural tones.

I can listen to these sounds forever. These sounds, all for me, all because of me.

Before he totally loses it, he places his fingers at my clit, rubbing, swirling, faster, faster. I'm so fucking slick, he's sliding all over the place.

It sets me off–BAM–and once again I'm floating, flying, but this time I'm with him, and we're riding it together, our bodies joined inside and out. For this moment, we are one, falling over the edge together.

When it's over, Emmett collapses against me, his large, muscled body sweaty and sliding against mine. His breath is rough and steady in my ear, and his lips brush my neck briefly. I want to hold on to him, to feel his skin as it calms, but I can't move. I think my arms are asleep.

Once he catches his breath, he places a soft kiss on my forehead, then pulls out. He takes the condom off, disposing of it in the trash in the head.

I need a moment to think. There are too many emotions swirling around inside. Too many of them that don't have a place. Not with us, not with what we're trying to do.

This is getting complicated.

This is getting dangerous.

Maybe for no one else but my heart.

In the waning tide of the orgasm, I'm starting to think clearly again.

"We can't do that again," I say to him quietly as I sit up, making a feeble attempt to cover my breasts. "I really mean it this time."

He stares at me in surprise. "Why not?"

"Because," I tell him. Suddenly the berth's cushions seem

infinitely interesting as I run my hands over them. "Because the more I have sex with you, the more things begin to blur. Things are already so confusing as it is. The last thing I want is to feel things for you."

When he doesn't say anything, I slowly look up and watch as he swallows, rubs his lips together like he doesn't quite understand. "Why is it so wrong to feel things for me?"

There's a quiet desperation in his voice that nearly catches me off-guard. I push on.

"Because I think, in time, you'll probably just break my heart. None of this is real Emmett. The last thing I need is to forget that."

He nods. Studies me. A flash of realization comes over his eyes, turning them cool. "You're right. In the end, I'd probably just hurt you. That's not what I want. That's not what you deserve."

Fucking hell. Even though those words pretty much came out of my mouth, it hurts something fierce to hear him say it, like a steel-toed boot to the gut. He can't even pretend that he can be the man I need him to be.

He's being honest with you, that's what you like about him, I remind myself. *Now tell your heart to go fuck itself and get back in the game.*

Sheesh. My inner pep talks are getting pretty harsh.

* * *

"CAN we have that table in the corner?" Jackie asks the hostess and then gives me a triumphant look when she starts to lead us that way.

It's lunchtime at a restaurant a block away from work and it's the first day Jackie has been back. The lucky bitch's honeymoon stretched on for almost two weeks before her and Will had to return with matching tans and big smiles.

She only works part-time at Mad Men so she can spare it, and Will, well Will only has to answer to Ted and we all know how Ted feels about it. I think he's just glad they came back at all.

While I've talked to her every other day while she was in Mexico, I still haven't been able to get down to the nitty gritty with her. Not that I particularly feel like it today. After the boating trip, my head has been all over the place and I'm really not sure what to feel anymore.

"I think Tiffany was a little upset that she wasn't invited," I tell Jackie after we order drinks, a Caesar for me and a virgin one for her.

"Hey," she says to me, giving me a steady look. "Remember when you needed to talk to me about Will, back when we were secretly dating, and you said she couldn't come? Just doing the same favor. We both love her to bits but you know she can't keep her mouth shut, try as she might. If word gets out about the truth about you and Emmett, it could ruin everything. The press would be so quick to jump all over that." She pauses. "Speaking of press, have you been keeping up with yourself?"

She takes out her phone and waves it at me. "I pretty much spent the whole honeymoon reading all the gossip sites. I think I learned more from them than I did from you. Alyssa, these people are fucking everywhere following you around. This must be driving you crazy."

I shrug. "To be honest, I'm getting used to it." I gesture around the restaurant. "And no one ever looks my way unless I'm with him. In a way, it's the perfect blend of fame and anonymity. With Emmett I know people will take pictures and we'll turn heads, I mean that's why I'm here. And when he's not here, well I'm just myself."

"So you're not yourself with him?"

Her question makes me pause. Am I myself with him? Or

am I putting on some persona? I dismiss the question with my hand. "It doesn't matter. The real question is, why were you looking at pictures of me on your honeymoon and not having sex with your new husband?"

"This isn't about me," Jackie says. "Don't even try to change the subject. We have our whole lives to talk about the baby and the honeymoon and how the husband is doing. What I want to know is every single detail about you two."

"Well what do you want to know?"

"Alyssa," she says sternly. "You're dating Emmett Hill. Do you know what they call you? The Bruiser and The Blondie."

I stare at her, slack-jawed. Seriously? Was that Carla's doing?

"Well it's highly unfair to call him a bruiser," I say. "That's just the media running with it because it rhymes with Cruiser. He's only gotten in like a handful of public fights."

"And your whole relationship is fake," she goes on, ignoring that. "So of course I want to know what the hell is going on. I mean, this is the most exciting thing to ever happen since…"

"Since you found out you were having a baby and getting married?"

She looks sheepish. "Well yeah. So are you sleeping with him?"

That's the one thing I haven't been forthcoming about in our texts. All the times I've slept with Emmett, which is technically three if you count the beginning, I haven't mentioned to anyone. I don't know why, I'm not usually one to shy away from sharing the details. I guess it's just the one thing we do together that's nobody's business but ours.

And it's something that won't continue, I remind myself. Though I'm starting to take these declarations less and less seriously. Kind of like when you promise you'll start your diet tomorrow and you never ever do.

"You are sleeping with him," she exclaims softly. "Holy shit."

"It's nothing. It's not a habit."

"Pretty nice habit if it was."

"He's good at what he does," I admit.

"You're selling him short."

I press my lips together trying to suppress a smile. Am I ever. Emmett is not just good at what he does, he fucks like champ. He's in it to win and nothing less than a million mind-blowing orgasms will do.

Crap. I know I have that sick dreamy look on my face and Jackie is delighting in every minute of it.

"But it doesn't matter," I go on, making my features blank, "because he annoys the living shit out of me."

"Oh, he does not."

"He's a cad, Jackie. A prick. An asshole. A player. A down-right scoundrel."

"And that's a problem for you?"

I give her a loaded look.

"Can't you just enjoy the wining and dining then?" she asks, desperate to find some sort of romance between us. "I mean, that's what helped Will win me over. That and the gifts."

"Yeah. And that's the huge difference here. For one, no one is winning anyone over. Except for us, together, winning over the general public. For second, you actually liked Will."

"I still don't believe you don't like Emmett, even a little." I stare blankly at her. She shrugs with one shoulder. "Okay, so then at least you like his dick."

"I do. And I can like a dick without liking what it's attached to." I pause. "Though I must say, his tongue and his hands are pretty fantastic too. Wouldn't be fair to leave them out. So I guess if there was some version of Emmett out there that was just tongue, dick and hands, I'd venture to say then that, yes, I like him."

A silence falls over us as we ponder this interesting phallic creation.

"You know what, I know you," she says with a patient smile. "I know you and I know you say you hate him but you don't. Not even a bit. In fact, the only thing you hate is the fact that you like him. I'd go on to say that you probably like him a lot."

I scoff and busy myself with the napkin. "You don't know what you're talking about."

"Oh, but I do. I do. All that time pretending I wasn't in love with Will was absolutely futile."

I glance at her in annoyance. "I'm not *in love* with Emmett."

"I'm not saying you are. But you like him and you're pretending you don't."

I swallow that down. "So?" I ask cagily.

"Love is a cliff. You're just steps from the edge. The fall is inevitable."

I let out a huff of air, blowing a strand of hair off my face. "You can like someone and not fall in love with them. It happens all the time. It's why so many people break up. They have the like. They want the love. And they expect the love. But sometimes that love doesn't show up. So you have to end it." I can't help but think about Emmett as I'm saying this, the way he was with his ex-fiancée.

"You're so cynical."

"I've been around the block a lot," I remind her. "And I'm not cynical, I'm a realist. I know what to expect, I know how it all works. The fact of the matter is the majority of relation-ships downright fail before they even get to the 'I love you stage', let alone after. And when it comes to Emmett and me, our relationship is one hundred per cent fake."

"I bet the orgasms are real," she says under her breath.

"And they are. I like Emmett. Okay? And I like having sex with him. No, I *love* having sex with him. But that's the extent of what we are and who we are to each other. It will never go beyond that. It's not in the contract. There are no cliffs of love for us to leap off of here. Just one big wall, signed with ink."

Jackie studies me for a moment before shaking her head and taking a sip of her drink. "You're a dream crusher, you know that? What the hell are you doing reading all those romance novels anyway? Don't you believe in the happily ever after? Don't you want that?"

I suck back on my straw and grin at her. "Honestly, I just want to get off."

She bursts out laughing and raises her drink. "Well okay then. Congratu-fucking-lations to that!"

"Cheers," I say as I clink mine against hers.

"Oh, by the way," she says after our food arrives and I've started wolfing down my gnocchi. "I was thinking that since you guys are officially dating, maybe the four of us could go on a date. Like a mini-trip together."

I take my time chewing before I swallow it down. "A mini-trip? That sounds serious. Do you think we're ready for that?"

She casts me a dry look. "Do you hear yourself? This isn't a real relationship, you said so yourself. Technically, you can't mess it up. You're already ready for anything."

Right. Fuck, it's hard to keep things straight. "Sure. A trip sounds fun." It would be the first time going away with Emmett but with Will and Jackie there, I think it could be doable. "Where, when?"

"Labour Day weekend is just around the corner. I was originally thinking Will's mother's campground in Tofino but she actually won't be there then. What about your mom?"

My mom. I'm immediately hit with a pang of guilt. Normally I'm driving over to Penticton once a month to visit her but Emmett's been sucking up so much of my time lately. The last thing I want is for her to meet Emmett and buy into the whole relationship thing, though I know she already knows about him. Then again, it would put her little heart at ease to at least think I'm in a serious relationship with a (mildly) respectable guy. At least a guy with money.

"That might work," I say cautiously. "I owe her a visit. But I don't want to stay in the house, there's not enough room for us all."

"Maybe Emmett or Will can rent some cabins down by the lake. Preferably one with a vineyard."

"You don't think you'll go crazy being surrounded by all the wine you can't drink?"

"I survived weeks of virgin piña coladas," she says, her brown eyes looking wistful.

"Well then that might just work."

"Oh come on, it will be so much fun."

"Will it?"

"Me, Will...the Bruiser and the Blondie."

I roll my eyes. "Please stop. That's all I see now. That and pictures of my fat ass and the headlines about me being a normal girl, said in the most belittling way. I'm terrified to read the comment sections, I know people are taking shots at me."

"Only because people are jealous and the world is a horrible place."

I laugh. "When you put it that way..."

"So we're in? Labor Day weekend. The lake."

"We're in."

"All in?"

I sigh. "All in."

CHAPTER 13

ALYSSA

*M*y mother was so excited to hear that I was taking my famous new boyfriend to visit her in Penticton that it almost felt terrible that the whole thing was a lie. I say almost because what she doesn't know can't hurt her.

Until the contract is up of course and Emmett and I part ways in what is sure to be a public break-up. Ugh. I hadn't really thought about that part, about what happens when this whole thing is over. I find myself entertaining the fact that maybe my contract will be renewed, like I'm a star on some show. And the show being Emmett Hill's life.

At first I was a bit wary of going away with him but that all changed when he took me out for sushi at one of the city's newest hotspots and broke the news to me: The CW network is having a party down in LA and the cast of *Boomerang* is required to go.

And Emmett insisted I come along as his date.

So that's why I'm currently sitting beside Emmett in the first-class section of an Air Canada flight, bound for LA. Forget about being nervous about the couples trip to Penticton, I'm absolutely jubilant that I get to go to Los Angeles for the first time in a long time. Too bad I'm not a huge fan of flying.

"Nervous flier?" he asks me, watching as my fingers tap dance along the arm rest between us.

"Just during take-off and landing," I admit.

"But we took off an hour ago."

"And we're landing in an hour," I point out.

He slowly licks his lips until they spread into an easy grin. "You're fucking adorable, you know that?"

Real or fake? Real or fake?

I'm going to pretend he's being real. Just for fun.

"Thank you," I tell him. "I try around you."

He laughs gently, his eyes searching mine. "No you don't. You don't try at all. That's why I like you." He then closes his fingers over mine and holds them tight.

I lean in close to him, catching a whiff of the fresh rosemary scent of his cologne. I whisper, "You just said you liked me and I think you might have meant it. I'm making a note of it."

He reaches over and gently cups the side of my face in his warm, broad palm. "It's never been a secret, sunshine."

Then he closes his beautiful eyes and brushes his lips against mine, a slow teasing kiss that deepens and blooms. I feel it slide over me like stepping into a warm bath, my tongue stroking against his until our mouths are aching and wild for each other.

Fucking hell, Emmett Hill. The man can fuck like a champ but he can also make out like no one's business.

The flight attendant clearing her throat is the only thing that makes us stop, though I can feel Emmett smiling against my mouth before he looks up.

"Would you like anything more to drink?" the flight attendant says with an overly warm smile, entirely fixated on him. And I can't blame her. Emmett's in black pants, an ice-blue button-down shirt that's open just enough at the chest, the color making his eyes come to life, his bronze hair artfully mussed up, thick and shining.

"Of course," Emmett says to her. "Keep them coming. A glass of white wine for each of us."

She nods and moves onto the next person.

"Sorry I ordered for you," he says to me, letting his fingers drift away from my face. My cheek feels cold without his skin pressed there. "I felt like it was a thing that we do."

"As is making out in public," I tell him. I poke my head up and glance around. No one in first class is paying us any attention. In fact, I think I recognize another passenger up here, some older man who used to play a demon on *Supernatural* or something.

Emmett shrugs and settles back into his seat, not apologetic at all.

I think I'm starting to figure out how we work. Anything physical is real. Everything emotional is fake.

Except for the fact that he just admitted he liked me. And he meant it. That much I know.

I'll take what I can get.

When we land at LAX, Emmett holding my hand tight during the entire landing, I'm completely unprepared for the onslaught of paparazzi at baggage claim. I mean, I'm used to the cameras in Vancouver but to be honest, most of the time it's the same two or three guys you see at every place. Everything else between Emmett and I seems to be documented by fans and strangers who cross our paths.

But here? Fucking eh! There's like twenty of them with huge cameras, all of them yelling our names like we're at some sort of cattle auction, a million flashbulbs going off until I'm practically blind. I'm actually doing that cliché pose that celebrities do where they walk while looking down, one arm out in front of them to shield their face, because if I didn't do that, I'd probably fall right down on the baggage carousel.

"Emmett! Emmett, you're looking great!"

"Emmett, can you tell us more about Alyssa?!"

"Alyssa how does it feel to snag one of the most notorious bachelors!"

"Emmett, has she helped you clean up your ways?"

"Emmett, how do you feel about your new nickname? Do you think it's accurate?"

"Is it true you sleep nude?"

"Alyssa, baby, you're beautiful! Give us a big smile!"

The yelling and the questions never stop but I do love how Emmett is turning extra-protective, trying to actually shield me from the cameras instead of showing me off. I think he's so blindsided by the attention that he's forgetting this is what's supposed to happen, what he's supposed to want for us.

"Give us some space, please," Emmett says through his smile, even though his eyes are flashing dangerously. He holds me tight, keeps me back from the cameras. I can totally see why actors end up breaking lenses because this shit is unreal and completely disorienting.

Somehow, we make it out with our bags and are ushered into a waiting Suburban hired by the network. It's only when we start pulling away from the airport and into the LA traffic, that I remember how to breathe.

"Are you okay?" Emmett asks me, holding my hand while he looks me over.

I nod. "Yeah. Just. Wow." I take in a deep breath, trying to get my head on straight.

"Fucking vultures." His voice is laced with anger. "They treated you like you were a piece of meat."

I personally don't see Emmett pissed off very often but I

have to say I'm touched by it. "I guess that's the good part about shooting in Vancouver, you don't have to put up with *this*." I gesture to the city as if it's some singular beast intent on harassing him.

He sighs and leans back in his seat, closing his eyes. "Yeah. It's funny. Working on Degrassi, I really thought it was my big break. I mean, it was. In Canada. But people quickly forget. And when it was over, I assumed I would go on to bigger and better things." He pauses, licks his lips. "You know, I wanted this. What happened back there. I wanted the fame and the glory and all of it. And now…is it really worth trading your soul for?"

I look him over curiously. "You traded your soul?"

He looks out the window and nods. "In a way. I think everyone does in order to get what they think they want."

"What did you trade away?"

After a few beats he says, "Respect."

"But people respect you." But as soon as the words leave my mouth, I'm not exactly sure if it's true. Autumn had mentioned how he isn't well-respected. And judging by the paparazzi show at the airport and what they write in the tabloids, the media certainly doesn't respect him either. "You're a good actor," I say feebly.

He gives me a wry smile. "Oh really? What have you actually watched me in?"

The truth is, it's been nothing lately. I can't even watch *Boomerang* because it's so damn weird to see him on the screen. "I liked an indie horror movie you did a long time ago."

He lets out a sharp laugh and slaps my knee. "The one with the killer bees?"

"Yeah. What was it called, Buzzed Off?"

He shakes his head. "Oh man, I'll never live it down. I do

have to say, working with bees all day did give me a deep appreciation for them."

"I'm sure it did."

"Well, let me tell you…it's not that people don't respect me. They do. I act well enough. The shows I do at least stay on the air. I'm not doing, like, porn. Bees aside, I'm not ashamed. But I lost a lot of respect for myself."

"Why?"

His tongue peeks out between his lips as his brows furrow, deep in thought. After a beat he says, "In hindsight, I should have stayed in London. I should have stayed in the theatre. That's really the only time I felt happy. I felt real and alive and fucking *thriving*, you know? It wasn't until you came along that I started to feel happy again."

Bam. My heart stills inside my chest, a cage of butterflies just dying to open.

Holy.

I swallow, the sound audible in the car. "You…I make you happy?"

He glances at me, a quiet smile tugging the side of his mouth. "Yeah. You do."

"Real or fake?" I ask whisper.

His features soften. "Real, Alyssa. Very, very real. I know this is…" he glances up at the driver who seems to be minding his own business before looking back to me with yearning eyes, "I know this is complicated and not necessarily what should happen but ever since I met you, I've had something inside me wake up. You don't know how grateful I am for it."

Holy crow. I don't know what to say. I don't even know how to feel. My heart is blossoming inside me, opening like a flower to the sun.

Don't catch the feels, I remind myself. But I think it's already too late.

"Anyway," he says after a moment, letting go of my hand and running his fingers through his hair. "That's the way it is now. You spend your whole life wanting one thing and then you get it and realize it's not what you want at all."

I clear my throat, still gobsmacked by his confession. "Maybe because what you want and what you need are sometimes totally different."

"That's true. So tell me, when this is all over...I mean, in the future...and you have what you want," he means the money, "will it really be what you need?"

I shrug and watch as the tall spires of downtown LA roll past. "I won't know until I try. But I have to try. And you had to try too. You'd never know otherwise. You have to go up for the role you want to find out if you need it in the end."

"So clever, tying this all into an acting metaphor."

"A clever blonde," I joke. "So rare."

"No," he says, his fingers pressing against my chin and tilting my face toward him, "*You're* rare, Alyssa."

The way he's looking into my eyes, so deep and searching and startlingly intimate, unnerves me to the core. I'm not even sure how to handle it.

"I'm not used to sincere Emmett," I joke, feeling like it's all too much. "When does the dirty-talking one come back?"

For a moment, I think I see a flash of disappointment in his eyes, but then they melt, all warm and crinkly at the corners as he breaks into a cheeky grin. "That will come later."

First though, we have a party to attend. Our plane landed in the afternoon, so as soon as we're checked into our pool-side cabana room at the Roosevelt Hotel in Hollywood, we immediately started getting ready. And by we, I mean me. I ordered a Glam Squad crew to come over and do my hair and makeup while Emmett relaxed out on the balcony, sipping on beer. And of course, all the girls wanted to talk about is Emmett.

I know I should have waxed on and on about our relationship and how great he is and how he's changing and all the things I've been getting used to saying. But the truth is, I didn't want to say that shit anymore. It didn't quite feel right. I didn't feel like I had to explain that Emmett was "better" with me, when he was fine before, just acting like a human being. I didn't want to go on about how in love we are, because suddenly the real concept of love between us seemed so fragile and sacred. Once upon a time, it didn't seem like a possibility at all, but I'm starting to realize that these feelings I'm trying so hard not to catch might be no match for my body in the end. I always assumed my heart had built up some sort of immunity but I'm no longer sure that's the case.

He's in my veins, in my system, slowly working his way to my heart.

I do have to say, all their questions and comments about Emmett made me forget how nervous I am about tonight, especially when I see the finished product in the mirror. I look pretty much as I did at Jackie's wedding, the night I first snagged Emmett, but a lot more…spicy.

"Wow," Emmett says to me as he steps in from the balcony, casually holding a Corona by the neck. "You look fucking fantastic."

The Glam Squad girls all coo and blush, as if he's complimenting them. I mean, I guess he is, it's their handiwork that's transformed me from average girl to Brigitte Bardot, but from the way his eyes stay fixated on me, I know I'm all he sees.

Then they leave and we're alone.

My pulse starts to quicken and I can't figure out if I'm nervous again because of the event we're going to or that for the first time I'm alone with him in a hotel room.

"I should get dressed," I say to him and start heading for the closet where I hung up my dress. I went shopping the day I found out about this event. Emmett was insistent on paying for it since it's his event and all, so I gladly took his credit card and had a field day at the mall. In the end though, I eschewed the high-end designer labels (that's more of Jackie and Will's thing) and settled on a long, neon-yellow dress from the department store. I know it's super bright but I figured it's LA and I'll probably stand out anyway in a sea of size zeros, so why the hell not make a statement?

But as I'm going, he grabs my arm and pulls me to him so I'm pressed against the taut muscles of his stomach and chest. Damn. I can practically feel the ridges of his abs against my skin.

"Would you be mad if I messed you up beforehand?" he asks me, a lazy look in his eyes. That look that actually means the opposite of lazy. Sex with Emmett is anything but.

"Then who will do my makeup and hair after?" I ask him as he grins at me, his mouth just inches away. "You?"

"I don't know," he murmurs. "Maybe we won't go to the party at all." He places his lips at my neck and my bare skin breaks out in gooseflesh. "Maybe spending the night right here will be far more entertaining."

I smile, my lungs breathless as his lips gently suck down the length of my neck, heading for my collarbone. Somehow, I manage to press my hand against his chest and push him back. "You have to go. It's in your contract. And by default, in mine. And I am not wasting my dress or this hair and makeup job." I pause, biting my lip before I realize I'm scraping off my orange-red lipstick. "Then we'll see what happens after."

He looks surprised. "Oh really. What happened to the whole 'we shouldn't do that again'?"

"I said *we'll see*," I remind him and hope he doesn't bring up the other thing I said on the boat. That I didn't want to develop feelings for him.

ALSO, my brain starts to yell, *remember he said that he'd probably hurt you in the end. You can't forget that!*

And yet I kind of did until that moment.

Things are getting dangerous.

I step away from Emmett, needing to get out of his orbit before it warps me. "I'm going to get ready. Are you putting on a tux or just going to stand around all day like that, drinking beer?" I take the dress from the closet and head into the bathroom to get changed.

I run the tap and take a good long look at myself in the mirror. I barely recognize the woman staring back at me, the one with the thick, shiny, Pantene hair and perfectly contoured face. But I do recognize the look in my eyes.

Fear.

Fear that maybe Jackie was right. Maybe the end isn't just a wall signed with ink. Maybe it's a cliff I have to jump off.

And what if I do something crazy, like throw myself off of it before I'm ready?

What if what I'm feeling is completely, horribly...unstoppable?

His words ring through my head. *In the end, I'd probably just hurt you.*

I just have to remind myself, once again, like I've been doing from the start, that I'm in it for money. I'm in it for fun. I'm not here to fall in love. I'm here because it's my ticket to a life I've been too afraid to go after. I mean, hell, here we are in LA, the one place I always thought my dreams would, or at least could, come true, and I'm going to a party with all the actors and crew and producers of a big network. Focus on that.

Not Emmett.

Never Emmett.

But that changes once I slip on the dress and step out of the washroom.

His eyes light up as he sees me and he lets out a low whistle. "You're trying to kill me, aren't you?"

I'm such a lost cause. It took a second and I'm totally giddy from the way he's looking at me. "What about you," I say, smacking him on the shoulder. "Mr. wears a tux like he was born in it."

"Such a complicated name," he says, still looking me up and down, soaking every inch of me in. Then he glances at his watch. "Too bad our ride will be here in a few minutes."

"Good," I tell him, quickly slipping on a pair of bright magenta heels. "I'm ready for whatever the night brings."

And the night turned out to be completely unforgettable.

It started off with a walk down the red carpet to the event, a red carpet lined with cameras and benches of screaming, yelling fans. It was totally different than it was at the airport. This time, I absolutely relished all the eyes on me, maybe because I was feeling good about myself, maybe because I felt I was in control. Maybe because Emmett didn't let go of my hand once. By the time we reached the end of the carpet, I actually felt like a total pro.

Then once we got inside the building, a huge ballroom, I was shuffled with a drink in hand over to every single power play and actor in Hollywood that you could think of.

Okay, that's kind of a lie. I mean, it was everyone that was part of the CW network. But even so, I saw a lot of the actors I crushed and drooled over (and by that, I mean masturbate to when I can't sleep at night), which was beyond cool.

What was also cool was the way that everyone flocked to Emmett. I know he feels like the world might not respect him in the way he wants, but even big-name actors were fawning over him, talking about his days on *Degrassi* with nostalgia, then congratulating him on his comeback. I still think the term comeback should be used rather loosely but the fact is, his peers look up to him, not necessarily as someone who is the master of their craft, but as someone who has consistently worked and never given up.

Later, when I'm done acting like a fangirl and have had one too many glasses of champagne, Emmett pulls me aside.

"I'm over all this," he whispers, holding my arm. "Are you over all this?"

I nod. "I'm ready to leave when you are."

"But you had fun right?"

"Oh, hell yeah I did. This was," I gesture to the ballroom where I think I might be looking at Archie from *Riverdale*, "a dream come true. I don't even think it's sunken in yet."

"I liked the way you handled yourself," he says, tucking a piece of hair behind my ear. "Like you've been doing it your whole life. Perhaps this acting thing really is in your blood."

"Hey, I told you I was serious about it. Serious enough to date *you*."

He chuckles and the sound makes me week at the knees. As does the amused grin he has on while he looks at me. "We don't fly out until late tomorrow night. How about we hit the beach in the morning, then in the afternoon see if we can do some improv."

"What do you mean, do some improv?"

"I have connections, sunshine. Ever heard of the Uptight Citizens Comedy Brigade?"

"Uh, *yes*." Like, totally one of the best incubators for comedians there is.

"Maybe we can get you on stage for a bit. I'll do it with you."

"You're joking," I tell him.

He shakes his head. "I'm not. I think it would be good for you."

I can hardly believe it. "Remind me in the morning…if you still mean it."

"You know I do," he says and pulls me away. "Come on, let's go back to the hotel."

But when we leave the venue and get back into the Suburban, Emmett wants to stop at a late-night taco place he loves.

While the Suburban waits around the corner, we get in line with the rest of the drunken patrons. The menu is pretty simple and I settle on a deep-fried chicken taco with pickled vegetables.

"So, I guess you know LA pretty well," I tell him, inching forward a step as the line moves.

"Did a lot of auditions here, even during Degrassi days."

At that, the person in line turns around to look at us and see who's doing the talking. Once they spot Emmett though, who just smiles at them, they frown, like they're disap-pointed, and turn back around. They were expecting Drake.

"Anyway," Emmett goes on. "I lived here for a few years before I moved to London. Did a lot of bit parts, some small roles, pilots, indie films."

"Would you move here if you had to?"

"Of course. I love LA. Love the sunshine. Love the vibe."

"But you still prefer London?"

He nods. "I know they're polar opposites but I think deep down, theatre speaks to me so much more than film or TV acting. It's…real. You're in the moment. It's scripted but it doesn't feel scripted, know what I mean? You're living it, like it's a reality. There is no performance, only passion."

No performance. Only passion. His words sink into me like stones.

Is that what we are? Are we living this, us, like it's a reality? Are we starting to throw the script away and just improvise on the fly?

It's so fucking hard to tell.

"So, when was the last time you went on an audition?" he asks me.

I know he expects me to say like ten years ago or something but that's not the truth at all.

"Um, last year?"

"What?" He's taken aback. "Seriously?"

I nod sheepishly. "Yeah. I go every now and then. Take a sick day, don't tell Will," I add. "I do it just to see if I still like it, to see where it could go. I still keep my headshots up to date too." I pause. "Obviously it never goes anywhere, but it makes me feel better. Like I'm feeding my soul, just a little bit. Honestly, I would take a Tampax commercial if they'd have me."

Emmett bursts out laughing. "I can just see it now."

"I'd be perfect," I protest. "I play bitchy so well and who the hell is happy on their period? Um, no one."

Emmett suddenly leans over and kisses me quickly on the lips.

"What was that one for?" I ask him. The oddly tender way he's looking at me makes me feel all warm and fuzzy inside.

"I have a feeling you don't tell anyone that. Not just your desire to be in a tampon commercial, but that you're still going on auditions. Still trying."

He's right. I haven't told a soul. My mother would support me no matter what I do, but she's been through so much and she was so happy when she found out I had gotten a steady job all those years ago and had put acting aside. My sisters don't really speak to me much, but they always thought acting was a joke. As for Tiffany and Jackie, I just get the feeling that they wouldn't understand. Or maybe they would, but they'd start asking me about it and cheering me on and I don't want that. I want it to just stay this private, secret thing.

Only now Emmett knows.

"I won't tell a soul," he says in a low voice, as if he can read my mind. "But for the record...I think it's great. Really. It takes a lot of nerve and courage to keep a dream alive when it's so much easier to give up on it."

I give him a shy smile. "Thanks."

Then it's our turn for tacos. We eat them at a brightly-colored picnic table under a buzzing streetlamp, the air warm and comforting. I don't even mind the smell of exhaust.

I'm just about to scrunch up the empty wrapper after I've scarfed down the last bite, when a man in a trucker hat with long, scraggly hair and a big belly stops at the foot of the table, camera at his side.

"Hey," he says loudly to Emmett and Emmett looks at him sharply. "You're Emmett Hill, right?"

"Who's asking?" Emmett says, not smiling.

The guy pats his camera. "Does it matter? I just have a question for you."

And then he raises the camera up and starts filming.

I glance at Emmett, not sure how he's going to handle this.

Emmett slowly gets to his feet. "I'd appreciate it if you didn't film us right now. My girlfriend and I just want some time alone."

"Girlfriend," the guy snorts but then doesn't elaborate. "Hey so, let me ask you something."

By now, some of the people in line at the taco stand are looking over at us.

Emmett stares at him with hard eyes, his patience starting to wear thin. I get to my feet and walk around the back of the table until I'm at Emmett's side. I take his arm, partly in comfort since this guy's vibe is totally messing with me, partly because I don't want Emmett to do anything dumb. Last time something like this happened, he broke someone's phone. If he does it to this guy's camera, he's going to raise a real stink.

"What?" Emmett asks deliberately, his jaw tense.

"Your mother," the man says and Emmett visibly stiffens, like he's just been punched. I hold his arm tighter as the man continues, "she was a heroin addict, died of an overdose. You're the one who found her, right?"

I stare up at Emmett. Holy fuck, is this true?

Emmett doesn't say anything. I don't think he can. He looks like he's frozen on the spot, every inch of him immobile.

"I'm just saying, you never talk about it and I was wondering if I could get a soundbite. Like, was she just a junkie or was she also a prostitute and was she on drugs when she had you, because -"

The man doesn't have a chance to finish his sentence.

Emmett lunges at him and with one swift, powerful movement, he grabs the camera with one hand while punching the man square in the face with the other.

It happened so fast, I couldn't even hold him back.

"Emmett!" I cry out. Not because I think he's in any danger, I mean, Emmett is strong like a bull and could probably take a beating and like it, but because he's throwing another punch at the side of the guy's head, just as the camera drops to the ground, parts breaking off.

If I don't do something, I'm pretty sure Emmett will kill him.

Somehow, I manage to wrap my arms around Emmett's waist and try and pull him back while an excited crowd starts to gather around. I'm pretty sure some of them are either chanting "Bruiser" or "Cruiser," I can't tell.

"You son of a bitch!" the guy yells, hands covering his bloody face. "I'm pressing charges!" He points at everyone around us. "I have witnesses, you're all witnesses! He attacked me! He attacked *me!*"

"Emmett, we have to go," I tell him, trying to pull him back. He's breathing heavily, his eyes wild, I'm not even sure he's hearing me right now. "Please, please, let's go."

"He's not going anywhere blondie," the fat pap says to me as he fishes his phone out from his pocket and starts to dial. He turns his back to us and talks into it. "Yes, I've just been a victim of assault."

"Oh shit," I swear, giving Emmett another tug. Finally, he yields to me and I pull him over to the street, looking around for the Suburban.

"We can't go," Emmett finally says to me, his voice hoarse. His eyes meet mine and there's so much anger and pain in them that I'm nearly speechless. "He's called the cops. They'll be looking for me."

"They're going to put you in jail," I whisper to him. "You can't go to jail."

He sighs and shakes out his hand with a wince, spreading his reddened fingers. "I'm really sorry," he says. "Really. I didn't mean for this to happen."

"The guy was asking for it, there's no need to apologize." I'm hanging onto him tighter and tighter, afraid to let go.

"I lost my temper. I shouldn't have."

Oh god, how I want to ask him about his mother, ask him if it's true what the man said.

God. Poor, poor Emmett.

But it's not long before the flashing lights appear and a police car arrives on the scene.

One officer talks to the man while the other comes over to us.

"Is it true you assaulted this man?" he asks Emmett,

nodding at the guy who is waving his hands wildly, trying to act out the scene.

Emmett opens his mouth to speak but I immediately remember every single TV show I've seen. "He's not saying a word until he speaks to a lawyer."

The cop rolls his eyes. "All right, all right. Look, between you and me, we have bigger things to attend to tonight than this. But I'm afraid I'm going to have to put you under arrest and take you to the station. If he doesn't press charges, you won't have to stay long."

"You can't arrest him!" I cry out. "He did nothing wrong!"

"Alyssa," Emmett says to me. "It's fine."

"It's not fine!" Where the hell am I going to go? Wait at the hotel to see if he gets bailed out or not? And who is supposed to bail him out? Is it me? Autumn? Will? How does this whole thing work?

"Ma'am, please," the cop says.

"But we're Canadian!" I plead. "You can't do this! We have an amazing Prime Minister!"

The cop doesn't care. "Then maybe your amazing Prime Minister will help bail him out when he's done cuddling panda bears and doing one-armed push-ups or whatever the fuck you crazy people do up there."

And then he's leading Emmett over to the cop car and cuffing him.

Naturally, the crowd around the taco stand has their camera phones aimed at him and the whole event, including the snivelling paparazzi man who is trying to pick up the pieces of his camera, moaning in pain for dramatic effect.

"The Bruiser and The Blondie," some girl says, speaking into her phone, "just got into a whole lot of trouble."

CHAPTER 14

EMMETT

I'd like to say I haven't been in jail before but that would be a lie.

After my mother died, I went to live with my religious aunt in this shitty town of Mission and though she tried to her hardest to keep her tabs on me during high school, after high school it was a different story.

Once, when I was twenty and hanging out with my friend Matt (this was a few months before I landed the role on *Degrassi*), we were feeling rather rambunctious and doing a few lines of coke. We were bored, as we often were, and hanging out at Matt's parents' place.

Matt's parents were used to me always being there and I think they felt a bit sorry for me because of my mother and my upbringing and my shitty aunt (she was the type of person at church who would watch how much money you were putting in the collection plate and then publicly chastise you if it wasn't enough), so they didn't mind me hanging out and we were pretty much left alone.

There's not much to do in Mission. It's a small town at the end of the road, lots of industry and a very religious slant. While I would work at the local video store and take the train into Vancouver for acting classes and the occasional audition, you had to make your own fun.

So we drank, did some drugs. That kind of thing.

This particular night, we did some lines and then let our boredom got the best of us.

My friend thought it would be hilarious if we went to the local donut shop and harassed the cops.

I know, I know. Made perfect sense at the time.

Then we decided it would be even funnier if we dressed up in his mother's clothes. His sister had some wigs. We melded the two together.

So after we got all dolled up, we went down to Tim Hortons and started hitting on the cops.

We thought it was hilarious.

"Oh, I do declare, officer," I'd say in my best Blanche DuBois.

They gave us plenty of time to back off and go away and yet we kept on pushing their buttons.

"My, aren't you fellas so big and strong?"

Finally, understandably, we were arrested. I remember clearly, like it was yesterday, the moment we were at the station being fingerprinted and I looked over at Matt, who was wearing a pink, floral dress and had a red, curly wig half-hanging off his head, and I said, "Matt, you look ridiculous."

Needless to say, we were let go in the morning, after spending a night in the cell dressed as women.

But the LA jails are no joke. Lucky for me, tonight I was shoved into the drunk tank with a bunch of frat boys who had passed right out and didn't give me any trouble.

Fucking hell though, what a hell of a night it was. To go from the high of having Alyssa on my arm at the party, actually having someone I wanted to show off, that I cared for deeply, that I was proud of, to losing my temper on the paparazzi. I had the night planned out so differently.

First, we would get the tacos and fill our bellies since I know from experience that the food choices at LA events are pretty skimpy since no one eats in this town, then we would go back to the hotel.

And I know that Alyssa had been standoffish after the last time we had sex and I also know I admitted that I might just be a rat-bastard in the end, but the fact was, I wanted nothing more than to get her naked and beneath me again. It was truly the only time I knew that what we had was real, that each moan, each look, each touch, meant more than anything either of us could ever say.

When I'm deep inside her, there is only truth between us.

The thing is…she's getting under my skin. She's slipping into my veins, a poison, a drug, and like most foolish men, I'm too weak to stay away, to say no.

I want her. Every day. Every night. I want her in my bed, I want her in my arms. I want her sitting across from me at the dinner table, not just for the next two months, but…for as long as I can. When I think about Alyssa now, it's no longer in terms of contracts. It's no longer in terms of what should be, what's supposed to be. It's no longer in terms of what's fake.

When I think about her, I think about just her. I think about what she does to me, what she means to me.

Honestly, she means the fucking world.

And I'm having a hell of a time expressing that to her because everything we have between us is supposed to be a lie. And if I was smart I would be keep it that way. After all, I told her about the kind of person I was, that I might hurt her in the end. But the truth is, I don't want to lie anymore.

I want every single moment we share to mean something.

The only problem is, she doesn't know the real me.

Though, fuck, she sure got a glimpse of that tonight.

I've always been very guarded with my private life. No one really gave a shit until I went on *Degrassi* and then the Canadian press started poking and prodding the boy behind Cruiser McGill. But that's the Canadian press. They're pretty bashful about it all. When they asked me about my parents, I told them both of them died when I was young and I was raised in Mission by my aunt. No one ever bothered to look into it. And there was no one from my previous life, the life on Vancouver's east side, that would ever argue. Everyone except Jimmy is pretty much dead.

That said, it doesn't surprise me that somehow someone would start digging and find the truth behind it all. I'm not ashamed. The problem with it all is that people get the wrong ideas. They start making assumptions. That's where it gets dangerous.

The right thing tonight would have been to address the guy's questions and set the record straight. But I just wanted to be alone with Alyssa and the fucker caught me off-guard, especially as he was the only reporter so far who knew the truth about my mother. I know my mother was clean when she had me, that she only started using a few years after my father left, and I'm pretty sure she wasn't a prostitute. She was more or less always at home and if she ever had guys over, I was allowed to hang out with them, if I wanted.

I rarely did. Even when you're raised around drug use, it never stops being a terrifying monster, one that doesn't live in your closet but out there in the open.

Fuck. Who fucking knows. What's worse is that even if I did try and set the record straight, the guy wouldn't have cared. No one would have cared. They only want the worst details from you as possible.

Well they have them now. Tomorrow, it will be known exactly what the man was asking me before I punched him, therefore, my truth will be laid bare for people to judge, as will my actions.

The only bright side to this whole damn thing is that at six a.m., the guard comes to the door and tells me I'm free to go. Obviously, I didn't sleep a wink.

I didn't even make bail–the assfuck who provoked me into this ended up dropping the charges for some reason.

When I make it out into the fluorescent lights of the police waiting room, Alyssa is there. Red-eyed and still in the dress she wore to the party.

This makes my heart ache more than I can bare. She didn't even go back to the hotel and get changed. She probably sat here the entire night, waiting for me.

I can't count on my hand anyone who would do that.

"How do you still look beautiful?" I say as I stagger toward her. I know I'm completely sober now, but there's something about walking out of a jail cell that makes you feel like you're part of *The Walking Dead*.

"Yeah right," she says, self-deprecating as usual. "How are you?"

"Well no one touched my privates, if that's what you're worried about," I tell her with a grin.

She doesn't laugh. "I hate that this happened."

"Me too," I admit and even though I shouldn't, I pull her into a hug. There are no cameras here and no one cares. But I care. I just want the feel of her warmth pressed up against me. She feels like she's my home.

Eventually we get an Uber who takes us back to the Roosevelt. Alyssa's phone died a long time ago, so she's not quite sure about the level of damage I've inflicted. I can only imagine that TMZ and the other sites are going ballistic with the information. Thankfully, it's a small town and it won't be long before some Kardashian ends up doing something stupid and then all the attention will divert over to them.

But when we get to the Roosevelt, there are no paparazzi to greet us. We slink in through the back entrance and over to the cabana rooms without anyone other than the valet and the front desk people seeing us.

Then the world gets a bit hazy…

I wake up to a tapping on my arm. I slowly open my eyes, wincing at the light streaming in the room.

"Sorry!" I hear Alyssa gasp and then feel a weight lift off the bed. The sound of curtains whirring closed and the light starts to fade.

"Please tell me this isn't prison," I mumble into the pillow.

"I promise you it's not. You're a free bird."

Moving slowly as to not disturb the molecules in my brain, I roll over and stare at Alyssa's sweet face as she looks over me.

Her makeup is all washed off and her hair is messy and it reminds me too much of the morning after we first had sex, when I showed up at her house and proposed to her the idea that we should date each other in order to fool the public.

It was Autumn's idea. It always was. And yet the moment she mentioned it, the moment I should have brushed it off as being one of her kooky schemes, was the moment it all made sense. I couldn't tell you why, it's just that when I was with Alyssa at the wedding, and particularly when I was deep inside her, she brought me a sense of peace that I was sorely aching for. A sense of realness when everything else I was chasing just seemed so fucking fake.

Because it was, I remind myself. *For the last few years, everything was fake until you found her.*

I reach up and gingerly stroke the edges of her cheek. "I'm not dreaming."

"You're not," she says. "You're here in this hotel and you're with me and you're safe and sound."

I smile at that and close my eyes again. I swear I drift off for a little bit because when I stir, the light seems to have changed in the room and I can smell bacon. Fucking delicious.

"Don't tell me you're a cook too," I murmur and I'm suddenly struck with the realization that I've never slept over with her, or visa versa. We've had sex in the yacht club's locker room, my living room, the boat, but we've never actually spent the whole night with each other, sleeping, until now.

"I wish," she says from across the room. "I ordered room service breakfast. I figured since you didn't have to spend any bail money, you might as well splurge."

"Speaking of, do you know why the asshat dropped the charges?"

"I think so. After the cops took you away, I was talking to the crowd and all of them were saying that the guy instigated it. They were all on your side. Someone even said they knew him from TMZ and would report him to the company. The guy got wind of that I guess. At least, that's what Autumn said."

At that, I slowly ease myself up. "You talked to Autumn last night?"

She nods. "I did. She didn't sound happy, I'll tell you that much. In fact, she told me if I wanted to, the contract would be revoked."

Now I'm awake. "What?"

Alyssa nods and brings the tray over to the bed. In her kimono-like robe and the wiggling way she moves, she looks like Marilyn Monroe come back to life. Marilyn who is now bringing me breakfast.

Focus, Emmett.

"Yeah," she says, lifting off the metal dome to showcase the bacon and eggs and ubiquitous avocado toast underneath. "She said she wouldn't blame me if I up and left, that some problems were too big for a PR company to solve."

"What the actual fuck?"

"Right?" Alyssa says, lifting off a piece of bacon from the tray and munching on it thoughtfully. "Anyway, I explained what happened, that it wasn't your fault. Then she reconsidered."

I stare at her openly. "You got Autumn to reconsider our contract?"

"I think I got her to reconsider all contracts," she says with a shy smile. "Yours, mine, hers. Anyway, it's all good now."

I don't know what to think about that. I don't doubt Alyssa is telling the truth so I'm sort of floored that Autumn would consider dumping me as a client over this. As she said, it wasn't really my fault.

But, at the same time, it was. I should have ignored the guy, I shouldn't have responded with violence, especially not in front of Alyssa, and most of all...I'm pretty sure Autumn is pissed that I never told her about my upbringing. She's strangely possessive over me at times, which is why I always thought it was odd that she suggested Alyssa and I get together. But she had the same idea about my past, whatever was presented on Wikipedia, and this whole time I was holding out on her like I didn't trust her.

And I don't trust Autumn. That's the whole thing. The only person I trust with all this is Jimmy and Alyssa. And Jimmy already knows the truth so...

Well, now I'm handing the truth to Alyssa with my bare hands and hoping that after all this, she'll still accept me. If not that, then at least be able to look into my eyes without disgust or pity.

"So," she says, nudging the plate toward me. "Are you going to eat?"

I nod but still push the plate to the side. "Listen," I tell her. "I want to talk to you about last night."

"I told you, I understand."

"No, not about the paparazzi. I mean, again, I regret hitting him. I know I shouldn't have done that. But I mean… why I was so upset."

She swallows audibly and nods. "Okay."

I breathe in deeply through my nose, sitting up straight and then look her right in the eye. "Most of what he said was actually true. My mother was a heroin addict. For all I know she wasn't a whore, and I know she wasn't using when I was born, but I did discover her when she had died and I did pretty much grow up on the streets."

Fuck. The words should be so simple in theory but the minute they leave my lips, they land between us like landmines. Maybe not going off now, but anytime someone missteps in the future.

But even so, she's staring at me with coaxing eyes, waiting for me to go on.

I sigh. "It wasn't as bad as it sounds. I know how ridiculous that seems, but when you're young, you don't really know what's wrong. You don't know you're poor, you don't know that you're living a life that's unacceptable for many. I guess I was just lucky. I wasn't often hungry; my mother was usually around. I went to school and saw my friends and played. After school I was either at the park or at home. I'd never been to someone else's place before so I never knew how it was supposed to look like, or smell, or feel. There were always junkies lying around but back then it wasn't nearly as bad as it is now. And again, being a kid, I just didn't know any different. I thought a man with a needle up his arm was just a man who needed medicine."

Alyssa's face crumples slightly. Not with pity. With compassion. Still, it's not easy to take.

I continue. "My only glimpses of the other life, the other side of the tracks, were what I saw on the TV. We only had three channels, but they were enough. They represented the fake world, the one I could escape into if I needed to. Maybe that's where my acting bug got started, who knows. Anyway, I'm saying all this because I don't want you to think what people want you to think. That I was suffering. I wasn't. I just happened to have a mother who loved the drugs more than me."

"Emmett," Alyssa finally says. "I'm so sorry."

"I told you, don't be," I tell her. "It happened. I'm sure I prepared for it in some way. I think on some level I knew the drugs would take her but I just thought everything would stay the same. When you're a kid, even when you're surrounded by death, you still don't think death will come for you. But it came right to our fucking door. I remember that evening like it was yesterday…" I shake my head, suddenly finding it hard to breathe. It takes a few minutes before I can continue. "I found her. My friend Jimmy eventually found the two of us. I couldn't leave her. He's like a fucking father to me, that guy. And before I knew what was happening, I was shipped off to Mission to live with my aunt. A woman who showed me a fraction of the love my mother showed me."

Silence hangs around us. It's not uncomfortable, it's just heavy. Weighted. This silence is the held breath of my mother and it demands our respect. I know we both can feel it.

After a moment I say, "I was happier before my mother died. I guess in some ways I've been chasing that feeling ever since, even though I know the last person I ever truly loved had left me." I suck on my bottom lip, trying to put my feelings in the tiny neat spaces where they belong. "So that's my truth. The son of a junkie. A boy who grew up on the wrong side of the tracks. Who grew up too soon. Who stared death in the face every day and didn't know it." I burst out laughing but it's a sour, bitter laugh. "I can see all those fucking headlines now, every single one of them, reducing my life, my love, into something quick and pithy enough to be devoured by the public."

Again, the silence. Alyssa lessens it by leaning over and putting her hand on top of mine. I can't help but meet her eyes, gaze deeply into them, wonder how the hell I got so lucky, wonder how the hell I'd ever let go.

"Your life is your life," she says to me, each word sounding as if she's handing them out with care. "No one else's. Not a single person on this earth is entitled to your life and what you've gone through. Even if you've never gone through anything. You have every right to protect your heart and soul and family from the things that people don't understand. And I will stand by you during every single step of the way. Contract or not, I'm here and I'm not judging and I'm not going anywhere. I'm just…yours."

Mine.

Maybe not forever, maybe not for real, but for now…she's mine.

I manage to give her a smile. "Thank you," I tell her. It's more than she'll ever know.

Even though I know I promised her that I'd take her to the beach, to the improv, even though I planned on ravishing her bare and naked here on this bed, all of those ideas have floated out the window.

Right now, all I want is to go back to sleep.

With the sun streaming through the window.

With her in my arms.

I lift up the covers, gesturing for her to join me.

I don't have to say a single word.

She gives me a sweet smile, places the tray on the floor,

and then crawls across the bed until she's settling beside me, pulling up the covers to her chin.

"I just want to sleep for a bit more," I tell her, stifling a yawn. "And I don't want to do it without you."

She smiles again and runs her finger gently over my bare chest before she nestles herself into my arms.

A few moments pass. I hear her breathing growing heavier, the air conditioner kick on.

Then she says, "Emmett?"

"Yes, sunshine?"

A pause. I can tell she's biting on her lip. "Is this real?"

I close my eyes and hold her tight. "It's always real," I tell her.

Then I fall asleep, wishing I could have told her more.

CHAPTER 15

EMMETT

*I*t's Tuesday evening. After we got back to Vancouver on Sunday night, tired to the bone, we agreed to spend Monday apart to give us both some space and get our heads on straight. After all, I had a bit of a PR disaster to try and deal with and Autumn wasn't being much help. But Tuesday is often a special night for me–when I'm not working–and I don't want to let this one go to waste.

That said, I don't tell Alyssa what I have planned until she's sliding into the passenger seat of my car. The only thing I said to her earlier was for her to dress down.

Of course, she totally overthought the word "down" just like she overthought "jogging" and "sailing." She's literally wearing a long-sleeved baseball t-shirt and overalls.

I don't think I've seen a woman wear overalls in a non-ironic way since I was in high school.

"Alyssa," I say carefully as I look her over, trying to hide a smile. "When you heard dress down, did you think going to pick corn at my grandpa's farm?"

She looks down at herself, defensive. "What? This is in. This cost forty fucking dollars at H and M!"

"Well if it's at H and M, then it's got to make sense," I say mockingly.

She crosses her arms in a huff. "Well it would help if I knew where we were going and what we were doing."

"You'll find out."

The truth is, I don't want to scare her off, not until we're at least there. I know Alyssa will probably take it all in stride, but still. She also has the tendency to build crazy ideas in her head into full-grown entities. I wanted to take her by surprise.

But Alyssa is smart. And as soon as my car takes a right off of Cambie Street and down Hastings, she knows. No one deliberately comes here. It's always by accident. And this is no accident.

I pull in to a parking garage and come to a stop and it's only then that she looks at me with soft eyes. "We're here, aren't we?"

I nod. "Yup."

I get out and open the trunk, taking out the plastic bag full of craft service items I took from yesterday. I know the soup kitchen does a really good job with tasty and nutritious meals, but I also know it never hurts to have extra, especially food that's portable. And yes, easy to trade, but at least the person then has a choice of whether to choose the drugs over hunger.

Alyssa gives me a slight smile and then grabs my hand, holding it tight.

Shit. I know she's nervous about all of this, that it's taking her out of her element. But the fact that she's here with me, that she's willing to see where I've come from, it means the fucking world.

"Did you know that four people die here each day," I tell her as we walk down the stairwell of the parking garage. It smells like piss and she's already wrinkling up her nose. It's only going to get worse for her going forward. "That one hundred people in BC died from drug overdoses last month? That 'Welfare Wednesday' this April resulted in 130 calls for overdoses just on that day alone?"

She shakes her head. "I knew it was bad. But I didn't think it was that bad. I'm a little ashamed to admit it but when I see this stuff on the news, I just tune it out. It feels so…hopeless."

"I know what you mean. I keep coming here and trying to help, volunteering, but it's like yelling into the wind. I wish I could shake them all, show them what happened to my mom, show them who I am and that I'm an example that you can come out of this world and live but…"

"At least you're doing something. Most people turn a blind eye."

"And I don't blame them. Because it's hard. It's hard to watch humanity self-destruct. The government has failed them. Our supposedly glorious health care system has waiting lists upon waiting lists for detox centers and rehabs, turning away people who actually want to get clean. There's no place for these people to go, no way to get help. It's a circle of death that never ends. Hell. There are even teams of Good Samaritans on the streets right now, finding those who have overdosed and saving them when health care workers can't."

I know I shouldn't sound so morbid about the whole thing but when we exit the garage and out onto the street, the depravity hits us tenfold.

Just like every time, it's like walking onto the set of a zombie film where the special effects are terrifyingly real. People are scattered everywhere, camped out against the buildings, wandering across the street and nearly getting hit by cars and buses. Some ask for money, some try and sell stolen goods, most just talk to themselves when they're not talking to each other. Every single soul here in need of help.

I feel a lump forming in my throat, a debilitating sadness that cancels out all the fear. There's so much I should be able to do and what I can won't go far.

I stop there in the middle of the sidewalk and wonder what's even the point.

But then Alyssa squeezes my hand, looks up at me with gentle determination and then starts handing out the food to the people.

I watch her for a few moments, humbled and awestruck by the sight of her being so kind, so compassionate, so brave as she meets and tries to talk to each and every poor soul she comes across. It's not an easy thing to do. The majority of them light up when they see her, even if she doesn't represent drugs, even if hunger is the last thing on their mind.

I know how they feel. That's what she does to me.

She lights me up inside, puts the sun in my sky.

Fuck.

I might be completely in love with her.

No.

Not *might*.

I am completely in love with her.

No doubts, no performances, no lies.

Just truth.

I blink at her there, standing on the darkened street, surrounded by the hopeless and yet now I'm brimming with love and hope from the inside out.

After she hands an energy bar to an old woman, Alyssa straightens up and looks over at me questioningly. I can tell she's still nervous about this whole thing, but she's doing it anyway. And I know she really doesn't want to do it alone.

You don't ever have to be alone again.

I nod at her, my smile spreading to an outright grin that probably seems horribly out of place.

Then I snap out of it and go to her side.

Together we walk up the street, handing out food until our bags are almost empty.

Then I take her hand, warm and small in mine, and lead her into the building.

"This is where I grew up," I tell her as we go up the stairs.

I take her all the way to the top floor and nod at the closed door down the hall. "That's where I was raised. And this is where Jimmy is."

I knock on his door. It's closed for once. And again, I feel that rush of trepidation, that I'm going to find something awful behind that door and I'm going to find it with Alyssa by my side.

I almost start to shield her but then the door opens and Jimmy is on the other side.

"Tetty!" he says with his gap-toothed smile. Then he looks at Alyssa in surprise. "And who might you be?"

"Jimmy, this is my girlfriend Alyssa," I tell him proudly. It doesn't feel like a lie anymore, even if I'm the only one who thinks it.

Jimmy gives her a charming smile. I have to say, I was hoping he wouldn't be like he was the last time I saw him and to my surprise, he looks great. He's clean-shaven, his thinning hair is slicked back and his eyes look bright. He's also wearing his uniform from the soup kitchen where he's supposed to be working tonight and where I usually volunteer on Tuesdays.

"Pleased to meet you, truly I am," Jimmy says, enthusiastically shaking Alyssa's hand. He grins at me, his cheeks growing pink. "Boy, Tetty. You really found the prettiest girl in the whole city. I am so happy for you. So happy to see you with someone. I was starting to worry about you, you know?"

"I was starting to worry too," I admit with a sheepish grin.

"Anyway, I thought we'd all go down to the soup kitchen together."

"Sure, sure, I was just about to leave," he says, looking back in the apartment as if looking for something.

I hand him my plastic bag. "First, some food for later."

"Thanks, thanks Tetty," he says, lifting up the bag in reverence before taking it inside and putting it on the kitchen counter.

As he does so, Alyssa turns to me. "He's adorable," she says, briefly leaning into my arm. "Thank you for bringing me to meet him."

Fuck. She's starting to unravel me, thread by thread.

I swallow and put my arm around her, holding her tight.

"Okay, let's go. Whoa. Look at you lovebirds," Jimmy says, closing the door behind him and locking it. "Boy, I remember what it was like to be in love."

Alyssa stiffens at that but I don't loosen my grip. I know what she's thinking, I know things are getting complicated, the edges are blurring, the lines are being crossed. But maybe she'll see the beauty in the change.

Or maybe she just wants her money. Maybe what you feel for her will in no way be returned. She thinks you're a cad, remember. A player. Someone like her daddy. Someone who will hurt her.

And you told her you would.

"You okay, Tetty?" Jimmy asks me.

I blink at him in surprise. "Oh, yes. Good. Let's go."

The three of us leave and walk the two blocks over to the soup kitchen. Even though I've been there enough, Jimmy introduces Alyssa to everyone there and everyone seems charmed by her, especially as she starts working alongside them, dishing out meals for the hungry. For being such a sassy, prickly woman at times, when that soft side comes out, it makes everybody melt. We're the lucky ones who see that side of her. It's why when I thought about bringing her here, showing her this part of my life, this part of my history, every ugly bit, that I knew she wouldn't balk, wouldn't run. She would be bold and brave enough to take it all on and do so with grace and compassion.

It also makes me realize why she's maybe been so unlucky in love. I have no doubt that every man that lays eyes on her thinks she's beautiful and, fuck, yes, undeniably sexy. I mean, that's one of the first things I noticed, other than her breasts of course. Her sexual confidence and strength. But there's something about that, and being an honest, strong-willed woman, that scares men off. It intimidates them. They want the woman that needs them. The truth is, we all need someone, including Alyssa, but some people require a little more than just scratching the surface.

I was determined from the start to peel back her layers, to slip beneath her armor. To discover the secret softness underneath, the places she keeps hidden.

I feel like I'm so fucking close.

It's in front of me, all within reach.

Now it's just a matter of her letting me in.

Something tells me it's not going to be easy to help her see past the lie.

But I'm willing to give it all I've got.

When we've put in a good few hours at the soup kitchen and it starts to close up for the night, I'm fully prepared to take Alyssa straight to her place.

But as we get in the car and leave the mean streets of downtown behind, she turns to me and says, "I don't want to be alone tonight."

I look at her in surprise, utter happiness fluttering through me. "No? Stay over at my place."

"That's okay?"

"It's better than okay, sunshine," I tell her. "I don't want to be alone either."

There's something about the reality and rawness that we witnessed today that makes me want to hold onto her even tighter. It makes me appreciate just how wild and real she is, that she's the fire in my life, the one that makes my heart beat. I want to bury myself deep inside her and never let go, let her light wash over all my darkness, let it dissolve my past. Alyssa is my sun, pure golden warmth that leaves only love behind.

My love for her.

Fuck, I'm in too deep.

But I don't care.

We get to my place and we're practically tearing each other's clothes off as we stumble through the courtyard. Once inside we move to the bedroom, articles being discarded to the floor, our mouths clashing against each other, lips, tongue, teeth. It's messy, it's urgent, it's a life force.

I push her down onto my bed, staring at her gorgeous body, the sly look in her eyes as I stand at the edge of the bed with my cock jutting out, already stiff as a board.

Her eyes widen as I knew they would. She loves my cock and I love her for it.

Her mouth parts sweetly and she turns around on her knees, shuffling to the edge. Her hands grab the back of my thighs, her nails digging in, and she stares up at me with burning eyes.

She doesn't break eye contact with me—I'm starting to think she gets off by watching me get off. I've been with my fair share of women, but none of them were as brazen as she is, not even close. It gets under my skin like nothing else.

Lucky, lucky, lucky.

She takes me in her mouth, working me softly, sweetly, but oh so fucking wild. I close my eyes and throw my head back, both wanting her to continue and wanting her to stop.

When I'm close to coming, I pull back, breathless. She stares at me, soulful, yearning, her perfect mouth open and glistening, practically begging for my cum.

I lick my lips and grab her by the arms, wanting her to feel my fire, feel just what she does to me, how mad with lust and desire she makes me feel. I pull her to me and kiss her urgently as the need, the lust, the want comes pouring out. I might just devour her right here. Everything she offers up is so beautiful and real and pure, but it's never enough. I don't just want to touch her and be with her, I want to fuse with her. Especially tonight of all nights. I want to sink inside her so deeply that she'll feel bereft without me there. I want to be everything to her, the way that she's become to me. I want her to feel that she'll never be alone when I'm around.

She's kissing me back, wild and untamed. She's clawing at me now, nails on my back, and I'm gripping her so hard I feel I might break her.

Quickly, I push her back until she's lying on the bed. I'll never tire of the sight of her beneath me, so perfect, every swoop and soft, plump curve that my lips and tongue and hands are so ridiculously addicted to. Her pussy is a fucking treasure, bare and wet, and for this moment, for every moment I've spent with her, I know it belongs to me.

Mine.

I move between her spread legs. It's almost painful, this desire, this need. Seeing my bare cock hard and ready, herself open, pink and soft—I feel like no man should ever be so blessed.

I want in deep and to never let go.

Slowly, so slowly, I ease myself into her as she raises her hips, pushing toward me herself, wanting that deeper purchase. Her mouth opens wider the further I get, her body stretching around me, holding me so impossibly tight.

Fuck.

I kiss her, melting my mouth into hers, wanting to be as close as possible.

Our faces are just inches apart as I slowly pull out and ease myself into her. Our gaze never breaks. Hers is full of lust and wonder, as if she's seeing me for the first time. I can only hope she likes what she sees, that I'm enough for her. The real Emmett, not the man on the screen. The one who came from filth, the one she somehow still sees as worthy.

When our hips meet, it makes me still, and I have to suck in my breath to regain control. There's something about her that makes me want to completely lose it and I've been losing my mind since the day I met her.

She confidently wraps her legs around my waist and rocks her hips forward, each movement pulling me further and further into her. Her hands are at my back and pushing into my muscles. Our skin moves against each other like we are one.

"Fuck, Alyssa," I croak out, sucking along her neck, to her tits. My tongue teases around the hardened peak of her nipple and I pull it into my mouth with one long, hard draw. Her moan is so loud, so uninhibited that I feel unstoppable. I'm in over my head for this, for the warmth, that damn, intoxicating warmth of being really, truly inside of her, of feeling her in every way I can.

"Harder," she says, arching her back. "Emmett, harder."

My name on her lips is a drug. I piston my hips to drive into her deeper, my knees burning as I pound her again and again and again. Her perfect tits bounce with each thorough thrust, and suddenly there are no thoughts. No pain. No past. That feeling of falling, of realizing how good it can fucking be when you actually care about someone.

When you love someone.

Shit. Fucking shit.

I don't know how much more I can hold on.

"Emmett," she whispers to me but never finishes her sentence. She just repeats my name with reverence, like I'm a prayer on her lips.

I keep working her, determined. The flush on her face spreads to her chest and her legs quiver around my waist. She's holding onto me like I'm about to fly and she doesn't want to be left behind.

I go to slip my hand down over her clit but she's already there and I barely have to trigger her. She cries out loudly, hips jerking upward, body shaking like a earthquake. She's so unbelievable when she's coming, this pulsing, writhing woman–*god, she's such a woman*–and I'm the cause of all of it. I'm the one who brings this force of nature to her knees, to the edge.

And she does the same to me.

My orgasm sneaks up on me, like being hit from behind. It's beautifully devastating and I'm loud when I come. I'm groaning and grunting as the orgasm wrings it out of me, but from the way she's gasping for breath and still holding tight, she still riding the same wave.

I collapse against her, sweat dripping off my brow and over my nose. I can hardly breathe but I don't care. I'm shuddering on the inside, completely unraveled.

This woman. This beautiful woman that I've just come inside of, this woman whose soft, creamy neck I'm kissing because it's the only thing to do.

She's my first act and she'll be my last.

There will never be anyone else for me.

I stay inside her for as long as possible, until she starts to adjust underneath me. When I pull out of her, the loss is deeper than I thought it would be.

I brush the hair back from her damp forehead. "Hi," I say softly. Because I feel like we're meeting again for the first time.

"Hi," she says lazily. Her hands ghost up and down my back, as if she can't quite believe what just happened.

"I like it when you stay over," I tell her.

"So do I."

"I could do that again in five minutes."

She laughs. Oh god, what a beautiful sound.

"Mmmm, you're ambitious."

"Only with you, sunshine. Only with you."

She reaches up and kisses the tip of my nose, giggling.

Everything inside me warms and blooms.

CHAPTER 16

"*W*hat is that?" Jackie asks as I walk toward their Land Rover. She gets out of the passenger seat and comes over to the take the Tupperware container out of my hands. I give her a grateful smile, slinging my duffel bag up on my shoulder as I take it around to Will who is opening the trunk.

"Cookies and brownies," I tell her.

"You bake?" Will asks with a grin, taking the bag from me, looking impressed.

"No but my roommate does," I tell them. "And I'll just say, Jackie, you're not allowed to have any."

"Why not?" she asks, totally confused. "Am I already that fat?"

Will rolls his eyes good-naturedly. "Dream girl, they're pot cookies," he explains patiently.

"I can't believe you're married and you still call her dream girl," I tease him.

He shuts the trunk and gives me a stern look. "And I can't believe I have to spend the long weekend with you." He glances at Jackie. "Tell me why this was a good idea again? I see her enough at work."

"Oh whatever, big boy, you love it," I say as I get in the backseat. We just have to pick up Emmett from his house and then we're off on a three-and-a half-hour drive to BC's sweltering interior and my hometown.

Will and Jackie recently got a Range Rover in preparation for their growing family and it still has that new car smell, even though I know their dogs ride in this thing a lot. I actually wish the dogs—Joan of Bark and Sprocket—were coming on the road trip with us, but knowing my luck with animals, they'd probably shit on me while I'm sleeping or something.

"So," Jackie says, eyeing me in the rearview mirror. "Are you excited? Nervous?"

"Why should she be nervous?" Will asks, his watch glinting in the sun as he drives.

"You don't understand women at all," Jackie says.

"Apparently not."

"I'm not nervous," I tell her. "I'm good. I'm excited. I think it's going to do us a lot of good to get away for a few days and just relax. You wouldn't believe the week I had at work, my stupid boss ran me ragged."

"Hey," Will warns. "No picking on your boss this trip. No mentions of the office or the word work either. As your boss, I'm making that an official rule."

"Or what? You'll fire me?"

"You'd probably like that," he says.

The funny thing is, I would. Not the actual firing part, that would suck. But as the end-of-contract with Emmett looms and that forty thousand dollars waves at me from the finish line, I really should start thinking about what I'm going to do next.

But as each day and date with Emmett goes on, as we fall deeper into this rabbit hole that is our quasi-relationship, the less I think about the future. My dreams are still as important to me as ever but I have a hard time focusing on them when Emmett seems to have taken over my life. It's not that I would dare put it on hold again, it's just that when I picture committing to the acting life, whether in Vancouver, LA, maybe even London, I see Emmett by my side.

It's just such a self-destructive thought.

Whatever we have, whatever this is, half-real, half-fake, it's going to come apart soon. There's an expiration date to this relationship, a point where I get paid and we part ways.

God. Just the thought makes my heart feel like it's coming undone, what once was a brick wall is now slowly crumbling to pieces.

Emmett is waiting at the curb when we pull up to his house, looking sexy as hell in his Timberland boots, his jeans, a faded Guns N Roses T-shirt that's almost a size too small. His skin is bronzed from the sun, his muscles looking effortlessly strong. Just the sight of him is like a balm on a wound and when he opens the door and sees me, his smile nearly breaks me in two.

"Hey sunshine," he says to me, throwing his bag in the back.

"Hi sugarbutt," Will says. He gives Emmett an exaggerated wink over his sunglasses.

Emmett rolls his eyes, nods a hello at Jackie, and then slides in the backseat.

He immediately pulls me in for an impromptu kiss. Quick and sweet.

When we pull apart, Jackie is watching us intently. "Hey. I thought you two hated each other."

Hate Emmett? That feels like so long ago. I try and put on a scowl but I end up smiling instead.

"Don't forget I'm a pretty good actor, Jackie," Emmett

tells her as he buckles in. "I only look like I enjoy Alyssa's company, but the truth is she's pretty intolerable."

"I hear that," Will notes.

"Shut up," I tell Will, and then smack Emmett on the arm. "And you shut up too. You're not that good of an actor."

"Ouch, my bleeding heart," Emmett says mockingly, grabbing his chest. "So this is what the weekend is going to be like, huh?"

"Alyssa brought pot cookies," Jackie points out. "So, yeah. That's the weekend. You'll all be high and drinking wine by the lake and I'll be beached up on shore like a bloated whale."

"Jackie, you're barely showing and even if you were, so what?" I tell her. "You're pregnant. You're going to show. And you're going to look absolutely beautiful every step of the way."

"This is what I keep telling her," Will says.

"You don't get it," Jackie says and then launches into a tirade about everything in her life right now that's falling apart because of her pregnancy. I do know one thing, she's moody as hell. One minute she's so in love with Will, her son, the baby, the next she thinks the world is ending. I would have thought a second pregnancy would be easier but who knows.

What I do know is that Will, as usual, has the patience of a saint. Though I often give him a hard time for being too nice, too charming, too handsome, he really is an angel when it comes to her. I don't think I've ever seen a guy so excited and ready to become a father.

I look beside me at Emmett as the car pulls out of the city, heading along the highway that will wind for hours past raging rivers and towering mountain peaks. He might be a self-proclaimed thirty-eight-year-old man-child but I no longer see him as that. In fact, it's hard to remember how I used to feel about him.

Of course, he's still a bit of a scoundrel, entirely focused on sex most of the time, with a flippant attitude and a knack for pushing all my buttons, good and bad. I know those parts of him won't change the more I get to know him. Because this last week alone, I feel like I've seen the real Emmett. The man behind the mask, living a life and not a role.

After his arrest in LA, where I spent the night waiting for him at the jail, praying that everything would turn out all right, he opened up in a way I'd never seen before. Every grimy, gritty detail of his life he shared with me, laid it all out on the table. As if that wasn't vulnerable enough, he then actually *showed* it to me.

I'll never forget that night. The east side is no place I would voluntarily go, I've been too afraid to face what's down there, to confront the things that make you question your privilege, the things you'd rather sweep under the rug.

And to think he grew up there. I picture Emmett as a little boy, tall, lanky, with light hair and that same smile, living in that filthy building. Growing up around the junkies and the homeless and the whores, seeing things that no one should ever see. The fact that he found his mother when she over-dosed…I can't even imagine what that would be like.

The man has issues, there's no doubt about that. I can kind of see why acting became an escape for him. I can also see why he doesn't get close to many people. It's not just that he's got a past he'd rather hide, but that he had to lose the one person he loved in the most horrific way. How can you not fear you'll lose everyone else?

But that's Emmett. And that's man I'm falling for.

He's shown me his deepest, darkest parts and it's only made me want him, admire and respect him more.

I don't even want to put up walls anymore. I don't want to keep him out. He let me in, I want to let him in, as scary as it seems.

And it is scary. It's terrifying. I saw firsthand what my father did to my mother, how it destroyed her, us, the whole family. And I've been with men just like that, who care about you one minute and toss you aside the next.

Emmett is supposed to be one of those men. He's supposed to be the player, the playboy, the love you and leave you type. He's even said so much himself.

As the saying goes, when someone shows you who they are, believe them.

And yet part of me doesn't think that Emmett is the one that's real.

The one that's real is the scared little boy with a dirty past and big shiny dreams. The one that yearns for respect, who wants passion over everything else.

But, god, please…if only he could also want me.

Want me, have me, not leave me…

Keep me.

It's interesting being with Will and Jackie. They're the only ones who know the truth behind the façade, know why we're together and because of this, we're free to just be ourselves. And in the backseat of the Land Rover, ourselves seem no different than the show we put on for the public. I lean against Emmett's shoulder, he plays with my hair, our arms and hands tangle against each other. We are as physical and intimate as two lovers should be, lovers not bound by rule or arrangement.

The drive passes quickly, maybe because time inside the car seems to still. Summer is coming to a close. It's already September. It's a reminder that what we have is coming to an end too. I feel like I'm trying to soak it all up, every single inch of him.

It's twilight when we arrive in my hometown of Penticton. The town lights twinkle, casting sparkles on the dark water of the lake. I've missed home so much, sometimes I forget how beautiful it is.

Penticton isn't a large town, about 33,000 people, and nearly double that in the summer. But what it lacks in size, it has in beauty. Unlike Vancouver, which is built along the ocean, Penticton is between two lakes, Lake Okanagan on one side and Skaha Lake on the other. Both lakes are pristine and warm and clay hills rise on either side covered in sagebrush and vineyards. It's hot, it's dry, it's fucking heaven.

We're going to have dinner at my mother's house tomorrow, who lives up on the hill just outside of town, so we stop at a grocery store for some camping provisions, pick up some booze and then get ourselves settled in.

Will had booked the cabin so I'm not at all surprised that it's more swanky than it is rustic. We're along the lake in an area called Naramatta Bench, where vineyards rise up from the lakeshore like verdant forests. The cabin we have is nestled in between a few famous wineries and has its own private beach and a dock with Adirondack chairs and a fire pit at the end. In the fading light, the sky going purple and gold, it's postcard perfect.

"Ugggh, I want to jump right in," Jackie says, fanning herself with a magazine she picked up at the store. "Who's in for a night swim? I think I'm overheating."

"How about we get settled in first," Will says, always the sensible one, as he leads us into the cabin.

It's not huge but it's new and has everything you need and then some, including a hot tub on the porch. Emmett and I go into one of the bedrooms, not knowing which of the bedrooms is better. It's always like Russian roulette in places like this. Whoever goes into whatever room first is the one who is stuck with that room, luck of the draw. And in our case, our room only has a twin bed and a bunk bed. Obviously Will and Jackie snatched up the master bedroom of the two.

"Guess we'll have to snuggle," Emmett says with a grin as he starts putting his stuff away in the drawers. "We can do that now because we like each other."

"You're such a dork," I tell him. Then I gesture to his unpacking. "And what is this? You're unpacking? We're only here for three nights."

He gives me an odd look. "You're an office manager, I thought you'd be all about organization."

"Only in other people's lives, not my own."

"Ah yes, I forget you like things a bit messy."

"I can't tell if that's innuendo anymore."

"Baby, everything with me is innuendo," he says. "Including having a little snack before dinner."

He then grabs my arm and pulls me over to the bed, throwing me down on it.

I giggle as I sink into the mattress and he prowls over me. He runs the tip of his finger down the middle of my forehead, over my nose, my lips, my chin, down my neck, all the way to my chest.

"You could at least close the door," Jackie says and I look over to see her and Will in the doorway, staring at us with absolutely no shame.

"Emmett's an actor, dear," Will tells her. "They're all exhibitionists." Then he jerks his chin at Emmett. "Help with dinner, will you? Let the girls relax."

"I was going to help Alyssa relax in my own way," Emmett tells him, but with a grunt, he rolls off of me and strolls out into the kitchen, adjusting his pants as he goes.

I sigh and get up, following close behind.

"Sorry," Jackie says, not sounding sorry at all. "Thank god our bedrooms aren't right next to each other."

I'm not sure if she's saying that for my sake or for hers but either way I have to agree.

While Emmett and Will get started on the steaks, Jackie and I scoop up all the materials we need for epic smores and head out down to the dock to start the fire.

"You're going to ruin your dinner!" Will yells out the window at us.

"You won't stop me if you know what's best for you!" Jackie yells back. As she settles into the Adirondack chair, she gives me a triumphant smile. "He knows not to mess with me when it comes to food. I'm not even craving strange things, it's just that when I do have a craving, I turn into a relentless she-beast until I get it."

I smile at that as I start up the fire, not exactly sure what I'm doing. Thankfully it catches easily and soon I'm sitting back in the chair across from Jackie and cracking open a tall, cold can of local cider. The sky is now completely dark and clear, a scattering of stars popping out above us.

I look over my shoulder at the cabin and see Will and Emmett inside in the kitchen, drinking beer and laughing about something. My heart does cartwheels inside my chest.

"What do you think they're talking about?" I ask her, watching as Emmett runs his hand through his beautiful hair. I'm so fucking in love with his face.

"You," she says emphatically.

"Will's probably talking about you and the baby," I point out, turning back around in my seat to face her.

"Nah," she says with a shrug. "They're talking about you. There's a reason that Will asked Emmett to help him in there. He's been complaining that he hasn't gotten the chance yet to properly grill him about you. You've been hogging up all of his time."

"Well we both know that's part of our contract."

"Ah yes," she says. "The contract. I still can't believe that's an actual thing that happens."

"I know," I tell her and open the bag of marshmallows. "Hollywood is so weird. You know, when he was in jail and I had to call his publicist, she said that stuff like this happens all the time."

"Fake relationships?" she asks.

"Yup. Usually it happens when an actual couple breaks up, if they have to do press together, the publicist will ask them to act like they're a couple for a long time after. By the time we hear about the break-up, it's been done and dusted ages before."

"Do you usually talk to his publicist? How much of a hand does she have in all this?"

"I just called her that night. I didn't know who else to talk to, what to do." I pause. "I hate to sound like a jealous, petty bitch but I don't like her. And it's not because she's stunning and gorgeous and successful."

"No?" Jackie laughs.

"No, well of course yeah. But I can't figure out what her deal is. And I have a feeling that she and Emmett used to be together."

"Have you asked him?"

"No," I say quickly. "I don't want to be *that* person."

"What person? You're his fake girlfriend, you can say anything, who cares."

But I do care. Because it makes me sound like the afore-mentioned jealous, petty bitch. And I have zero *real* claim to Emmett.

"I don't know. It's just...I don't trust her. I don't trust her relationship with him, I don't trust her intentions," I admit, as I gather up the long metal poker I got for marshmallow toasting.

"But you said it was her idea, this whole stunt."

"I know, it was. That's why it's so weird. Anyway, I guess it doesn't really matter."

"Why not?"

"Because eventually the contract will run out and we'll part ways."

"Alyssa...you know it doesn't have to be that way. Stop pretending you don't have feelings for the man. It's obvious."

Ugh. Is it really? I hate that it is.

"Is it obvious to Emmett?"

"I don't know," she says with a shrug. "Men are so dense sometimes."

"Sometimes or always?"

"You know, you could just have an actual conversation with Emmett about all this."

"I do have conversations with him."

"I meant about your actual, real relationship. How you feel."

"Well, that has come up once."

"And?"

"And I told him he was a player and he owned up to it. He didn't deny it. I said I didn't want to have feelings for him because he would just hurt me in the end and he fucking agreed with me!"

She holds out her palm. "Wait. How long ago was this?"

"I don't know, three weeks ago?"

"And is it possible you both feel differently now than you did a few weeks ago?"

God, yes. Every single feeling I have about him has been driven in deep, embedded into my skin and bones.

"Maybe," I warily admit.

"And could it be because *you* brought up the fact that *you* didn't want to have feelings for him because of the way *you* say he is, that he just agreed with you to save face."

Ah. Shit.

"Maaaaaaaybe."

"I bet that's what it is. No one wants to hear that another person doesn't want to develop feelings for them. Alyssa, that's harsh."

"I'm prickly," I say feebly by way of explanation. "And he's a man who has probably been in my shoes a million times and he can take it."

"Just because you see Emmett as a player and a man doesn't mean he doesn't have feelings himself. That's all."

I close my eyes and exhale. Could that be right? Could he have just said all that because he thought it was pointless to argue with me? Because he didn't want to be the one saying, please feel something for me?

Who knows.

"Man. This shit gets more confusing day by day," I tell her.

"No kidding. I honestly don't know how you do it. Why you even agreed to this ridiculous contract to begin with."

"Right. Well here's the thing." I take in a deep breath. "I haven't been exactly honest with you."

Her frown deepens in the shadows. "What do you mean?"

"Well," I say as I fish out a marshmallow and stick it on the end of the poker, "the whole fake relationship thing with Emmett? There was an incentive to go along with it."

"What kind of incentive?"

"Money. Lots of money."

Her brows raise. I lance the stick into the fire and sparks dance into the air.

"How much?"

"Forty thousand."

She blinks at me for a moment and then lets out a dry laugh. "Wow. Okay. Why didn't you tell me that before?"

"Two reasons. I didn't want you to think I was, like, a whore or something."

"But you were paid to date Emmett for publicity, not sex. Right?"

"Yes of course. But still. It was hard to explain." I rotate the stick when one side gets perfectly charred.

"And the other reason?"

"I wanted the money so that I could quit Mad Men Studios." I glance at her. "Please don't tell Will that. You can't. You have to promise."

"I won't tell him," she says after a beat. Her eyes look sincere in the fire light and I know she'll keep it secret, even though I'm sure that's the last thing she wants to do this early on in her marriage.

"I promise I'll let him and your father know soon. I'm just waiting for the right time."

She nods, chewing on her lip for a moment. "Honestly, I'm not surprised. And Will won't be either. He's told me on more than one occasion that you're too good for the job, that you're not being challenged. I'm sure my father feels the same way too. But...what are you going to do instead?"

I hesitate for a moment, bringing the marshmallow out of the fire and blowing out the flames. "Don't judge but...acting."

"Acting?"

"Yup."

"Didn't you used to do that?"

"I did. And sometimes I still do. I still have head shots, I still go on auditions sometimes. I take those damn Master Classes online with Kevin Spacey." She laughs at that one. "I do what I can to keep the dream alive. But it's not enough. I want to quit so I can devote my time to it, full-time. I want to give it one last shot. And if it doesn't work, then at least I tried."

Silence envelopes us. The crickets are starting up again.

"I'm not judging," Jackie says slowly. "And I think it's great. But you're almost thirty…"

"So? Who says you have to have all your shit figured out when you're young? I'd rather try and find myself now and see what happens than wait and let it pass me by."

"I guess. And if it doesn't work out?"

I shrug. "Then I'll have no regrets. Oh, come on, admit it, it's a crazy idea but it makes sense for me."

"You're kind of right about that. It *is* crazy."

"But you only live once. I'm not expecting the world but I am expecting something I can look back on and be, wow, I'm glad I did that. For a while there, I really fucking lived. And Just Jackie, so far, I haven't felt like I've been living. Just going through the motions, doing the things we're told we should do, the things we're supposed to do. In fact, the only time I've felt remotely alive is…"

I trail off. I realize that I'm about name Emmett and I know that on the plane, he pretty much said the same thing to me.

"It's Emmett," Jackie fills in. "I know it. Ever since you started dating him, fake or not, you've changed. For the better, of course. Even Tiffany and I were talking about it the other day."

I give her a sharp look. "She still thinks it's real, right?"

"She thinks it's real because it *is* real. Alyssa…that cliff we talked about? You're so far over it, you can't even see it anymore."

I take a long sip of my cider and sigh. "There's no point in hiding it anymore, is there."

"Nope. Welcome to the Love Club." She raises her can. "Though I have to say, I didn't make forty grand when I fell in love with Will."

No, but he probably spent that much trying to woo you, I think to myself. "The thing is…I didn't just do it for the money," I tell her. "That wasn't enough, really. The real reason I went out with Emmett was…because it felt like the right thing to do. I know how nuts that sounds but for such a crazy situation, being with him just made sense."

A slow smile comes across her lips. "No. I get it. Your soul was familiar with him before you were."

I eye her in surprise. "Well ain't that poetic."

"I am a writer," she points out. "And I'm still in the romantic stage of our marriage. Anyway, I'm sure Will and my father will miss you deeply, but I have to say that I think you're doing the right thing. Whether the acting thing works out or not, no matter what you end up doing, it's pretty obvious that your future isn't as an office manager of a visual effects studio." She pauses. "But I will also tell you that your future *does* belong with that man who is waiting for you, right now, in that kitchen. And no. I don't mean Will. I mean the other guy. Your bruiser."

Just then, Will pops his head out the window and yells. "Dinner's ready!"

His booming voice seems to carry across the lake.

"Wow, the people over in Peachland probably heard that," I tell her, getting to my feet. Before we walk off though, I pass the marshmallow to her. "For you, Jackie-O. The pregnant one gets the first roasted marshmallow."

She gives me a charmed smile and plucks the marshmallow off the end of the stick, popping it into her mouth.

Then we walk back to the cabin, ready for dinner with our men.

* * *

As much as Jackie wanted to go for a night swim in the lake, as much as I wanted to drink cider and eat marshmallows, as much as Will and Emmett seemed adamant we have a poker tournament, all of us ended up going to bed early. Maybe it was the bottle of red wine at dinner (which Jackie stared longingly at) or the fact that we had a lot of steak and potatoes, but the only thing anyone was in the mood for was bed.

Even Emmett didn't try any moves on me once we settled under the covers and before I could even comment on it, we were both out like a light.

We all slept in the next morning too, only getting up just before lunch to make a big meal of bacon, eggs, hash-browns and toast. Then Jackie and Will went into the lake to try stand-up paddle-boarding, while Emmett and I walked up the street to the nearest vineyard to do some tasting.

Of course, the closest vineyard happened to be called Cockburn and had a five-foot tall ceramic rooster outside.

"What is your fascination with giant cocks?" Emmett jokes as we stroll hand in hand through the gates. Even though it's just after noon, the parking lot is packed with cars and bikes from people doing vineyard tours.

"What can I say, they make a girl happy," I tell him.

"As long as it's just my cock making you happy." His grip on my hand tightens and a strange flash of heat comes across his eyes. "It has just been me, right?"

I look at him strangely. "What do you mean? You mean have I been sleeping with other guys?"

He shrugs and pulls down his aviator shades.

"Emmett," I tell him, pulling him to a stop. "I'm with you all the time."

"You did say there was that Casey guy at work, the one who maybe took the pictures."

I let out an acidic laugh. "Casey? Casey is a creep and also he didn't take the pictures. I can tell. Besides, it is in our contract that the both of us can't go around screwing other people."

"I know what the contract says but it doesn't mean you don't want to."

I'm not really sure what's come over him and I'm also not sure how to respond. Do I play it cool or not?

I go for something in-between. I lean in close to him and when I'm sure no one is looking, I reach down and grab his crotch. "This is the only cock for me. All you and all the time."

Finally, he breaks into a grin. I guess all I needed to do was stroke his ego. Or his cock.

"Oh my god, isn't that Emmett Hill?" a girl says to her friend as they walk past.

Right. Back to being on. And as much as it's not out of place for the world to see us like this, I really could do without a headline that says Alyssa Martin Loves Cock This Much or something like that.

I pull my hand away and give him a quick smile. "Let's go inside."

The winery is busy but it's also fairly large so it's not long before we find ourselves lined up for a tasting. The guy doing it seems completely enamored with Emmett and keeps giving us large pours, which is great. The cabin is in stumbling distance and I have plenty of time to sober up before dinner at my mom's. On second thought, I might want to stay buzzed. Bringing Emmett to meet her is a bit nerve-wracking, no matter our relationship.

"So Emmett," the sommelier says. His name tag says he's Eric. "Can you give me the inside scoop on Boomerang? Is Doctor Death really going to steal Boomerang's power? I have a theory that because Boomerang can go back in time by one minute, Doctor Death is going to develop a formula to do the same. But he'll be able to do it for like a whole day. Essentially beating Boomerang at his own game."

Emmett lets out a low whistle, seeming both humbled

and flattered. "Impressive. If I didn't know any better, I'd say you took a look at our scripts."

The guy beams. "I'm clairvoyant," he says and I'm pretty sure he's not joking. "I can see into the future, in bits and pieces. Nothing significant."

"Maybe there should be a superhero show about you," I tell him.

Eric gives me a faint smile and then fixes all his attention back on Emmett again. "Seriously though. I think that's what's going to happen. But I still think Doctor Death will die."

Emmett shrugs, apparently not put off by it. "It depends on my contract," he says.

I give Emmett a look, like I'm not sure if he should be talking about this stuff but he doesn't seem to notice.

"So you're not permanent," Eric notes.

"Nah, man. Never was. I was supposed to be there for a few episodes but they loved me so much they kept me on. But I still think I'll get written off at some point, maybe even soon."

"Really?" I ask him.

Emmett nods, looks between the two of us. "Yeah. But it's okay. This was never supposed to be my real comeback. You said so yourself."

"I know but–"

"So then what will you do?" Eric asks. "And what happens to Boomerang?"

"Boomerang will find some other villain to tussle with. Look," he says, adjusting himself on the stool, "we all know my character isn't the Joker. He's not even Klaus. He's good for now but eventually there will be someone better. Or the show will get canceled." He laughs when Eric looks horrified. "Anyway, I'll find something. Probably go back to London and do theatre again."

"What?" I whisper. This is the first I'm hearing of this. What the hell is he talking about, moving back to London to do theatre? When?

"Uh oh," Eric says, starting to pour us all more wine. "Looks like you guys are in for a break-up."

I practically snarl at Eric. "Mind your own business," I tell him.

He stares at me with wide eyes and slowly backs away from our glasses. "This is the merlot. Enjoy." Then he promptly turns around and starts dealing with other people.

"Hey, he was pouring good," Emmett complains, swirling the wine around the glass.

"When were you going to tell me you were going to move back to London?"

His features go slack. "I don't know. At some point."

"But when?"

"I don't know," he says again and takes a sniff of the wine. "Not bad."

"Emmett," I hiss. "Please. I can't believe you've been thinking about this and you didn't have the courtesy to even tell me."

His eyes narrow. "Courtesy? Why would I have to tell you?"

"Because."

Because I'm me. And aren't I something to you?

"Alyssa," he says, lowering his voice, "we're not an actual couple, you know. I don't have to tell you everything."

Oh my god. Ow.

OW.

I can't help but wince at his words.

He sighs. "I didn't mean it to come out so harsh," he says. "I just…I don't know, I've been thinking about it and that's it really."

"But you think you might have to leave Boomerang."

"I know I will. My contract with them is only so long. It's up pretty soon and from the way people have been talking and the way the scripts are going, the ratings, I don't think I'll be there for much longer. And it's fine. For once, it's truly fine. This is a good thing."

"Yeah, for you."

"Why not for you? Nothing changes. We'll still fulfill our contract, you'll still get your money. Don't worry."

"Yeah but…," I trail off. *But it's not about the money. It's about you.*

Ah, shit. I'm thinking back to my conversation with Jackie last night and how carried away I was getting thinking there was more to us than there is. This is a perfect example of the fact that everything so far has just been in my head, wishful thinking.

I put on a brave, completely fake, smile. "I guess if I still get paid, that's all that matters. I wouldn't have wanted all of this to be for nothing."

If my words hurt him in any way, he doesn't show it. "You know, it wasn't until I met you that I had the courage to realize what I really wanted. I think going back to my passion is the right thing to do. Maybe some people will say it's failure or that I'm moving backwards, but I don't see it that way."

Well that's good for you. You'll move forwards, backwards, wherever, but it's going to be without me.

He warned me. He really did.

"Come on," he says to me, grabbing my hand. "I've had enough of this cockamamie place. We should probably go check on Jackie and Will, make sure she hasn't drowned him or anything. Man, I haven't seen a woman so easily affected by *hanger* before in my life."

I nod absently and let him lead me out of the winery.

When we're back in the sunshine and strolling down the road back to the cabin, he still doesn't let go of my hand.

"The sky here is so blue," he says, staring up. "You must have loved growing up here. Fucking eh, it would have been so hot in the middle of summer but with having that lake right there I bet it was just bliss."

"Yeah," I say quietly, so confused. So, so confused.

He looks to me, tilting his head. "Are you okay?"

You might move back to London and you didn't even tell me!

"Yeah," I give him a big smile. "I'm fine. I guess I'm just taking it all in."

"Would you ever move back here?" he asks me.

"Maybe to settle down."

"Oh really. And who does Alyssa Martin see herself settling down with here? A winemaker?"

"Who knows," I tell him honestly. Maybe he would have played one on TV.

CHAPTER 17

ALYSSA

"*B*aby!" My mother cries out, throwing open her arms and practically running down the path to see me.

Before I can even say hello, she's scooping me up in her arms. My mother has gotten skinnier and I swear shorter over time, so much so that I resemble a giant fluffy pillow next to her, but somehow, she's still strong, like freakishly strong. Like, she might just bench-press me, I don't know.

"Oh, you look so lovely," she says once she pulls back and examines my face. "No need for Botox yet either."

I roll my eyes. My mother is extremely vain, probably brought on by the fact that my father was a philandering dickhead. I'm pretty lucky though that by the time I was born, she didn't care so much about appearances. Not like she did with my sisters. They all got the brunt of it, which is probably why they all went off and married so young. It was pretty much what they were conditioned to do.

"And here is the rest of the gang," she says, letting me go and turning her sights to Emmett, Jackie and Will.

She goes to Emmett first, sauntering over to him and wagging her finger. "I know you from all the pictures in the magazines. I have to say, you're a lot more handsome in person. In the pictures you look kind of, I don't know, gay I guess."

"Mom!" I cry out, completely embarrassed.

"Well that's what happens when you do gay porn," Emmett jokes.

"Emmett!" Now I'm admonishing him. "She'll take you seriously."

"Oh, come now, I know when people are joking," my mother says. "And don't get me wrong, if you were gay Emmett, I wouldn't have a problem with it. For all I know, this could be one of those beard relationships, you know. Like with George Clooney."

"What about George Clooney?" Jackie asks in a shocked whisper.

My mother dismisses her with a wave of her hand. "Oh, you should hear what the girls at the beauty parlor say. I'm telling you, if you want to know the inside scoop on things, you go down to Barbara's on third street and you'll get all caught up. Of course, they had stuff to say about you, Emmett. I do have to wonder if it's true."

"Like what?" Emmett asks but I detect fear in his voice. I'd forgotten how overbearing my mother can be when she first meets people. It will take her a few hours to calm down.

"They say you're a playboy, you know. Always with a flavor of the month, until you met my Alyssa, of course. Which does make me wonder, what could she possibly offer you that the other girls couldn't? More of her to love, I suppose."

"Oh my god," I mutter, rubbing my palm into my forehead. "Make it stop."

"It's okay," Emmett says to me. "It's a fair statement. I guess I liked to have some fun, no harm in that, but when you meet the right person, nothing else really seems to matter anymore."

His words sound more flippant than serious, so I'm trying not to let my heart get carried away again.

"They also say you like to get in fights. I heard you were arrested in LA. I have to say, good for you. I like a man who can fight for what's right." She's smiling and then suddenly stops. "But if you really do turn out to be an asshole to my Alyssa here, I'll be the one fighting you, so don't even think about it. I know your type."

Emmett looks both insulted and scared.

I try to give him an apologetic smile and then point to Jackie and Will who have been standing behind me this whole time, wide-eyed and open-mouthed.

"And these are my friends Jackie and Will," I tell her wearily.

"Oh, Will the boss," my mother says, fixing her attention on him now. "My, you're a handsome one too. I suppose I should thank you for keeping my daughter employed for this long, I know what a pain in the ass she can be."

"Yes, she is, but we love her anyway," Will answers with a wide smile. "I suspect she gets her tenaciousness from you, though."

"You have no idea," she says with a wink and then starts back to the house, waving her hands in the air for us to follow, her bracelets jangling.

I let out a heavy sigh. I think I forgot to breathe that entire time.

Jackie looks at me, shaking her head while biting back laughter and then pushes me toward the house.

This isn't the house that I grew up in. My mother had that until I left home and then promptly sold it. This place is a small two-bedroom, located far up on the hills above town. It's at the end of a cul-de-sac too so it's extra isolated and has beautiful views of the town and both lakes. I worry about her living alone all the way up here–though my mother acts bossy and tough, she's really quite fragile at heart–but she's stubborn and says she's going to stay here until she dies or she gets bored. Whatever comes first.

Because the house and property are small–the backyard is just a slice of yellowed grass and porch before it drops off down ragged clay cliffs and gullies–there isn't much of a tour. Thankfully my mother has already prepared dinner for us, so there isn't a lot of sitting around and having small talk.

We eat in the narrow dining room, my mother at the head of the table, and she calls us to say grace before we feast on her famous lasagna recipe. My mother has never said grace a day in her life, so I think she just decided to do it for the sake of Emmett.

Then I know it's true when she tells him she hopes it reminded him of growing up.

"Come again?" Emmett asks as she passes him a dish.

"After your mother died, you were raised by your aunt, were you not? She was very religious and you went to church a lot."

I exchange a look with everyone else. How did my mother know this?

"Don't look so shocked, dear," she says to me. "I told you I know all the dirt."

Emmett clears his throat, looking uncomfortable. "You're right. She was religious, we did say grace a lot."

"Such a shame what happened to your mother, you poor boy."

"Mom," I warn her, though I'm practically whining. What is it about being with your parents for five minutes that turns back the clock to when you were a petulant teenager?

251

"Oh, come now. He's your boyfriend, sweetie. There are no secrets here. If he wants to know about everything your terrible father did to us, he's welcome to it. There's no shame in it, it's just the reality. Everyone has something, don't they?" She looks at Will and Jackie. "You're both the perfect looking couple, but he's far older than you. I bet that caused problems at some point."

Will and Jackie look at each other, brows raised. My mother doesn't even know the half of it.

"I'm not ashamed," Emmett speaks up. "It's all true. And it was horrible. And...it's caused problems. In my personal life. In my professional life."

Now we're all watching Emmett. It sounds like he's about to go into confession time. I don't want him to say anything he doesn't want to though, not for the sake of my nosy mother because she's putting him on the spot.

"But as you say, that's the reality, isn't it?" Emmett goes on. "And the truth is that it's taken a lot for me to realize what's real and what's not. Being an actor, you're used to living in the grey zone, the space where you start to believe your own lies."

At that he looks at me. And it hurts. It hurts because I feel like I know what he's trying to say.

That we're a lie. We're a lie that he started to believe.

And now he's realizing that it's nothing more.

Even though it's absolutely everything to me.

I swallow hard, my pulse kicking against my veins, preparing for the worst.

"That's probably why you like my Alyssa," my mother says delicately. "She's very honest. Just like me. She'll tell you the truth. She's not your fake Hollywood actress or flavor of the month. She's real."

A small smile tugs at Emmett's lips. His eyes soften as he stares at me.

"She is real," he says, his voice low. "She is the most real thing in my life. Honestly, I don't know what I'd do without her. What I do know is that I am deeply, madly and ridiculously in love with her."

Beside me, Jackie gasps and kicks me under the table.

But I can't feel anything at all.

Because it's all a lie.

It's a lie I want so desperately to believe.

"I tell her this all the time," he goes on, and each word is like a kick in the teeth, "how much she means to me, how much I love her. Sometimes I don't think she hears me, or knows it, but it's true. She has my heart and always will. And there is nothing more real than that."

The worst part of this all is the way he's saying it.

With so much passion and conviction and disarming tenderness that it's rendering me stupid. It's fileting me apart. It feels so fucking *good* to hear him say this.

And the reality of it all, of how cruel this is, is too much to take.

"Will you excuse me," I say and abruptly get to my feet, leaving the table.

I don't know why but the urge to cry and run and scream has taken over.

I've got to get out of here.

I head straight out of the house and up a ragged path that skirts the hill. I'm gulping for air, the sagebrush and desert shrubs pulling at my dress as I walk.

Everything inside me feels hollow and sick and I keep rubbing my chest, my stomach, trying to make the feeling go away, the horrible, misleading, teasing feeling that keeps building and building.

I know I shouldn't have left, I should have just stared back at Emmett and given him the fake smile and gone on pretending as I have.

But I'm so fucking tired of pretending.

I don't want to do it anymore.

I'm so close to the end but being with Emmett in this way is starting to kill me.

"Alyssa."

And there's his voice.

I figured someone would have come to check on me, but I thought it would have been Jackie. I wanted it to be Jackie.

Instead it's him.

I stop and turn around and see him approaching me, his eyes wild and filled with concern.

"What happened?" he asks me. "Back there, what happened?"

I shrug. "Wasn't feeling well."

He grabs my arm, his eyes growing more intense by the second. "Why are you lying to me?"

"Why are you lying at all!" I yell at him. "Why did you have to tell my mother that?!"

"Because I wanted her to see that you were happy. That you had someone. And that I wasn't like your father."

"But you are like my father!"

He balks at that, frowning, pissed off. And rightfully so. "What? Do you have any idea how insulting it is to hear you keep saying that? Look, I don't know your dad but it's more than unfair to keep comparing us."

I can't help it, even though I know he's right.

"Do you want me to be like that?" he asks. "Do you want me to be the player, the playboy, the manwhore? Is that the box you want to put me in?"

I shake my head, wrapping my arms around my chest. "No."

He places his body so he's right in front of me. "Because I'll tell you one thing," he says. "The more you tell someone what they are, the more they'll believe it."

I glare at him. "Is that a threat?"

"Fucking hell, Alyssa? Why does everything have to be so complicated with you?"

"Because I'm complicated!" I yell. "You're complicated. We're complicated. Okay?"

"Okay," he says, placing both hands on my shoulders and wrangling me in place. "Okay, so we're in a complicated situation. But if you just...talk to me, tell me how you feel."

"Why?" I cry out. "Why would I tell you how I feel? What good would that do?"

"Because I care about you," he says. "So much. I want to know how you feel and I especially want to know how you feel about me."

"Why? You decided you may go back to London and you didn't even tell me."

He closes his eyes and exhales loudly. "Look, that was just...I was just thinking. And I didn't tell you because I didn't want to scare you. I don't know what you want. And to be honest, I am not used to being in a relationship. I'm not used to the way it works, to sharing my life with people."

"But this isn't even a real relationship."

"You keep saying that," he says bitterly. "And the more you say it, the more I think that's what you want. That you're trying to convince yourself that it's been fake from the start."

"I don't know what's real!" I cry out.

"I'm real," he says. He takes my hand and places it on his chest. "My heart is real. What I feel for you is real. It always has been. Only the formalities have been fake. But every single word I've said to you, in public or not, has never been a lie."

I try to swallow the lump in my throat but I can't. "What about what you said back there. To my mother. About me."

His mouth lifts, a soft smile. "It wasn't a lie. That was

real." He puts his palm to my cheek, rests his forehead against mine. "I love you."

Everything inside me dissolves.

I'm both floating and drowning and flying all at once, my heart pulled into so many directions that I don't even know how I feel.

"I love you," he goes on, his voice choked with emotion, "I love you and it's terrifying the shit out of me, because I've never loved without losing before, but I love you. It's the most real thing I've ever felt in my life. And I know that no matter what happens, I'm not going to let go of it." He pauses, runs his thumb over my lips. I'm absolutely breathless. "I don't want to put any pressure on you either. You don't have to say a word. But I can't let you go on thinking that what we have isn't the one true thing. Passion over performance, remember? There's only passion here. Only truth. Only you and only me."

Tell him you love him. Tell him you love him.

But for some reason, I can't even speak.

I'm just so damn overwhelmed with it all.

I'm free-falling so far off that cliff that I don't know what side is up.

"Emmett," I whisper to him, my fingers digging into his shirt. "I…"

"Don't say it," he says. "Just feel it."

Feel it and be free.

He kisses me softly. "Let's go back to the dinner. I think your mom is worried sick."

I nod, almost dizzy from it all. I manage to swallow. "Yeah. Yeah…sorry about her."

He laughs gently. "She's quite the handful. I can see where you got all your thorns and prickles from. Armor against her."

"Pretty much," I tell him.

He loves me.

He loves me!

Now it's starting to sink in for real.

Now I can't stop smiling.

I let out a soft laugh, staring at Emmett with new eyes.

Every single cell inside me is warm and glowing. I'm made of a million sunbursts.

I'm about to tell him that I don't even think I'm hungry anymore when I hear a snuffling sound from behind me.

In unison, both Emmett and I turn around.

There's nothing but trees and sand and yellow flowers and brush and rocks and...

A raccoon pokes his head around a ponderosa pine and looks at us.

At me.

That masked fucker looks me dead in the eye.

We don't spend any time figuring out if this is the desert-dwelling cousin of Cyril Sneer or not.

Emmett grabs my hand and looks at me. "Run."

We both start running down the hill, leaving the raccoon in a cloud of dust.

THE DRIVE back to the cabin after dinner is quiet. Jackie is the designated driver, so she's concentrating on the directions from Siri. Will wasn't sure how to handle my mother while Emmett and I were gone, so he had a lot of wine and is now snoring lightly in the front seat.

Emmett and I are tangled together in the backseat.

But we're not tired in the slightest.

In fact, I can't remember the last time I felt so alive, that every cell inside me was pumped and ready to go.

By the time the car pulls up beside the cabin, Emmett and

are running inside to grab another bottle of wine and some towels and then start heading down to the beach.

"Oh, so now you want to do the night swim," Jackie says warily as she and Will head inside the cabin.

"Clothing optional!" I yell at her as I start to pull my dress off over my head.

I know it's dark out and we're slightly visible in the cabin's porch light, but I honestly don't care that I'm going in naked or not. Both Emmett and I have stripped completely nude by the time our feet hit the water and we splash into the lake.

"Ahhhh!' I cry out, laughing. The water is a bit colder at night and it's bracing in the warm night air.

Emmett splashes beside me, grabbing my hand and pulling him to me. "Come here you gorgeous sea creature you."

"It's a lake, Emmett," I tell him, kissing him on the tip of his nose. "I'm a lake creature."

"The Ogopogo?"

I nod, giggling. "That seems about right."

"Have you ever seen the Ogopogo?" he asks, wrapping his arms around my neck. I wrap my legs around his waist, feeling his cock jut between us.

"Is talking about the Ogopogo turning you on?" I ask him slyly. "Because that's a weird fetish if I've ever heard one."

Every deep, dark lake has a legend about it. Loch Ness has the Loch Ness Monster. Lake Okanagan has the Ogopogo. They both look roughly the same, have the same amount of (feeble) evidence to support their existence and there's a lot of people who truly believe in them.

"I've heard there's a million-dollar reward for hard evidence," he tells me.

I reach down and grab his cock. "I've got some hard evidence right here."

He bursts out laughing, even as I feel him grow hotter and larger in my hand. "I'm just thinking, with your luck with animals, perhaps we could use you as bait."

I bite my lip and grin at him, his beautiful wet face dimly lit by the cabin lights behind us, the dark lake stretching out as far as the eye can see. "Oh. I'm Ogopogo bait now, am I?"

"Stop saying Ogopogo. The word is ceasing to lose all meaning."

"You started it."

He grins and twirls around so we're moving faster and faster in a circle, the water splashing around us.

Above us, the sky and the stars dance.

The water gets deeper.

I'm about to tell him I'm getting dizzy when something brushes against my ass.

"Ahhhh!' I scream.

"What is it?"

"Something touched me!"

We both exchange a look.

I yell out, "Ogopogo!" while he starts laughing and together we start swimming until we're closer to shore.

"I think the solution is to never let you go," he says, burying his head in my neck. "Never let you out of my sight. Stay with me forever."

As simple as his words sound, they mean the world.

"I would be okay with that."

He pulls back and looks at me with all intensity. "Yeah?"

And then I realize he still hasn't heard what he needs to hear. What I need him to hear.

I put my hand at his cheek, feeling his wet skin, his rough stubble, and gaze deeply into his eyes until all he sees is me. All he sees is the real me. All he sees is my heart.

"Emmett," I whisper to him. "I love you."

It takes a moment for my words to reach him, like they

get lost in time, or are swallowed by the lake. But then, slowly, the biggest, most breathtaking smile stretches across his face.

"I love you," I tell him again, his smile making me whole.

And I tell him again and again.

CHAPTER 18

"*Y*ou, my friend, are impossible to get a hold of," Autumn says as she steps into my trailer.

I look up from the tattered copy of *Watership Down* I'm reading–found it when I last visited Jimmy–and give her a wane smile.

I am hard to get a hold of. On purpose. The last three weeks or so, ever since we got back from Penticton, I've been spending as much time with Alyssa as possible. It has nothing to do with the contract anymore. The fact is, I can't stand days without her. If she's not in my bed, I'm in hers. It feels fucking good to kiss her in the morning when either of us go off to work, like we're actually in this real, breathing relationship and one that fucking works.

I've been going to work less and less, as it is.

In fact, in the last three weeks, my life has changed fairly drastically, even though it's all for the better.

My role on *Boomerang* has come to an end. Today was actually my last day on set and I've just finished up my scenes but am hanging around in my trailer, waiting to see if I'm needed for a reshoot before we're done for the day.

I'm not sad about it at all. In fact, had they not told me when I got back from Penticton that Doctor Death was meeting his death, I probably would have brought it up at some point. Things have been slowly shifting into place and I'm looking at my life with a new perspective, even if I'm unsure how to make things happen. What I do know is that I'm like Alyssa in some ways, ready for something new even if I don't know what it is.

The leap of faith.

Ratings on *Boomerang* have been slipping, so they think that by bringing in a new villain, they'll win back their audience. The one thing I did ask the producers though is if my leaving the show had anything to do with my supposed reputation.

Boy, you should have seen their faces.

"Emmett, your personal life is your personal life," Gary Edwards, one of the producers, had said to me. "I don't care if you're kicking puppies or helping little old ladies cross the street. As long as you show up on time and do the work, that's all we care about. That's all any producer cares about."

So, it turns out that my bad boy reputation as a bruiser didn't have much bearing at all.

It's one reason why when Autumn managed to get me on the phone today, I agreed for her to stop by. It's petty but I want to rub it in how no one gives a shit about my reputation except for her.

But as it is my last day on set, I shouldn't be surprised that she has a fancy bottle of rye in her hands, a Crown Royal reserve with a bow wrapped around it. I find myself looking at it more than I am at her.

"I got it just for you," she says smugly, walking toward me. "Shall we toast?"

I put the book down and sit up. She's always wearing something sexy and today is no different. High heels, minis-

cule black shorts, a silk tank, no bra. Not exactly professional nor practical since September is almost over, but I
suppose it is Friday night and she has somewhere to be
after.

Autumn and I have always had a complicated relationship. She literally only signed on with me by the recommen-
dation of Julian when I started on *Boomerang*. I know Alyssa
has grilled me about her a few times, assuming we've been
physical with each other, wanting to know the truth
about her.

Truth is, I did sleep with her. The first day we had a meeting, last year. We hit it off and then it just sort of…happened.
I'm not proud of it, but somehow we were able to make it
work afterward. It didn't mean anything to me, it was just
physical. And it didn't mean anything to Autumn. We were
able to start working with each other after that, like it never
happened, and we never did it again. I guess we just got it out
of our systems.

But even though I've told Alyssa this and assured her that
there's nothing going on between us–I can appreciate
Autumn's beauty but it honestly does nothing for me now–I
know she's a bit cagey about us being together. I'm sure if
Alyssa had a choice, she'd prefer I don't work with Autumn
at all.

I'm half-inclined to agree with her. It's not that I don't
like Autumn or think she's a shitty publicist, but if it makes
Alyssa uneasy, then she's got to go. The only problem is this
contract. Autumn is overseeing it so I'm pretty much stuck
with her until it's all done.

It's also one reason why I've been avoiding Autumn's
calls. The only reason I even answered today was because she
said she had big news for me. Now that she's here, I'm
wondering what it is.

"Emmett?" Autumn asks, shaking a glass at me. "Come on,

you have to celebrate your last day. You can't be all mopey and depressed about it."

"Mopey?" I frown. "I'm the opposite of mopey."

"I don't know. You're in your trailer, alone, reading a book. I know how hard it is to say good bye to an era."

"I was on the show for less than a year. It was a short era."

"Even so. Toast with me."

I glance at the clock on the wall. "They might need me for a reshoot."

"Nope," she says with a big smile. "They said you're all done."

"Really?" Hell, they could have told me that. I would have tried to meet up with Alyssa.

"When they're done shooting, they said to come over to Julian's trailer for a goodbye toast but I thought I would beat them to it. So drink up."

She hands me the drink and raises her glass to mine.

We cheers.

I drink.

Damn, it's good.

And then…time just kind of slips by.

Autumn keeps refilling my glass, sitting beside me in the trailer, until I'm not sure how much I've drunk.

"So," she says to me and I'm barely conscious of the fact that her leg is pressed against mine. Warning bells are going off in my head but I'm not sure why. "What do you think your next role will be? What do you want me to help you campaign for? If I work side-by-side with your agent, I think you could have pretty much anything. Even a movie role. A big one."

"I'm moving to London," I tell her, aware that I've slurred my words. Also aware that I'm not sure if I'm moving to London at all but it seems the thing to say right now.

Autumn stills beside me. Her hand goes on my leg. "What?"

"I said I'm moving to London and taking Alyssa with me."

I look up at her face and she's staring at me in horror. "Alyssa? You…the contract is almost up, Emmett."

I shrug. "I'm in love with her. What can I say."

"You're what?!" she hisses.

"In love." I hold out my empty glass and wave it at her. "More please."

She watches me for a second. My vision starts to double on itself so I see two sets of blindingly white teeth. Then it comes together again.

"Emmett," she says, pouring me another glass. "You can't go to London. What would you do? Theatre again?"

"Why not?"

"Then what use am I to you?" For the first time, she looks absolutely hurt.

Shit. She's taking it personally.

"It'll all work out," I tell her, taking a drink.

She grows silent for who knows how long until she mutters to herself. "Well I'm glad I saw this coming."

"Huh?"

She gets to her feet. "Come on. We should go join the party."

"Party?"

"At the other trailer. Julian's. Your goodbye party." She then pours me another drink. "Finish that first."

I stare at the bottle. "Shit. I've almost had most of it."

"You're very drunk," she says. "Finish it."

I do what she says. Who am I to argue.

When I'm done the glass, I have a hard time getting to my feet. She has to haul me up.

I almost fall over on her. I can't stop laughing. "I'm so

sorry, I don't think my feet work. How am I going to do musical theatre again if my feet don't work?"

"It's fine," she says, laughing in response. It's nice that she's back to being nice again.

She opens the trailer door and the parking lot where all the trailers are parked is dark, no one around. The air is crisp with fall. The giant studio looms beside us. In the distance I hear Julian's laugh and some cheers. There really is a party going on. If it's for me, I should be there.

Hell, Alyssa should be here. She's my forever date. I wish I'd known.

I should call her.

"Alyssa," I say but I don't know what I expect. For her to appear?

At that, I nearly stumble down the trailer steps and she's holding me up once again.

"Wow. You're stronger than you look," I tell her as she puts my arm around her shoulder.

We walk a few feet until we're between two trailers, then we stop.

"You're drunk, Emmett," she says again, her voice lower now.

I lean back against the trailer, trying to get my bearings. Holy shit. What is even happening.

My hands are going down her sides, skirting over her waist, hips, thighs.

Her hands are cupping my face.

Then she's kissing me.

I kiss her back.

It takes a second for me to realize.

This isn't Alyssa's mouth. Not her lips, not her tongue. This isn't her skin beneath my hands.

"No," I blurt out and try to move my head back. The world spins. I nearly lose my balance.

Autumn is holding me.

Autumn is not letting go.

This is all Autumn, not Alyssa.

"I'm sorry, I can't," I mumble, trying to keep my head up straight.

Autumn is pulling my face towards her, trying to kiss me again.

"No one can see us, it doesn't matter," she whispers to me as I move my face out of reach.

I put my hand on her chest and push her back. I fall back against the trailer and raise my head.

She's staring at me, enraged under the dim lights of the parking lot. "What's wrong with me, Emmett?" she asks. "What is it?"

I don't know what to say. I try and swallow. "I'm flattered."

Oh, she doesn't like that. "Flattered?"

"Yes. Yes, I'm very flattered you tried to kiss me and you like me but it's not mutual. Nope. I'm with Alyssa and you're not Alyssa and I'm sorry but…"

"That's a fake relationship Emmett," she snipes harshly.

"It isn't. I don't think it ever was," I admit. "I love her."

"You don't know love," she says. "That's not who you are."

I flinch. "I'm sorry. I don't think…I need to go home."

"Emmett," she warns.

I start walking off and when she tries to grab a hold of me, I push her off.

"Emmett!" she yells after me.

I manage to get my phone out of my pocket and dial a cab before I lose all capability.

Then I stumble out of the studio, skipping my goodbye party and leaving my publicist behind. I need to be alone. I need to sober up.

Then I need to tell Alyssa exactly what happened.

* * *

I WAKE up to a knock at my door.

I think I've been listening to it for a long time but I thought it was my heart pounding in my head.

My mouth feels like I've swallowed sawdust.

I am in *bad* shape.

Gingerly I roll over and groan. My curtains are closed and soft light is filtering in through the cracks. I have no idea at all what time it is.

I reach over and pick up my phone.

It's dead. Figures.

I take in a deep breath, trying to bring feeling back into my body.

Fucking hell. What did I drink last night?

Oh yeah.

Oh…fuck.

It all comes rushing back.

What a mess.

The knock at the door again. Louder this time.

Pounding, actually.

Fuck, fuck, fuck.

That's never a good sign.

I get out of bed and pull on a pair of jogging pants as I head over to the door.

I look through the peephole.

It's Alyssa. She's looking down at her phone.

I quickly swing open the door.

"Hey," I say to her, squinting at the light. Even though it's cloudy, it still hurts my eyes. "My phone's been dead, I–"

And then I see her eyes.

She's been crying.

She also looks like she wants to slice my head clean off.

"What happened?" I ask, immediately fearful.

She tries to swallow, her jawline growing tight. "How could you?" she whispers, her words caught in her throat, her red-rimmed eyes filled with pain. "How could you do this to me?"

I blink at her. "What?"

I wish I could think faster, that my hangover didn't have a hold on me.

Autumn. Is it Autumn?

Does she know that Autumn kissed me? But how?

"Come in," I tell her, gesturing to the house. "Please. Let's talk."

She hesitates. She's almost afraid. It's now that I realize she looks like she just crawled out of bed. She's in her pajama pants, flip flops, an oversized Mad Men Studios hoodie. She's got no makeup on, her hair is a mess. She's so completely vulnerable, fragile yet brimming with so much animosity that I'm not sure how to handle her, what to do.

"Please tell me what happened," I say.

At that her eyes narrow. "I can't believe you," she mutters bitterly.

But at least she walks inside.

I quickly shut the door as she walks into the middle of the room, looks around.

"What are you looking for?" I ask her.

"Is she here?"

I run my hands down my face and sigh. "Is who here?"

"Autumn."

I give my head a slight shake, knowing I have to tread carefully now. "No, Alyssa. She's not. Why would you think she's here?"

She sniffs, her face crumpling. "How could you do this to me?"

"Baby, please…"

269

"Don't baby me!" she cries out, back to vicious. "Don't play dumb!"

"I just woke up, Alyssa! I don't know what you're talking about."

"You haven't seen your emails?" she asks, nearly breathless.

Now I'm extra worried. "No. Phone is dead. Why? What…?"

She folds her arms across her chest. "Go and look. I'll wait."

It feels like my heartbeat is doubling up as I stride across the room and pull out my MacBook from the shelf. I bring it over to the kitchen island beside her and open it, then open my emails.

There's an email there from a name, Kristoff Gantz, no subject but an attachment.

I glance at her.

"Open it," she says in a hard voice, eyes like steel.

I click on it.

There's only a few lines of text. A few lines that turn my world upside down.

I HAD the pleasure of taking these photographs last night. I know that is your publicist, not your girlfriend Alyssa Martin. If you don't wire me 50,000 to the bank account below in forty-eight hours, I will release the pictures to the public.

Kristoff Gantz.

MY HEART SINKS.

Do I even dare click on the attachments?

I look over at Alyssa. "Alyssa…"

"Look at them," she says.

Her voice is practically shaking.

I ready myself and click.

There are four of them. All taken from the same angle, a low angle, like he was crouching at the edge of the other trailer.

Every single one looks completely incriminating and in every single one we're kissing.

It doesn't matter that I know that the kiss only lasted a few seconds before I broke it off.

It looks like it lasted a hell of a lot more than that. The photos only tell half the story.

But is that a story that Alyssa is willing to believe?

I look at her, feeling my heart hanging in the balance.

This can't be over, not because of this.

I lick my lips. "You have to let me explain," I say quietly.

She stares at me. "I don't want to hear your explanation. You said you were working last night, Emmett! Your last day on the job! I was hoping that maybe when you got home, I could take you out to celebrate. But you never called me. And now I know why. Jesus…"

With each word, it sounds like she's dying.

"Alyssa," I say, putting my hand over hers but she yanks hers away.

"Don't touch me," she sneers. "Don't you dare touch me after you kissed her. You…god!" she screams and pulls at her hair. "I'm such an idiot! I am such a fucking idiot, I actually believed you. I actually believed in us. And it was all a lie."

"You're jumping to conclusions."

"You're fucking kissing her! Tell me those photos are manipulated then!"

"They are!" I yell. "We only kissed for a second."

"Oh my god, you admit it!" she shrieks, turning her back to me and walking across the kitchen. "I can't believe you."

"Well if you just let me explain what happened," I cry out

weakly. There's nothing but pure panic rising in my chest, fluttering around in a flurry of wings. Holy shit. Is this really happening?

"Explain?" she says, whirling around. "Explain what? You just said you kissed her, what else could you have to add to that?"

"For one, she kissed me."

"Oh she did? She took advantage of you, is that it?"

"I was drunk."

Fuck. That was not the right thing to say.

She stares at me, blinking, her mouth open. "You were drunk," she eventually says. "So when you're drunk, you go around kissing girls. So that's a thing you do."

"No," I protest. "It's not...I thought she was you for a second."

Alyssa's laugh fills the room, so bitter, sour, laced with hatred for me.

"Well I am so fucking flattered. Emmett...I wanted to expect more from you, I really did, but somehow I'm not surprised."

Now I'm starting to get mad. "Wait a minute, that's a low blow."

"You deserve a low blow."

"You expected me to do something like this?"

"And you just did it!"

"Alyssa," I say, breathing heavily now. "Please just...listen to me. Okay? She came over to my trailer and she brought rye to celebrate." She rolls her eyes, scoffs. "And so we did. I had too many drinks and then we left to go join the party in Julian's trailer, the goodbye party for me. I could barely stand. I thought I should call you. I remember even saying your name out loud and then the next thing I knew she was kissing me. And yes, I kissed her back for a second, that second you see captured on film. And then I realized what was happening. I broke it off. I pushed her back. I told her no. It pissed her off. But I told her no, that I love you and I can't, and I left. I called a cab and got in that cab alone. And then I wake up here to this…this fucking bullshit!"

"Don't start yelling at me!"

"I'm not yelling at you, I'm yelling because it's bullshit! Of course there was some fucking vulture hiding around the corner, of course there's someone fucking blackmailing me right now. Blackmailing us."

"Oh they aren't blackmailing me," she says. "This is your problem now. Whatever we had, it's over. Fuck the contract, I don't want your fucking money and fuck your reputation too. You obviously reap what you sow."

I wish what she was saying wasn't flying into my chest like shrapnel, but it is. It fucking is.

"No," I tell her, but fuck it's hard to speak. This can't be happening. "No. You have to understand. Everything I said is true."

"But the pictures say otherwise."

"The pictures lie!" I yell. "It's all a lie. You have to believe me." I press my hand into my chest. "Me, Alyssa. We've been together in this crazy world of real and fake for so long now, I get that it's confusing, I get that you don't know what to believe, I get that you might think it's an act. I'm not blaming you for thinking the worst."

"What? *Thinking* the worst?!" she cries, throwing out her arms. "Again, Emmett, the pictures. Your words. You kissed her. You were drunk and thought it was me. That doesn't make it okay. Not even a bit."

I put my head in my hands, pinch my eyes shut, hoping to drown out the world. "I know. I know it's not okay. I fucked up." I breathe in deep but everything hurts. "I fucked up."

"Yeah," she says quietly. "You did. And I'm sure I should just give you the benefit of the doubt but…I can't. I just can't.

These pictures they're…I'll never stop seeing them. Never stop picturing you with her."

I stare at her, imploring her with my eyes but I already see the wall between us. "This can't just end. It was just beginning."

"It was a role to you Emmett, that's all it was."

"It was never a role. It was always real. Alyssa…I love you. More than I can even say. Please, don't leave it like this, leave me like this. How I feel about you is the only true thing I have."

God, please, let these words get through to her!

She breathes in deep through her nose, shaking. "I need to go."

She heads to the door.

I need to run after her.

I need to stop her.

I need to cry and plead and beg.

But I don't.

My heart hurts too much to even move.

CHAPTER 19

ALYSSA

*B*roken.

There's no other word for it.

There are other words for how I'm feeling. Humiliated. Embarrassed. Ashamed. Angry. Sad. Depressed.

But the word that says it all right now is…*broken*.

I'm no longer a whole human but one that's splintered and fragmented and made up only of jagged parts.

On Saturday morning I got the email that was addressed to both me and Emmett. The email that ruined us and everything we shared together. It ruined the future I thought we had. It ruined a love I thought we had.

It broke me into a million pieces before I even heard the truth from Emmett's mouth.

Him with her. Autumn, who represents everything I'm not. Tanned, tall, skinny, effortlessly beautiful. Successful. She's the polar opposite of me in every way.

And she's Emmett's type. Not just in the fact that he dated and screwed so many actresses and models that looked just like her before I came around. It's the fact that he specifically slept with her before. He says it only happened once…I believe him. But I also believe that's why when she kissed him, he let it happen.

The thing is...I know that Emmett was probably telling the truth. He's an honest guy, especially about his misdeeds and shortcomings but...

Fuckity fuck *fuck*.

He just broke my fucking heart.

Is he that easy to take advantage of when drunk? How many times has this happened before?

And...what if I never showed up at his door, if we never got that email...would he have told me what happened?

That's what I have a hard time wrestling with. Because as honest as he is, I can't forget his type, the person he was before he met me. I believed him when he says he loved me, I really did but...I just think maybe his idea of love is skewed. I couldn't even blame him for that, not with his upbringing and losing his mom, not with his job and essentially lying for a living. After all, how can loving *me* really change a person? How can I make him stop being the person he was and become someone else?

I'm just Alyssa Martin.

And I don't think I have that kind of power over him, over anyone.

How can a relationship built on a lie ever feel like the truth?

And how the fuck am I ever going to get over him when it feels like I don't even possess my heart anymore. I left it at his house, where it lays shattered on his floor. Now I'm just scooped out inside, hollow, a space that only darkness can fill.

It's killing me.

Honestly, I don't know if I've ever really loved, ever really hurt before.

Not like this, never like this.

I walked straight off that cliff.

Why am I even surprised I hit the ground?

"How could he?" I cry out suddenly over my glass of wine.

I'm plopped down on my bed, the wine having already spilled twice as I try to balance drinking and lying down at the same time. I want to float away to oblivion and I can't even sit upright to do it.

Tiffany and Jackie don't say anything and when I lift my head to look over at them, Jackie in my armchair and Tiffany sitting on the floor, knees drawn up, hand in the middle of the popcorn bowl, I realize they're exchanging a look. That look pisses me off.

"What?" I ask. "What is it?"

Their look deepens.

"Well…" Tiffany says slowly.

Yeah, Tiffany knows the truth now about Emmett and me and our whole relationship. I told her the moment that my life went to fucking hell. She wasn't even insulted that she was kept in the dark for so long. She just said, "You're smart, I probably would have told everyone. Accidently, of course."

"Well what? Come on guys," I plead. "This is part of the grieving process, isn't it?"

Jackie shrugs. "Me and Will never broke up."

"Ken's the only boyfriend I've ever had," Tiffany adds.

"What the fuck?" I glare at them, rolling over on my side. "Neither one of you have an idea what I'm going through? That's it. Carla!" I yell. "Get your ass in here!"

Within seconds my bedroom door opens and Carla appears, her hair wrapped up in a bandana, holding a bottle of beer. "Are you finally inviting me to join your pity party?"

"Are you high?" I ask her.

She shrugs.

"Anyway, tell me about the last time your heart was broken."

She leans against the doorway, eyes staring off, tapping her finger against the bottle. "It was July, 1994. We had met at the waterpark, shared a stick of Juicy Fruit…"

"Just sit your butt down and make me feel better," I tell her.

She sits on the edge of the bed and looks me over. "I think you're being too harsh on him."

"What?" I exclaim. "*I'm* being too harsh? Do you even know the rules of a pity party?"

"I mean, the guy has to pay you forty thousand dollars, right? And now this blackmailer fifty thousand? And he just lost his role on Boomerang? The dude is out close to a hundred grand and just lost his job. Give him a break."

I'm slack-jawed. "First off, I'm not taking the money. And, Carla, he cheated on me!"

"Kissing isn't cheating," she says with a scoff.

But both Jackie and Tiffany make urgent sounds of protest.

"I would cut off Will's balls if he kissed another woman."

"I would put Nair in Ken's hair oil," Tiffany seethes, "and then I'd switch his toothpaste with hemorrhoid cream, and then I'd cover him in honey from head to toe and push him off a plane straight into a bear's den, throwing down a bottle of bear spray that I actually filled with salmon-scented water. Cuz bears love that shit."

We're all staring openly at Tiffany and I'm making a mental note to never cheat on her.

"Anyway," Carla says slowly, turning her attention back to me, "the girl wanted him, you suspected this yourself. She gets him drunk, she kisses him. Now you can believe he pushed her back right away or you can believe he had a full-on make-out session with her. Which one do you choose to believe?"

I still, thinking it over. "I don't know. Both are bad."

"Both are bad. One is worse. You can't possibly tell me that you haven't gotten so drunk that some guy hasn't kissed you and it took you a few seconds to be like, whoa, no, this is wrong. Or at least a situation similar. Isn't that the important part? The fact that Emmett stopped it?"

"But the pictures…"

"The pictures tell a half-truth, just as the pictures with you both, the pictures that started you all, told a half-truth."

Holy crow, that feels like a whole lifetime ago.

"Now it comes down to you and Emmett," she goes on, "it comes down to trust. Either you trust Emmett or you don't. If you don't well…then you needed to break up. Because there is no relationship without trust, not a real one anyway. But maybe you guys have been so busy faking it that you've both forgotten what it's like."

Carla looks to Jackie. "Tell me, Miss Pregnancy Pants, if someone sent you pictures of your husband kissing, like, your housekeeper or something–"

"We don't have a housekeeper."

"In this scenario you do. And she's super *hawt*. That's hot with a W. Anyway, you get the pictures and Will is all, look she got me drunk, she kissed me, I broke it off, I told her no, I told her I love you, I swear the moment I realized what was happening I was disgusted, I would have told you the first thing but I was sleeping, etcetera, etcetera, would you believe him?"

"Of course I would," she says.

"Without a doubt?"

"Without a doubt. I trust Will with all my heart. He would never ever do anything intentionally to hurt me. He would never even want to kiss another woman. He wouldn't do that to me."

And then all three of them give me a weighted look.

I chew on my lip for a moment, mulling it over. "So now the problem lies with me?"

Carla nods. "It comes down to trust. What he did was stupid but…if you believe him, you should have nothing to worry about. If you believe him, it's something you'll get over. It's not something to end your relationship over. Not when you truly love a person. You don't give up that easily."

Ah, fuck.

"What do I do?" I ask, looking down into my wine glass. I feel like I could sink to the bottom of it and never come out.

"We can't answer that," Carla says. "You have to search within yourself to find the truth. And then you should probably talk to Emmett about it."

Because he was my truth.

I take in a deep breath.

All the hurt and humiliation and pain and shame isn't just going to go away. Even if I do believe Emmett, even if I have faith in this new him, that he wouldn't let this happen again, how do I deal with my feelings? How do I deal with this hurt? I can't be with him and secretly hate and resent him at the same time. I can't go back to him until I've worked it out, until I'm ready.

And what if that never happens?

What if I find the real truth about us and discover that nothing was real to begin with?

CHAPTER 20

EMMETT

*R*ain.

It's one of the things that make Vancouver what it is. It's what the tourists and locals both complain about, it's what keeps it beautiful and green. It shows up on long weekends and tends to rain out concerts and weddings. And it's the perfect soundtrack for a ravaged heart.

As emo as that sounds, that's all I have right now. The rain pouring outside this coffee shop window and the ache in my heart that hasn't subsided for the last forty-eight hours.

Actually, it's been forty-four hours.

I still have two more hours to figure out if I'm going to pay this blackmailer's ransom or not. If I pay it, he'll free the photos. If I don't, he'll sell them to the highest bidder.

Either way, he wins. He gets the money.

And I lose.

But fuck, I've already lost Alyssa.

What else is there?

Take it all. I really couldn't care.

The chime above the coffee shop rings and I look over.

It's Autumn, right on time. Despite it being eight on a

Monday morning, she's all dressed up like she's going to some party. Now I have to wonder why. Is it to try and win me over? The next guy? Who knows.

All I know is that she's about to be very, very unhappy with me.

I haven't seen her since she kissed me.

And I don't have the best news.

"Hey," she says to me, sitting down in the armchair across from me. If she's embarrassed about what happened, about the way she came on to me, she doesn't show it.

I pick up my coffee cup and gesture to the baristas. "You're not going to get anything?"

She shakes her head. "No. I want to get right down to it."

I open my mouth, about to tell her my plan, but she plows on through.

"I think you're making a huge mistake."

"What?" I ask.

"You're leaving this down to the wire. The guy is going to flip soon, he could flip at any minute and sell those photos."

"Okay."

"Okay?" She flinches.

"Yeah. That's why I wanted to talk to you. I don't want to pay him."

"Emmett, you have to."

"Why?"

She lowers her voice, leaning over, her eyes lit with fire. "There are pictures of us kissing."

"I'm aware. You kissed me. Someone caught it on camera." I wait for her to protest and say I kissed her or some lie but she doesn't. "But I'm not paying it."

"The world will call you a cheater."

I shrug. "I'm not a cheater. I know this. The world can think what it wants."

"Think?" she cries out softly. "There is proof of you and me together."

"But it's not real."

"Nothing has been real in your life!"

A few heads in the shop look our way at her outburst.

"Do you want to attract more attention?" I ask her dryly.

"Then why did you pick this place?"

"Because I knew you couldn't lose your shit here. The fact is, I'm not paying. And I don't care what people say. I know the truth and that's all that matters."

"But does your girlfriend? Sorry, I guess I should say ex-girlfriend."

Heat drums through my veins, my face growing hot. "How do you know we broke up?"

She shrugs. "I figured. Why would she stay with you after what she saw? You were thrown to the curb like garbage, weren't you?"

I jerk back, staring at Autumn with new eyes. There's something off here about all of this, something I can't put my finger on. An unwarranted viciousness. If only I could think faster.

"Whatever is between Alyssa and I stays between Alyssa and I."

"If you don't pay, you'll shame her all over the world. People will laugh at her. Do you really want that?"

Fucking hell. No. I don't. And that's the only thing that's been holding me back on all of this. I don't want her to be humiliated. But I've tried to get a hold of her ever since she left my place, I even stopped by her apartment but her room-mate was adamant she wasn't home. I can't figure out what she would want me to do.

But I think I know what I have to do.

"Alyssa is tougher than you think. Far tougher than you.

She'll handle it with grace. She's not the bad guy here anyway, I am."

Autumn's eyes narrow into slits. "If you do this, you void the contract. I'll make sure of that. And you'll still have to pay her."

"Fine with me. She earned it."

"And you'll have to pay me my bonus early. That's in the contract too."

I raise my brow. I'd forgotten that bit. It wasn't much, ten grand, but it's odd that she's reaching for it. Guess she knows what's coming next.

"That's fine."

"And then I'm no longer representing you as a client."

"That's fine too."

She stares at me in disbelief. "So just like that, you'll let me walk away?"

I frown, puzzled. "I guess so. Your services are no longer needed."

She shakes her head, a strange look of pain across her face. "You can't do this. You can't do this to me. You have to pay the fifty thousand and then you can walk but you can't… this isn't…"

Jesus Murphy. Is this what I think it is?

"Emmett…," she whimpers, leaning across and putting her hand on my knee. "I've been a part of you since the beginning. I've helped you and you've helped me and I know you care, I know you do. You don't have to pretend anymore that I'm just your publicist, you can drop that act. You can walk away from her, but you can't walk away from me, you can't."

I stare down at her hand, frozen for a moment, until I move my legs to the side and slowly get to my feet. "It was you," I say softly as everything slides into place. "You got me drunk, you kissed me because you knew a photographer would be there. You knew because you hired him. You hired him because you are Kristoff Gantz, you wanted the money because you knew I'd leave you."

It feels like I'm reaching here. It feels like I'm just pulling this out by the seat of my pants and hoping for the best. But as crazy and ridiculous as it all sounds, I know it's the truth. You know the truth when you hear it, when you see it, and it's right in front of me.

She just shakes her head, tears spilling down her cheeks. "Emmett," she says, but she can't say anything else.

And that's the whole truth. For all I know, she probably arranged for the photos of me and Alyssa to be taken to begin with, a lucky guess I'd hook up with someone, who knows. Something to endear me to the public, to make her more important, to make me more important, to further the both of us at the expense of Alyssa.

But I don't have time to sit here and figure it out. In a way, this has made a shitty problem a little less shitty.

"Go ahead and post the photos," I tell her as I pause behind her chair on my way out. "Do whatever. But I'm not paying it, I'm not paying you. Everything between us, real and imagined, ends right here and right now."

"I love you Emmett," she says through a quiet sob.

I let out a dry laugh. "No you don't. You love the role you think you play, that's all."

Then I step outside into the rain and leave that act of my life behind.

* * *

"DAMN, SON," Will says before taking a lazy sip of his drink. "You definitely need that after everything." He nods at the Manhattan in my hand.

I exhale, my breath causing ripples in the liquid. I'd just

spent the last hour with Will at the bar, unloading everything single thing that happened over the weekend, including what happened with Autumn this morning. I know he probably heard Alyssa's side of things from Jackie, but I figured he should know the actual truth and the play-by-play from me.

"So how do you know Autumn won't post the photos?" he asks me as he leans on the bar. When the bartender looks our way, Will signals for two more drinks.

"I don't know. But I don't think so. It's been nearly a whole day since I told her I wasn't paying and if she were to do it, I think she would have done so by now. Besides, those photos incriminate her. It's not exactly smart to be seen kissing your client. It would only damage her reputation in the end."

"Fucking eh. So, she ended up being a bit of a nutter who was in love with you? Man, you get all the interesting stories, don't you?"

I shrug. "I don't know how interesting it is. She always seemed a bit…off. But you know how hot girls are."

"Do I ever."

"I mean, Alyssa is no different. But she's an off that I can understand. We gel. We get each other." I glance at Will, hoping I don't look too pathetic. "Please tell me you're here to talk about her."

He gives me a sympathetic smile. "I'm here because you're my friend and you especially need a friend right now. I'm not sure how much I should say about her."

"Why wouldn't you say anything?"

He scratches at his chin. "Well, you see, the missus…she told me not to."

"And you listen to her?"

"I have to. I'm her husband."

I sigh loudly. "I just want to know what's going on. I would know myself but Alyssa won't return a single text, call or email and yes I've shown up at her apartment. The only thing I haven't done is show up at her work. Can I show up at the office?"

Will looks uneasy as he takes a sip. "Well if you do that, you won't find her there."

"What do you mean? What happened?"

"She gave her notice today," he says.

"Gave her notice? As in she quit?"

Holy fuck. She actually did it.

"Yup. Called a meeting with me and Ted and laid it all down. I wasn't surprised of course. Jackie warned me it was coming. But it was still quite a loss."

I stare straight ahead, my eyes absently taking in the bottles behind the bar. "I can't believe it. I mean...did Jackie tell you about the money part of the contract?"

"Sure did. And I know you didn't give it to her yet. I know she doesn't want it." He gives me a look. "If you two end up talking again, don't push it. You may think she's earned it by putting up with you, hell, I may think she's earned it, but she doesn't want it." He pauses. "That said, I have no idea how she's going to afford London."

"London!" I exclaim.

"I wasn't supposed to tell you that," he says sheepishly. "Anyway. Yes. London. England. She only gave one week notice too, which Ted and I aren't too happy about. She flies out on Saturday. But Tiffany is more than eager to take over as office manager, so I know we aren't too screwed. It could be worse."

It could be worse? "For me, Will, this *is* the worst. How the fuck could it get any worse?"

He winces. "Yeah. I'm really sorry about that. I wish there was something I could do but...you know Alyssa. Once something is set in her mind, it's hard to break. Honestly, I first thought that she'd just need time and maybe that's still the case but this whole moving to London thing has really thrown us all off-guard. Says she wants to try her hand at acting again. I don't know why she doesn't do it here or even in LA but...well, I'm not going to try and figure her out."

I shake my head and finish my drink. "I'm not giving up on her."

"I admire that."

"She's just so fucking...prickly."

"You got that right."

"I just don't know how to get her to talk to me."

"Well if you can talk to her between now and then, then you have to convince her not to go."

"That won't be easy."

"It won't. And that's even if she talks to you. She's really hurt, Emmett. You got to see it from her side."

"I do see it from her side. That's why...that's why I don't want to push her too much either. I want to explain what happened, I mean I have before, but I really need her to see it. See that I love her, that I would never do anything to hurt her. That everything has been nothing but real. But I don't want to push her. If she honestly doesn't want me, if she can't trust me...I'll back off."

"I don't think that's wise," Will says after a few beats.

"Why?"

"I don't normally give advice because, well, what do I know? But I have learned a few things over the years. And that's that women like the grand gesture."

I raise my brow. "What?"

"The grand gesture. You can't just show up at their door and tell them how you feel. You have to do it with a boombox over your head, blasting Peter Gabriel."

I make a fist. "Fucking Lloyd Dobler, that movie ruined it for the rest of us."

And then Will launches into a long story about a girl he

took to see *Say Anything* when he was in high school and how in love she was with John Cusack but I'm not really listening.

I've never done a grand gesture for anyone. Never really had to, to be honest. Never even been in the situation where I wanted a girl back.

But for Alyssa, I'll do anything.

I've never felt as whole-hearted as I do when I'm with her, never felt so…full. Of life, of love, of passion. It's not a matter of being complete and incomplete. It's about being the better version of yourself.

She made me better.

And now I'll have to prove it.

CHAPTER 21

ALYSSA

*I*t's been seven days since Emmett and I broke up.

He's come to my apartment four times.

He's texted me 38 times.

Called me seven times.

Written me five emails.

And in the last three days, I've heard absolutely nothing.

Which is something I should be happy about. The fact that he's stopped bugging me. That he's letting me be, giving me space.

The problem is, the space between us is about to get larger.

As large as Canada and the Atlantic Ocean.

I'm standing at the Vancouver airport just outside security. Jackie, Will, Ted, Tiffany and Carla have gathered around to say goodbye and I am trying my hardest not to start crying. I don't know why, I've been crying all week long, why not start now?

But I want to show them that I'm brave and that I'm doing the right thing.

Lordy, though. I have no idea if I'm doing the *smart* thing.

The whole London move was completely impulsive, as was quitting Mad Men. I know I had been talking about leaving for a while now, even telling Jackie about it, but I thought it would happen after the contract was over with Emmett and I had gotten my money. That was the original plan from the start.

But now the contract is void. Or at least I'm assuming it is. I know via Will that Emmett and Autumn are no longer working together and I also know I'm not being held to the agreement anymore. I know I could get the money if I wanted, that Emmett would gladly hand it over, but I don't want that. Not even a bit.

It was never about the money. Of course, I'm now heading to one of the most expensive places in the world with just my meager vacation pay and a bonus cheque that Will and Ted gave me for my years of service because they obviously felt sorry for me. Not that I'm complaining, though. It will be just enough for me to get by for a month, no more, but it's something.

I'll struggle. That's a given. But that's also part of the experience. I'm not going to London so that I can carve out the same safe and boring life I had in Vancouver. I'm doing it so I can truly live for once.

If anything, Emmett has been a big inspiration. The life he had over there, that's what I want. I want to be busting my chops while trying to make it. I want to get a waitressing gig and run around to auditions and go to plays and drink beer and just be in a place where no one knows me, where I can be anonymous and be myself. Start over. No expectations. Just everything that's real.

That's why I'm doing this. And as last minute as it was, as crazy as it seems, it's what's right. I do feel bad about leaving Will and Ted so abruptly but Tiffany has been a great help in more ways than one. She's not only moving into my role as office manager, something I know she's had her eye on for a while, but she's also moving into my role as roommate.

Yup. I felt like shit leaving Carla high and dry, even though she insisted she'd find a roommate pretty fast, though not one as awesome as me, of course. And then Tiffany said she'd be interested. She's been dying to move out of her parent's house for a while now and with the office manager job, she can finally afford it. I think what she really wants is to be able to bring Ken over without her parents breathing down her neck, but hey, whatever works for her.

So, while it sucks to be leaving Vancouver and my friends behind, I also know that I'm leaving them all in a good place. Tiffany will help Will, Ted and Carla. Jackie is definitely going to miss me but with the baby coming up, she's got a lot to focus on.

That of course leaves Emmett.

He's the one person not here.

He's the one person I thought might show up at the last minute.

You know, a grand gesture?

That's why I'm trying to stall things at security.

Even Will keeps looking over his shoulder like he expects him to come.

"Looking for someone?" I ask him hopefully.

But he just gives me a wane smile and doesn't say a word.

"You better catch your flight, sweetheart," Ted says, nodding at security. "I hope you packed all your knives in your checked luggage."

Fuck. I'm going to miss these people.

"Are you going to cry?" Tiffany asks, inspecting me closely.

I dare to meet her eyes. Thank god she seems amused by all of this. I can't even look at Jackie because she's been sniffling and sobbing for the entire ride to the airport.

"Okay," I say, taking in a shaky breath. "This is it."

Jackie starts bawling. "This is all happening so fast," she sobs.

"Oh, you overly emotional hormonal mess." I pull her into a quick hug. "Hey, I'll be back to visit. Hell, I might be back in a month."

"If you come back early, you can always sleep on the couch," Carla says, wrapping her arms around the both of us.

"But don't think you can get your room back," Tiffany says, throwing herself at us until we're just a ball of hugs. "Or your job back."

When I think I've had my share of the touchy-feely stuff, I break apart from them while they still hold onto each other. Sheesh. You'd think I was boarding a spaceship to a galaxy far away.

Will and Ted are naturally more reserved.

"Have a good one," Ted says, shaking my hand and giving me a slap on the shoulder. "Give those Brits hell."

"Goodbye Alyssa," Will says, giving me a quick hug. "Break a leg, will you?"

Ugh. Jackie's got a good hugger in this one.

I squeeze him back. "Thanks Will. I'll do my best."

I break apart and look at the faces of all my friends, wondering how the hell I'm leaving them behind.

But it's happening. And no amount of doubt or sadness will change that.

"Bye," I say, wiggling my fingers as I walk into the line. "Cheerio."

"Top of the morning to you," Tiffany responds.

I just shake my head, roll my eyes, and go through security.

There's nothing like the airport to distract you from all your woes. While my heart is continually sinking, something else inside me is rising. Hope. Excitement. And yet having to battle security lines and getting to your gate and not losing your passport, really pushes all of that to the side.

It isn't until I get on the plane that reality hits me.

And by the way, reality sucks.

Because I booked last minute through a super budget website, I didn't have a choice of seat.

So, of course, my seat on this British Airways jumbo jet is in the very back of coach, in the middle of the middle.

I'm going to be sandwiched in a row of stinky strangers for ten hours. How will I even sleep? I can't seem to stop battling either person on both sides of me for control of the armrest, leaving me completely squished in the middle. This is hell and we haven't even taken off yet.

This is when I have time to think, of course.

And while I'm sad thinking about Jackie and Tiffany and the gang and I'm excited about what adventures London might bring, my heart is absolutely bereft about Emmett.

The truth is…I miss him deeply. And the fact that I'm flying far away without even saying goodbye, well, it hurts. It hurts like hell. I should have at least picked up the phone, read the emails. I should have at least listened to what he had to say.

I know that what he did was wrong and he knows it too. But Carla was right–it all comes down to trust. And while the images of him and Autumn are still seared in my mind, I'm starting to realize that it's something I can overcome and move past. It's something worth getting over if it means having Emmett back in my life.

But now that won't happen. I was too stubborn and too impulsive to even give us a chance. The only thing that was ever really real.

Oh, please don't start crying here. Not with these people. They don't deserve your tears.

"Miss Martin?" the flight attendant says to me in her prim

British accent, bringing my attention over to the aisle. She gives me a bright smile.

"Yes?" I ask. Oh shit. Am I in someone else's seat? How embarrassing.

"You've been upgraded to first class," she says.

Ding, ding, ding, ding! It's like winning the fucking lottery. Every person around us is looking at me like *you lucky bitch* and, hell, I can't blame them.

Still… "There must be some mistake," I tell her. "I booked my ticket on FlyLow." Which is a lousy name when you think about it.

"No mistake," she says. "Please come with me."

Now, wait a minute. Is "upgraded to first class" really just code for "you're being kicked off the flight"? Is it because I'm wearing yoga pants? If this was United they would just drag me out by the hair but since this is British Airways, maybe they do things a little more discretely. Trickery and all that.

I'm nervous now. Hesitant. Until the guy next to me breathes a bunch of heinous salami breath in my face and says, "If you don't take the first-class seat, love, I will."

Oh, hell no you won't. As quickly as I can, I grab my purse and get to my feet and then I wait while everyone else has to get to their feet and exit the row. Then I grab my carry-on from the overhead bin–which nearly slams into my head and takes me out–and awkwardly follow the flight attendant up the aisle.

Everyone is looking at me like I really am getting kicked off.

Oh shit. What did I do? Is it the pants? Yoga pants aren't leggings.

But when we get to the door I came in through, she keeps walking.

Through premium economy and past the stairs that lead up to the upper deck.

All the way to first class, at the nose of the plane.

Nearly every seat is taken but thankfully no one is paying any attention to me.

The girl in size-too-small Lululemon pants who obviously doesn't belong up here.

The attendant points to an empty pod in the middle and takes my bag from me. "Here you go."

"Are you serious?" I whisper to her.

She just gives me a quick smile and walks off.

I slowly ease myself down in the seat. There's a pod right on the other side of me but with the partition up it feels like I have my own damn bedroom.

I put my purse beneath the table, flip over the menu, press some buttons, adjust my seat.

Oh my god. This is fucking heaven.

I start fiddling with my seat, making it go into a bed and then back up again.

This is the *best*.

"Having fun over there, sunshine?"

I freeze. Blink.

I didn't just hear that…did I?

I look around. We've just pushed back from the gate and the attendants are about to go into their safety demonstration. No one is looking at me.

But that voice, his voice…it didn't just come from nowhere, did it?

With my heart galloping in my throat, I unbuckle my belt and very slowly stand up until I'm peering over the partition at the seat on the other side.

Emmett is staring up at me.

"Ahhh!" I cry out and immediately flop down into my seat.

Now everyone is looking at me.

Slowly the partition comes down.

I think I might just die.

Emmett is sitting right beside me, a wry grin on his face.

Oh god, his beautiful face.

His face that feels like home.

"Hey," he says softly, then peers over at my lap. "You better buckle up."

I can't take my eyes off of him. I don't want to. I'm afraid if I do, he'll disappear. I don't want to let him go. Not now, not ever.

How is this real?

Somehow, I manage to buckle myself back up without looking but the words just don't form.

"I hope you like the upgrade," he says to me, watching me warily. "I had to pull a few strings to make it happen but luckily the flight attendant was game."

My mouth flaps open. Closed.

"How are you…how are you here?"

His mouth quirks up. "I heard you were leaving. I thought I would leave with you."

"But…but…"

Oh my god. I can't believe this for even a second.

And the crazy thing is, I imagined if I saw Emmett again that I would just see him and Autumn kissing in my mind. That I would feel pain and anger and shame.

But I don't feel any of that anymore.

None of that matters anymore.

Because it was never ever true.

The only true thing is him, right here, with me.

Holy crow.

"Is this really happening?" I ask him softly.

He places his hand on the ledge between us, palm up. "It's real." I put my hand in his and close my eyes as he holds it tight. "It's real, baby. Everything. All of this. You, me. I know you're still mad and you're hurt and I get it, I really do. I know I fucked up. But I couldn't just let you walk out of my life. I love you, Alyssa. More than I ever thought I could love anyone. More than I thought was possible. I love you and I am not letting you go without a fight."

I swallow hard, the tears finally bubbling up. "I love you too," I whisper, opening my eyes. "I'm so sorry I ignored you, I–"

"No, I get it," he says, leaning forward, his beautiful eyes searching mine. "I get it. I don't expect you to take me back, not after what happened. Not after everything. But I had to make sure. I had to have a shot. I had to try. Alyssa, our relationship was built on a lie, it was fucked up from the start. It's never been straight forward or easy. It's only been complicated. And while I know that it tested us, I just want to start again. From the beginning. I want to start over, you and me. One hundred per cent real. Only passion, no performance." He breathes in deep. "I don't know how to make it up to you, or what to say. But I figure I have a captive audience for the next ten hours and I'm going to use every single second to convince you to come back to me."

I can't help but smile. "Well, if you've had a whole play planned out, then I'm sorry to disappoint you."

"I had you at hello?"

I laugh. "You had me at a first-class upgrade."

God. I'm giddy. Giddy!

"Well then," he says, giving my hand a squeeze. "I'm glad that won you over. You put someone in coach, crammed in like cattle in a feedlot, and then bring them up here and they'll promise you the world."

"Seriously though," I tell him, feeling so much bubbling through me, I don't know what to do with myself. Gah. "I'm…I'm so glad you came after me. I didn't want to leave it like I did, I just didn't know what to do. I was so hurt."

"I know."

"And now I know that it doesn't matter. I believe you, Emmett, and more than that, I trust you. And I want to be with you, always, forever. Just us." I pause. "And now we're both flying across the world together. I didn't really see that one coming."

"I did," he says simply.

"How?"

He shrugs. "You kept talking about acting. I kept talking about going back to London. I figured at some point we would go together. This whole thing with Autumn was a horrible wrench thrown in the plans but this…" he gestures to the plane, "us. It was all supposed to happen."

"The grand design?"

"Something like that. More like, I know you and you know me and this makes sense."

"Well I'm glad it makes sense to someone because I left a bunch of shocked people behind in Vancouver."

"Nah, they get it. They all want what's best for you. They know you'll never be happy unless you head out and try to find what you're looking for."

"But what if I've just been looking for you?"

"Then you have me." He raises my hand to his lips and kisses the back of it. "You have me, body, heart and soul. And for whatever else we're looking for in life, the *passion*, we'll look for it together." Then he leans across the divider and kisses me, soft and sweet and achingly beautiful. "I love you, sunshine," he says against my lips.

"I love you, too."

We hold hands while the plane taxis down the runway.

And then we're flying.

EPILOGUE

ALYSSA

A YEAR LATER

"*B*loody hell, he's good."

I glance over at my friend Jodi who is leaning forward in her seat, her eyes glued to Emmett as he moves fluidly across the stage.

Emmett's only had the role of Professor Henry Higgins in the musical *My Fair Lady* for a few weeks now and already most of London is flocking to see him every single night. The headlines here have been calling him the sexiest professor ever, and there's no question why. Emmett's true calling isn't playing some dopey spineless teenager or the villain of a superhero (which, can we just say, has the lamest power ever). Emmett's true self is on the stage: acting his heart out, singing, dancing. Being one hundred per cent him.

The man can move, that I've always known (especially in the bedroom) and manages to make dancing both elegant and masculine. And then there is his voice. Bold and deep, it's like when I first saw Ewan McGregor in *Moulin Rouge*, how when he opened his mouth, I was floored at all the talent I didn't know was inside him.

It was the same with Emmett. He blew me away. And even though over the last year of us living in London he's been having prominent role after role, singing his way into my heart, it still leaves me in awe every time I watch him.

Tonight, I got my friend and I front row tickets to the always sold-out show. Normally I would watch from the wings, but since this was Jodi's first time at this show, I thought this would be the better experience.

Jodi and I work on the same play together. It's at a tiny theatre in east London that can only seat a couple hundred people tops, but we're doing *The Crucible* and despite the seriousness of the play, it's been an amazing experience. Jodi happens to have one of the main roles, I'm pretty much a secondary character, but even so I'm finally living my dream.

As is Emmett. We found our dream together.

After we landed in London it took us a while to get into the rhythm of things. Even though I had Emmett now to help support me, I still wasted no time in getting a job. I ended up working as bartender at the pub located below our apartment, which worked out perfectly as I used the days to go and start my acting career. It was a hard slog, still is, but I was really, truly, doing what I set out to do. I was finally going after my dreams.

The apartment we share is a modest two-bedroom in the Shoreditch area–Emmett sold his Vancouver house for several million dollars but we're still renting in London for now. There are so many amazing neighborhoods that we don't want to be tied down to one place just yet.

There's also the fact that property here is outrageously expensive and Emmett used most of the money he made on his house to start a non-profit organization back in Vancouver. With the help of Will, Ted and some of his fellow actors as investors, Emmett bought the building he grew up in and created Play for Hope, a shelter that provides beds, food, employment plans, and hopefully, a clean and controlled injection site. There are still some logistics regarding that that Emmett is working through, mainly government restrictions considering how controversial injection sites are, but we're happy to say it's been a success story.

At least it's a success story in the fact that Emmett finally feels like he's doing more than just handing out food and a hope and a prayer. With the programs he has in place, people really do get a chance to get back on their feet. Even his friend Jimmy is helping to run it. The best part is that once a month, the first floor of the shelter turns into a mini-playhouse where those in need can come together and put on shows. We've seen a few on YouTube and they're adorable, if not a bit chaotic at times. Still, it gives them a sense of purpose and passion outside of the drugs. It gives them hope.

We have plans to go back soon and visit anyway, as soon as Emmett gets a break. My play only runs for a few more weeks and then it's back to auditioning and trying to find something else. But you know what? As instable as the business is for me, I wouldn't trade it for anything else in the world. The way I look at it is that I never know what role is coming next–it might just be the role of a lifetime.

Plus, I get flexibility to travel. Jackie and Will had their daughter a few months ago and the Facetime sessions I've had with them just aren't enough. The baby, Lauren, is so cute she actually makes my often-ignored uterus have jealousy pains. When I finally see her, I'm going to spoil the crap out of that kid. I've already picked out a whole tiny wardrobe for her that matches the ones Kate and William dressed their baby Charlotte in.

"You're a lucky girl, you know that?" Jodi says to me as the curtain comes down at the end of the show. Both of us get to our feet and start whistling like mad, even after Emmett has left the stage and the other actors are taking their bows.

"I know," I tell her, smiling like an idiot.

"No…you have no idea," she says and there's something about the tone of her voice that makes me pause. What is she getting at?

Before I have a chance to ask her what she meant, Emmett comes back on stage, the spotlight following him until he stops right above us.

He glances down at me, gives me a wink, and then addresses the audience.

"I just wanted to thank you all for coming to see me night after night after night. It feels like I've been doing this forever, even though I haven't, and it's only because this play, this role, this theatre, is such a joy to come to every night. But there's another reason why I'm able to sing and dance about being an ordinary man. It's because I have an extraordinary woman in my life." He smiles at me and in his old-fashioned suit and top-hat, I can scarcely breathe.

"I'm an ordinary man," he starts to sing "Ordinary Man," his rich voice soaring across the audience, "who desires nothing more than an ordinary chance, to live exactly as he likes, and do precisely what he wants." He stops singing, looks at me and says, his voice low, "And, sunshine, what I want is you. Always you. Forever you."

He drops to one knee on the stage and I gasp.

The audience gasps.

He fishes out a ring from his front pocket.

I gasp even louder.

The audience gasps even louder.

And for all the people around us, the spotlight on Emmett's face, his eyes as they search mine with so much hope it nearly breaks me, the moment is somehow just between us. I barely even look at the ring he's holding out for me, the diamonds catching the light and sparkling like crazy.

All I can see is him.

Emmett is proposing to me. In front of everyone.

Still on stage, still in costume, still in a play.

A performance?

"Real or fake?" I whisper to him.

"Real, always real," he says.

I take a step until I'm pressed against the stage and I give him my hand.

"Alyssa Martin, will you marry me?" he asks.

I can't even swallow the lump in my throat. I can barely say, "Yes."

But I say it.

I say it. I mean it.

Because it's us.

And it's real.

"Yes, yes, yes."

Always, always, always.

THE END

- I WOULD LOVE TO HEAR WHAT YOU THOUGHT ABOUT AFTER ALL! IF YOU HAVE A FEW MINUTES TO LEAVE A REVIEW ON AMAZON, I WOULD BE OH SO GRATEFUL. JUST SEND ME THE LINK TO YOUR REVIEW TO AUTHORKARINAHALLE@GMAIL.COM AND I'LL THANK YOU PERSONALLY.

To get updates and stay connected with me (I would LOVE it)
- Join my exclusive readers group on Facebook where I have awesome giveaways, sneak peeks, fun trivia, great people and

lot's more. Seriously. We're the best group of readers on the internet: Karina Halle's Anti-Heroes

- Sign-up for my newsletter to get alerts when new books come out, plus exclusives such as FREE books, excerpts and cover reveals!

- Watch my daily adventures on Instagram (I practically live here)

ALSO, I HAVE WRITTEN OVER THIRTY-FIVE NOVELS IN A RANGE OF DIFFERENT GENRES, FROM CONTEMPORARY ROMANCE, TO ROMANTIC COMEDY, TO ROMANTIC SUSPENSE, TO PARANORMAL ROMANCE. WANT A LIST OF THEM ALL? VISIT MY AMAZON AUTHOR PAGE HERE AND GIVE ME A "FOLLOW" WHILE YOU'RE AT IT SO YOU CAN STAY UP TO DATE WITH NEW RELEASES!

WILD CARD

Looking for your next read? How about Wild Card, releasing August 1st, 2017.

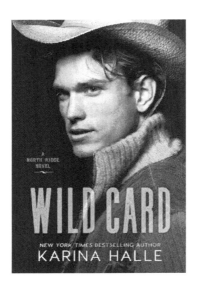

Wild Card is a standalone novel and the first book in the North Ridge Trilogy about rough and rugged Canadian mountain men, the Nelson brothers. Canada's never felt so hot.

She swore she'd never go back home.

She swore she'd never see the man who broke her all those years ago.

But you don't always get to choose your path.

And sometimes that path is as wild and rugged as the heart.

Rachel Waters thought she saw the last of the small mountain town of North Ridge, British Columbia, when she left six years ago. But while her advertising career blossomed beneath the skyscrapers of Toronto, her mother's sudden illness has the 26-year old returning to North Ridge to care for her, putting her career on hold while dealing with family secrets, regrets and unresolved goodbyes.

Shane Nelson has always been a bit of a wild card. The youngest of three brothers, Shane's spent most of his life being underestimated and misunderstood. With his quiet intensity, classic good looks and thoughtful demeanor, he's an enigma on horseback, managing his father's sprawling ranch on the slopes of North Ridge.

But while Shane remains the quintessential brooding cowboy, complete with an arsenal of inner demons, all of that changes when Rachel steps back into his life.

She was the girl he pushed away.

Now she's the girl who wishes she could leave.

Despite the odds, Shane will do everything to convince Rachel he needs a second chance that he doesn't deserve but when the two of them head off into the wilderness together in search of lost cattle, more than just their hearts are at stake.

Whether it's love or lives on the line, one thing is for sure: always bet on the wild card.

ALSO - HAVE YOU READ **BEFORE I EVER MET YOU?** THAT TELLS THE STORY OF HOW WILL AND JACKIE MET (BEFORE THE EVENTS OF AFTER ALL). BELIEVE ME, YOU DON'T WANT TO MISS IT.

BEFORE I EVER MET YOU IS AVAILABLE AT ALL RETAILERS! KINDLE: bit.ly/BIEMY-Kindle

ACKNOWLEDGMENTS

There are the usual suspects I'd like to thank for this book: Nina Bocci for her PR work and getting the word out and the book into the right hands, all the bloggers and readers who have taken a chance on Emmett and Alyssa, my FB group admin team, my street team, my Anti-Heroes, proofing superstars Roxane LeBlanc and Amanda Cantu.

Bruce. Of course. You're the best pibble there can be (though you are nuts, let's face it).

AND always the biggest thanks goes to Scott Mackenzie. While I was tinkering with After All here at home here on Salt Spring Island, to writing during our trip to Iceland, Berlin and London, you were supportive every step of the way. I don't know how many "vacations" I've worked on but I love that you always understand.

Thank you for being real and keeping it real.

PS Justin Trudeau's butt is MORE than okay.
PPS Ketchup chips are awesome.
PPPS I say Jesus Murphy all the time.

PPPPS The Ogopogo is real and BC wine is awesome

PPPPPS Vancouver's addiction problem is truly as horrible as described. If you want to help or get further info, I suggest here for a good starting point!

PPPPPPS That "Run To You" song really pisses me off.

ABOUT THE AUTHOR

Karina Halle is a former travel writer and music journalist and The New York Times, Wall Street Journal and USA Today Bestselling author of The Pact, Love, in English, The Artists Trilogy, Dirty Angels and over 20 other wild and romantic reads. She lives on an island off the coast of British Columbia with her husband and her rescue pit bull Bruce, where she drinks a lot of wine, hikes a lot of trails and devours a lot of books.

Halle is represented by Root Literary and is both self-published and published by Simon & Schuster and Hachette in North America and in the UK.

Stay in touch

www.authorkarinahalle.com
authorkarinahalle@gmail.com

ALSO BY KARINA HALLE

Sins and Needles (The Artists Trilogy #1)

On Every Street (An Artists Trilogy Novella #0.5)

Shooting Scars (The Artists Trilogy #2)

Bold Tricks (The Artists Trilogy #3)

Donners of the Dead

Dirty Angels (Dirty Angels Trilogy #1)

Dirty Deeds (Dirty Angels Trilogy #2)

Dirty Promises (Dirty Angels Trilogy #3)

Veiled

Black Hearts (Sins Duet #1)

Dirty Souls (Sins Duet #2)

43846075R00190

Printed in Poland
by Amazon Fulfillment
Poland Sp. z o.o., Wrocław